The
Other Life

The
Other Life

ⶠⵌⵌ

Ellen Meister

G. P. Putnam's Sons
New York

PUTNAM

G. P. PUTNAM'S SONS
Publishers Since 1838
Published by the Penguin Group
Penguin Group (USA) Inc., 375 Hudson Street, New York, New York 10014, USA •
Penguin Group (Canada), 90 Eglinton Avenue East, Suite 700, Toronto, Ontario M4P 2Y3,
Canada (a division of Pearson Penguin Canada Inc.) • Penguin Books Ltd, 80 Strand,
London WC2R 0RL, England • Penguin Ireland, 25 St Stephen's Green, Dublin 2, Ireland
(a division of Penguin Books Ltd) • Penguin Group (Australia), 250 Camberwell Road,
Camberwell, Victoria 3124, Australia (a division of Pearson Australia Group Pty Ltd) •
Penguin Books India Pvt Ltd, 11 Community Centre, Panchsheel Park, New Delhi–110 017,
India • Penguin Group (NZ), 67 Apollo Drive, Rosedale, North Shore 0632, New Zealand
(a division of Pearson New Zealand Ltd) • Penguin Books (South Africa) (Pty) Ltd,
24 Sturdee Avenue, Rosebank, Johannesburg 2196, South Africa

Penguin Books Ltd, Registered Offices: 80 Strand, London WC2R 0RL, England

Library of Congress Cataloging-in-Publication Data

Meister, Ellen.
The other life / Ellen Meister.
p.   cm.
ISBN 978-0-399-15713-4
1. Married women—Fiction.   2. Pregnant women—Fiction.   3. Marriage—Fiction.
4. Motherhood—Fiction.   5. Mothers and daughters—Fiction.   6. Domestic fiction.
7. Psychological fiction.   8. Love stories.   I. Title.
PS3613.E4355O75   2011   2010028958
813'.6—dc22

Printed in the United States of America
1   3   5   7   9   10   8   6   4   2

Book design by Meighan Cavanaugh

This is a work of fiction. Names, characters, places, and incidents either are the product of
the author's imagination or are used fictitiously, and any resemblance to actual persons,
living or dead, businesses, companies, events, or locales is entirely coincidental.

While the author has made every effort to provide accurate telephone numbers and
Internet addresses at the time of publication, neither the publisher nor the author assumes
any responsibility for errors, or for changes that occur after publication. Further, the
publisher does not have any control over and does not assume any responsibility
for author or third-party websites or their content.

For Max, Ethan, and Emma

The
Other Life

PROLOGUE

———+———

1973

On the day that Nan Gilbert decided to kill herself, she awoke sometime after noon to the sound of her neighbor playing the radio in his backyard. The song was new to her, but the voice was familiar. It was Paul Simon singing without Garfunkel. And though "Kodachrome" was a rueful song about the bright-colored days of youth, it seemed quaint to Nan, who couldn't imagine that people still experienced the world in any kind of light.

Her life had become colorless. She'd been depressed before, Lord knows, but the darkness had never been so complete. It was as if the pregnancy had made everything utterly opaque. Sitting up, sipping the water by her bedside, rising—each action existed within a black box. There wasn't a pinhole of light anywhere, and the concentration required to find her way from the beginning of a task to the end depleted her.

She stood in her bedroom trying to remember what it was she had set out to do. There was something . . . something.

Nan closed her eyes to shut out distractions and it appeared to her as a glint of silver. And there it was, her X-Acto knife. She could picture it—the chrome cylinder with a disposable triangular blade. It was in a can in the back room with her paintbrushes. She went to it.

Sitting in the easy chair by the window, she held the thing and examined her own reflection in the narrow tool. She could see only a single sliver of her face at a time. Her eyes. The middle of her nose. Her nostrils. Her lips. Pieces of who she used to be. Already she was thinking like someone on the other side.

No sense in even going into the bathroom to do it. She'd leave a mess either way. If she let herself bleed into the soft cushions of the chair, he could simply throw the whole thing away. Nothing of her would be left.

The flesh of her wrist looked gray in the sunlight, but the diagonal blue line was as vivid as a road map leading her away. She stuck in the tip of the blade and shivered at the sharpness of the pain. The sensation was so precise, it was close to pleasure. She drew the knife downward, opening her vein with glorious ease. Nan spread her knees so that she could lay her wrist on the cushion, letting the blood travel into the absorbent batting.

It didn't take long for her toes and fingers to go cold. This is good, she thought. Soon she would fall asleep, and that would be it. The baby started to move in her belly. It was a small kick at first, and then a massive wave as it turned completely around.

"Shh," she said, resting her good hand on her belly. "You won't be alone."

Nan closed her eyes and the baby turned again. It was a bigger movement than she'd ever felt. "Please . . . don't fight this," she said, or maybe she just thought it. She couldn't tell anymore if she was speaking or not. She started to drift and felt a great pressure as the baby pushed downward. I'm giving birth, she thought, right here, right now.

"Push, Nan!" someone said. "Push!"

She opened her eyes to a bright rectangular light. Beyond it, she could make out her husband's features. Her legs were in stirrups.

She closed her eyes and was back in the easy chair, dying. She opened them, and was in the delivery room, giving birth in beautiful Technicolor. The two realities made perfect sense to Nan. The decision to live and the decision to die were simply playing out simultaneously. To be or not to be. The choice was spectacularly hers alone.

Nan shut her eyes and floated in the darkness, letting it take her. Somewhere, a phone rang. She opened her eyes and the delivery room was gone. She was in the easy chair by the window, blood pooling between her legs. The baby was still now. She reached with her right hand and picked up the phone.

"I need help," she said.

Present

QUINN BRAVERMAN HAD TWO SECRETS SHE KEPT FROM HER
husband. One was that the real reason she chose him over Eugene, her neurotic, self-loathing, semi-famous ex-boyfriend, was to prove her mother
wrong. She *could* have a relationship with a normal, stable man.

The other was that Quinn knew another life existed in which she had
made the other choice. The two lives ran in parallel lines, like highways
on opposite sides of a mountain. There, on the other side, the Quinn who
had stayed with Eugene was speeding through her high-drama, emotionally exhausting, childless urban life. Here, the Quinn who had married
Lewis lived in the suburbs of Long Island, drove a Volvo, and was pregnant with her second child.

But the important part of the secret—the part that terrified and thrilled
her—was that she knew it was possible to cross from one life to the other.
There were portals.

Sometimes she discovered them by accident. Like last month at
the supermarket, when she had her hand deep in a bin of string beans,

groping for the fresh ones on the bottom. She saw Isaac, her six-year-old, eyeing the Lucky Charms in someone else's cart, and could tell from his expression that he was considering making a grab for the box. He glanced at her—his conscience—and she simply shook her head.

"Why?" he whined.

"Because we don't take things that don't belong to us."

It was an important lesson and she meant to be stern about it, but when he folded his arms and pouted, Quinn laughed. Something about his naked petulance was so guileless that it melted her heart. When adults behaved like that, it was just plain obnoxious, though she had always excused it in Eugene, her ex. His neediness brought out her tender side. He was anxious, prickly, and so often miserable that comforting him was practically a full-time job. But of course that was Quinn's nature—she was a caregiver. All those years of handling her mother's moods had taken root in her psyche, and Quinn grew toward the troubled like a plant seeking sunlight.

She thought about that as she picked through the string beans. The first cousin of that need to be needed was guilt, Quinn's constant companion. Her conscience gnawed at her continuously. Was she doing enough for Isaac? For Lewis? Had she done enough for Eugene, or had she ruined his life by leaving him when she did? As she turned that thought over in her mind, the solid mass of raw vegetables beneath her fingertips seemed to push away on their own, like a magnet repelled by its opposite. She knew then that she was touching the edge of the other side, and that if she moved the string beans she would find a fissure in the bottom of the bin, a rupture in her universe that presented itself during these moments, when the choices she made to alter her own destiny intersected with the choices she hadn't. Quinn wiggled her fingers, thinking about the life she hadn't chosen. If she wanted to, she could leave Isaac in the middle of the produce section of Waldbaum's and slip through to emerge somewhere else, with a whole different life.

She also knew there was a portal in the basement of her house, behind the ancient built-in ironing board. She never opened it, didn't even like to look at it. But from the time she first walked in and saw it folded up against the foundation wall, she knew.

They'd been house hunting for months, and this hundred-year-old colonial on the North Shore had nearly everything they were looking for. When the real estate agent was out of earshot and Lewis whispered that the place felt like home, Quinn paused. He was right, of course, but was it smart to live in a house with an escape hatch? Would she wake up one night after some stupid fight over who parked on which side of the driveway, and be tempted to slip away?

She didn't think she would. But the very possibility was enough to keep her from telling Lewis about this or any of the portals in her life. Surely he would want assurance that she could never be lured away, and Quinn didn't know if she could make that promise.

In the beginning of their relationship, she was tempted to tell him about this other life she knew existed but had never dared visit. But she asked herself how she would feel if Lewis had such an escape hatch in *his* life, and it made her shudder in fear. Quinn had spent her entire childhood trying to cope with her mother's unpredictable disappearances into depression, and had managed to fashion an adult life for herself safe from such worries. She simply couldn't burden Lewis with such a terrible torment.

Eventually, the secret worked itself so deep into the tapestry of their relationship that it became easier to ignore than to focus on, and Quinn knew it was her lot in life to protect her husband from this dangerous truth forever.

Ultimately, of course, she agreed to live in the house despite the escape hatch. And in the four years since, she never even opened the antique ironing board to get a good look at what she had sensed behind it. Today, though, while Lewis slept, Quinn sat on the edge of the bed, thinking about the news they had gotten from the doctor, and contemplated tip-toeing into the basement and slipping through.

It was the day of her amniocentesis. Lewis had taken time off from work to come with her for the test. In the morning, Isaac sat in front of his cereal bowl, dipping his finger into the milk and using it to paint shapes on the table.

"What are you doing?" Quinn said, pulling a paper towel off the roll.

"Making chickens," Isaac said. "See?"

Quinn stopped to peer at what her son had created. The milk lines were running together, turning whatever he had painted into an amorphous blob. "Is that a beak?" she asked.

He nodded. "And these are the hands."

She stifled a laugh. "Your chickens have hands?"

"Where else would they put their wristwatches?" Lewis said as he walked into the room. He kissed Quinn on the mouth. "How do you feel?"

"So far, so good."

They were talking about her morning sickness. Quinn didn't like to complain much, but nausea was her own version of hell. And at the beginning of the pregnancy, even the most benign smell could send her to the bathroom, gagging. Now, at thirteen weeks pregnant, she was starting her second trimester and having more good days than bad.

"Sweetie," she said to her son, "next time you want to draw, get your crayons and paper. The table is for eating."

"The table is for eating?" Lewis said as he rapped his knuckles on the hard surface. "No wonder he's missing his front teeth." He winked at Isaac, who laughed, causing a spoonful of Honey Nut Cheerios to dribble out of his mouth.

"I got it," Lewis said to Quinn as he grabbed a napkin.

She paused. It was the kind of domestic moment that usually triggered her "go away and let me handle it" response, but today was different. She was edgy and running late. She nodded and went upstairs to get dressed.

Quinn tried on three different shirts, getting crankier with each one. Nothing was loose enough to flatter her expanding frame, and she wasn't quite ready for maternity clothes. She studied herself in the mirror, trying to be more objective. Her straight, dark hair had the luster of pregnancy, which pleased her. And the navy top was pretty with her fair complexion. But would anyone notice that faint grease stain down the middle?

She thought about the blouse hanging on the dryer rack in the basement, waiting to be ironed. It was clean. It was roomy. It was comfortable. Only problem was that she didn't want to go down there. Not today, when she was feeling this shaky. Usually she could walk right by that ancient ironing board without much trouble. But on high-anxiety days like this she hated to be reminded that she could so easily slip away.

Quinn was thirty-six, old enough for amniocentesis to be imperative. But she'd also had the procedure seven years before, when she was pregnant with Isaac, because her obstetrician was the cautious type who believed pregnant women should take advantage of every test medical science had available. So she knew exactly what to expect. She would be in a small, darkened room, the image of her baby on a screen tilted so that she could make out certain aspects of the shapes while a radiology technician freeze-framed different views, taking measurements. After that was done, Sally Bernard, her obstetrician, would be called in to perform the amniocentesis. Dr. Bernard would use the screen as a guide so that the long needle used to extract a sample of amniotic fluid would miss puncturing the baby. This was the part that scared Quinn. What if the doctor was distracted? What if she forgot for a moment that the baby was a real and fragile human being, and got careless?

Hormonal madness, Quinn told herself, as she took a deep breath and let it out slowly. Her body had pushed her into maternal overdrive.

Quinn went back to the kitchen, where Lewis was at the table having his breakfast. Isaac sat next to him, drawing—on paper this time—with a blue crayon. It wasn't until her son started preschool that Quinn understood he had unusual artistic abilities. His teachers always wanted to know where he got it from, and Quinn would explain that her mother had been an artist. What she left out was that she hoped artistic talent was all he had inherited from her. Quinn's mother suffered from bipolar disorder, and became so depressed after she and Lewis got married that she killed herself by overdosing on prescription medication. As evidenced by the scar on her wrist, it hadn't been her first suicide attempt—just her best.

Lewis looked up from his newspaper. "Do you want me to pack his lunch?"

"I've got it," she said.

He went back to his reading. "You know your shirt is stained?"

Quinn looked at her top, realizing it was foolish to think a stain right in the middle of her expanding chest could go unnoticed. She went down the basement steps quickly, as she always did, trying to pretend it was the most casual act. Quinn had long ago decided that keeping her secret required behaving as if there were nothing at all peculiar about her circumstances. That way she could live as normal a life as anybody else.

The washer and dryer were in a small, square laundry room Quinn and Lewis had built in the far corner of the basement. The two walls that were part of the foundation were concrete, and the other two were the drywall that had been erected to create the space. Lewis had painted the whole thing a pale peach, leaving the dark wood ironing board untouched. He had offered to oil the hinges so that Quinn could actually use it, but she made some excuse, telling him that it was too close to the corner to be practical, and she preferred to just leave it intact as a historic artifact.

She opened the ordinary, freestanding ironing board and laid her purple blouse over it. As she worked the hot iron over the seams and nosed it around the buttons, her back to the wall, she sensed the opening in the foundation like another presence. It was as if her other life—the one where all her energy was spent trying to keep Eugene from coming unglued—were buzzing by just a few feet away.

She finished ironing the blouse and changed into it, dropping the stained one into the empty washing machine. Quinn put her hand on her swelling tummy, excited to think that in a matter of hours she and Lewis would see their new baby on the sonogram screen, a fuzzy image in shades of gray. A little brother or sister for Isaac. She closed her eyes, picturing a newborn swaddled in soft cotton, and her nipples tingled in anticipation. Funny how trained her body was to react this time around.

LATER, AS SHE LAY in the small, darkened room in the radiology department of the hospital where her amnio would be done, the technician squirted heated jelly onto her stomach, and Quinn reached for Lewis's hand.

The radiology technician, a small woman with a Caribbean accent who had introduced herself as Jeanette, ran the transducer over Quinn's flesh. Immediately, the quick *whoosh-whoosh-whoosh* of the baby's heartbeat filled the room, and Lewis smiled.

"You don't want to know the baby's gender, is that right?" Jeanette asked without taking her eyes from the screen.

Quinn hesitated. She had told her doctor she didn't want to know, but that was more for Lewis than herself. In fact, she would have found it helpful to know, so that she could get everything ready before the baby was born. But when Lewis told her how excited he was about the idea of being surprised, she capitulated.

It wasn't out of weakness, but generosity. In fact, she considered the ability to give her greatest asset. It took a certain power of will, she reasoned, to put her own needs last and take care of those she loved.

Her mother, who had often been the recipient of this self-sacrifice, had labeled Quinn "a pleaser." It was clear to Quinn that this was intended as neither an insult nor a compliment, but the acceptance of an unfortunate flaw, such as astigmatism or lactose intolerance.

Quinn looked at her husband, wondering if he might change his mind about finding out the sex of the baby.

"We want to be surprised," Lewis said to Jeanette.

"Can you already tell from these images?" Quinn added.

Jeanette smiled. "Mama, you shouldn't ask what you don't want to know."

Right, Quinn thought, and smiled back. She couldn't believe she had almost let curiosity get the better of her.

Jeanette continued working, pushing the probe around Quinn's middle, occasionally stopping to press into one section or another.

"Is that the hand?" Lewis asked. "I thought I saw a little hand."

Jeanette's expression dropped. "Just a minute," she said. She continued running the wand over the same section of Quinn's stomach, staring hard at the screen. She pushed a button to freeze the picture, and Quinn thought she heard a small intake of air. Was it her imagination, or had Jeanette gasped?

"What is it?" Quinn said. "Is something wrong?"

Jeanette moved the transducer and took another picture. She put the equipment down and gave Quinn's lower arm a squeeze.

"I'll be right back," she said, and left the room, shutting the door behind her.

Quinn propped herself up on her elbows. "What the hell was that?" she said to her husband. "Is something wrong?"

"I don't know," he said.

The room was too dark for her to make out her husband's complexion, but she knew him well enough to sense he had gone ashen.

"I'm about to freak out," she said.

"Don't freak out," he said. "I'm sure it's nothing."

"For 'nothing' she sure ran out of here fast."

He brought her hand to his mouth and kissed it. "Let's not worry yet. She'll be back in a minute."

"Your hand is cold."

He rubbed his palms together, creating heat from friction, and then took her hand again. "That better?"

"I have to pee."

By the time Jeanette came back into the room with a black-haired man in a white coat, Quinn's armpits were damp, despite the fact that her extremities were now even icier than Lewis's hand had felt.

"Is everything okay?" Quinn asked. "Where's Dr. Bernard?"

"She'll be here soon," he said. "I'm Dr. Peng."

"Are you an obstetrician?" Lewis asked.

Dr. Peng sat in front of the monitor. "Radiologist," he said. Jeanette leaned over him to press something into the keyboard. The doctor stared at the screen and picked up the transducer. Jeanette squirted more warm gel on Quinn's stomach and Dr. Peng began swirling the probe over it. The technician positioned herself behind the doctor, her hand over her mouth as she watched the screen.

"There," she said quietly.

"I see," the doctor said. He pressed the wand harder and harder into Quinn's stomach. She felt the sweat run from her armpit to her back and swallowed against a hard lump.

What's wrong? she asked, but only in her head. She didn't want to say the words out loud. She couldn't bear hearing them. At last Lewis said them for her, but the doctor was evasive.

"Let's wait for Dr. Bernard to arrive," he said. "We can chat in my office after the amnio."

"Please," Lewis said. "Tell us now."

Quinn knew that bad news was supposed to be delivered across a desk, not in a diagnostic examination room with the patient flat on her back and half-undressed. But the doctor paused, clearly weighing whether the situation warranted a breach of protocol. Quinn held her breath.

Finally, he sighed. "We think there's a problem," he began. "It looks like the fetus's skull hasn't fused properly. The ultrasound indicates an abnormality in the forehead." He ran his fingers from the bridge of his nose upward, as if to illustrate the exact location. Then he turned the screen toward Quinn and Lewis, and pulled a laser pointer from his pocket, using it to indicate a hazy spot on the screen. "It's hard to tell at this stage in development, but part of the brain or the brain's cover is likely extending beyond the opening, preventing the bone from being able to fuse. We call this an encephalocele."

Quinn's fingers and toes went numb. "I don't understand," she said.

"Think of it as a fissure in her skull," the doctor said. "We can see something extending beyond it, but it's difficult to tell whether it's brain matter or the brain's cover and cerebrospinal fluid. We'll have to do more testing, schedule you for a targeted sonogram."

"And then what?" Lewis asked. "Will the baby be okay?"

Lewis's voice sounded distant to Quinn, and she became aware that the whole room seemed to shrink, as if she were viewing it through the wrong end of a telescope. She closed her eyes. *This can't be happening.*

"At this point," the doctor was saying when she opened her eyes, "it's impossible to make a prognosis."

"But can it be treated?" Lewis asked.

The doctor licked his lips, his eyes scared and somber. Quinn could tell he was thinking hard about how to phrase his answer, and she knew that if he had the power to disappear at that moment, to slip through his own portal, he would. "Sometimes," he said. "But I'll be honest with you. This is a very serious condition. On the other hand, an encephalocele in the frontal region, where it appears with your baby, is more treatable than one in the posterior region."

"Treatable how?" Lewis asked. "Surgery?"

Dr. Peng nodded. "Sometimes surgery can be performed either shortly after birth or even several years later, depending upon the circumstances. The surgeon repairs the damaged area and closes up the abnormal opening."

"What about brain damage?" Lewis asked.

"I understand you have a lot of questions," Dr. Peng said. "Let's wait until Dr. Bernard arrives and we'll discuss it further, figure out a game plan." He turned to Quinn. "Do you want to sit up while we wait for her?"

She nodded, and Jeanette placed a towel over the gel on her stomach while Lewis helped her to sit up.

"This could be a mistake, right?" Quinn said. "I mean, you could be seeing shadows or something. I've heard about that happening." She looked at Jeanette as she said it, hoping for a sympathetic nod. But the woman glanced down, avoiding Quinn's gaze, and she knew.

2

ALONE AND AWAKE IN BED THAT NIGHT, QUINN STILL FELT emotionally anesthetized, her numbness now blocking even her cognitive functioning. There was something she'd meant to tell Lewis, but what was it? During their crisis-fueled dance of asking questions, making medical test appointments, and gathering information from whatever sources they could, Quinn and Lewis had successfully avoided talking about the big issues, such as whether they would consider terminating the pregnancy, and what it would be like to raise a disabled child. But there was something more immediate she kept reminding herself to bring up when she and Lewis were alone. Now she couldn't remember what it was.

She looked at the clock. It was ten after one, and Lewis needed to get up at seven a.m. for work. He was, she knew, in the spare bedroom they used as a home office, researching "encephalocele" on the Internet. *Come back*, she willed him. *Come back to bed*. But nearly an hour later, when the anxiety nipping at the edges of her consciousness could no longer keep her awake, Lewis had still not returned. So she drifted off to sleep, remembering at last the words she had wanted to say to her husband all day: *The doctor said "her skull." Her. It's a girl, Lewis. Our baby daughter.*

WHEN QUINN AWOKE in the darkness a few hours later, Lewis lay next to her, locked in the heavy breathing of deep sleep. It would be cruel to wake him, since he was only getting a few hours of sleep as it was, but she was burning to talk to him, to tell him what was racing through her mind. She just wanted to share her vision, to let him know that this abstract baby they were talking about was a girl, a tiny bundle who would be swaddled in pink-trimmed receiving blankets. If they aborted the pregnancy, or if the baby died in utero, or was stillborn, or lived a short while before being taken from them, they'd be mourning a daughter. And if she lived—fine or disabled or terribly sick—she'd be their little girl, Isaac's baby sister, and they would love her fiercely.

She wondered if Lewis knew how much he'd love her. He would. Of that Quinn was sure.

She got out of bed and went into Isaac's room. He was asleep, curled onto his side, his mouth open to compensate for a stuffy nose. His complexion looked bluish in the dim light seeping in from the window by his bed, and though she could hear the soft, steady burst of each exhale, she put the back of her hand by his mouth to feel his warm breath. She wanted to touch him, to stroke the soft hair over his ear, but she wouldn't risk waking him. Instead, she leaned in, closed her eyes, and deeply inhaled off the top of his head. Sometime in the last year his infant smell had dissipated completely, replaced by another distinctly Isaac scent, barely discernible beneath the smell of shampoo, laundry detergent, pizza, Play-Doh, or whatever else he had gotten into on any particular day, but there. Always there.

Quinn's brother, Hayden, had once teased her that women were much more animalistic than men. "I don't know why you females are always insisting that guys are such beasts," he had said. "There's nothing more feral than the human mother. You're all leaky messes, driven by hormones and scents and blood and breast milk. It's a little disgusting, to tell you the truth."

She had laughed and told him the only reason he thought women were so savage was because he wasn't familiar enough with the heterosexual male. But Hayden had snorted, insisting that macho bravado was mere posturing, and that women were the true evolutionary throwbacks.

He was right, of course. There was something about motherhood that switched on the animal brain. She knew it the moment she took her first whiff off the top of Isaac's newborn head. She was no different from a lioness or mother bear. When it came to their babies, they were sisters in ferocity.

Quinn padded her way down the hall to the home office, where Lewis had left the computer on. She tapped the space bar and the screen bounced to life, the Internet search page he had been reading reduced to a tab on the bottom. She clicked on it and the page opened on the screen to reveal photographs of horribly deformed children, huge tumors growing out the back of their heads, or worse, the front, contorting their small faces into monstrous parodies of human forms. Faces that weren't faces at all. She quickly closed the page and collapsed into the chair.

This isn't my baby, she thought. It can't be. When the doctor had described the condition their baby had, he never mentioned that she'd look like some sort of monster.

My baby, a monster?

Quinn rose from the chair then and began pacing the perimeter of the room, repeating a single phrase in her head over and over, like a mantra: I can mother this child, I can mother this child. But all the while she pictured that escape hatch in the basement. Her heart pounded wildly.

Quinn stopped at the doorway and closed her eyes against the vision of that other life in which none of this was happening. She heard her husband stir.

"Hon?" he called out gently.

Quinn went into the bedroom and stood by the door.

"Are you okay?" he asked, lifting his head. "What's wrong?"

When she didn't answer he looked from her face down the center of her body, as if searching for a clue. His eyes reached her crotch and paused.

She knew what he was thinking, what he was hoping. Miscarriage.

"Quinn? What is it, honey?"

"Nothing," she said. "I'm okay. Go back to sleep."

"Were you online?"

She nodded.

"I'm sorry. I should have closed that tab."

Quinn folded her arms. "You don't need to protect me."

"C'mere," he said, putting his arms out as if a hug would make it all better. She didn't move.

"I can mother this child," she said out loud.

He adjusted his pillow and sat up. "You know . . . you're not in this alone."

"But you want me to have a miscarriage."

"What?"

"Admit it. You want this to go away."

"I don't know *what* I want," he said.

Didn't he? Quinn folded her arms. "You're not being honest," she said.

"Are you?"

"What is that supposed to mean?"

He shook his head as if he shouldn't have to explain it. "You don't have to be strong one hundred percent of the time."

Easy for him to say. How else could she be expected to get through this?

"All I'm saying is," he continued, "it's okay to have doubts."

Doubts? She knew all about doubts. There wasn't a day in her life that she didn't wonder if she could have done something to prevent her mother's death. Would it be the same with this baby? If she had an abortion, she could spend the rest of her life regretting it. She wouldn't do it. She couldn't. Quinn would save this baby as she hadn't been able to save her mother.

She swallowed hard. "I have to do laundry," she said.

"Now?"

"Go back to sleep. We'll talk tomorrow."

Quinn padded down two flights of stairs to the basement. She wasn't going to slip through the portal. At least she didn't think so. She just wanted to face it once and for all. To get a clear vision of what her escape hatch looked like.

Quinn flicked the light switch in the dim laundry room and the fluorescent overhead bulbs washed the room in clinical brightness. The hinged part of the contraption was waist level, and Quinn had to reach up to grasp the top of the ironing board. She pulled it slowly at first, just an inch away from the wall. She stopped, not sure if she wanted to proceed.

You're just looking, she told herself. *You're not going to do anything. Just open the damned thing.*

She pulled it another inch and the hinge groaned. Quinn realized then that she'd actually need some muscle if she was going to get it open. Was that a sign that she shouldn't? That the thing wanted to be left alone?

Excuses, she told herself. *Don't be so fearful.*

She tightened her grip and pulled hard. It budged less than an inch this time, and Quinn knew it could break if she forced it. She would need to oil the hardware before going any further. She turned, expecting to bolt up the stairs and into the garage, where Lewis kept a can of WD-40, but almost ran smack into Isaac, who stood before her in his rocket-ship pajamas. The sleeves were already two inches too short, and the sight of his narrow wrists exposed made her ache somewhere near her womb.

"My mouth hurts," he said, his hand on his neck.

"You mean your throat?"

He nodded once and she felt his head. It was cool. "You probably just have a cold."

Quinn knelt and folded Isaac into her arms. One of the very first things her obstetrician had told her when she tested positively for pregnancy was that she shouldn't pick up her son.

"You'll be tempted to," Dr. Bernard, a mom herself, had said. "But he's a big boy now and you have to think of the baby."

It was a revelation to Quinn, who hadn't considered that the new territory she was entering would require weighing the needs of one child against another. Could mothers really do that? Did they instinctively know which child needed them more at any given moment? Would *she*?

"Anything else hurt?" she whispered, smoothing Isaac's hair.

"I don't know." He laid his head sleepily on her shoulder and she inhaled.

That smell. Quinn hugged him tighter, ready to pick him up. She closed her eyes and imagined climbing two flights of stairs, Isaac's fifty-pound body pressed against hers. If she reached the top landing and felt a terrible cramping followed by ominous spotting and, ultimately, miscarriage, would anyone blame her? Of course not. *It wasn't meant to be,* they'd all cluck.

"Let's go upstairs," she whispered to Isaac.

He hugged her tighter. "Carry me."

Quinn didn't respond.

"Mom?"

She released him and looked at his delicate face. "You're a big boy," she said. Then Quinn took his hand and they went upstairs together, side by side.

3

"You sure you're okay?" Lewis asked.

He was getting ready to leave for work and had offered to take all or part of the day off, but Quinn said she was fine. Besides, she would need him home tomorrow morning to come with her for the follow-up ultrasound, and she knew the business couldn't spare him that long.

Like most people who owned their own companies, Lewis found it hard to take time off. Sure, he had staff who could run things, but as Quinn understood it, one crisis or another seemed to crop up every day, and his presence was required.

Lewis ran a family business he had inherited from his father, who had inherited it from *his* father. It was, essentially, a fleet of New York City medallion taxicabs, though the way the cars were owned and operated bore little resemblance to the business his grandfather had run. Over the years, skyrocketing insurance and gasoline prices had had such a devastating impact on the business that most owners had been forced to sell out, leaving few fleets in operation. Lewis's father—who had more perseverance in business than in his own marriage, which he had walked out on when Lewis was five—had hung in through near bankruptcy. Now, with the value of each medallion exceeding the price of most middle-class homes, it had turned lucrative indeed. Lewis's skills were well suited to the day-to-day operations, which required near-constant innovation, not to mention an uncanny ability to see straight through to a person's character. The latter was particularly helpful when job applicants came from all corners of the globe, bearing exotic cultural differences.

It was the taxi business that had first brought Lewis and Quinn together almost ten years before. She was living with Eugene then, and he had come home apoplectic about having left his briefcase behind in a taxi. Quinn spent an hour trying to calm him down, jotting down notes as she tried to piece together what was in the briefcase so that she could take steps to make replacements. Her sense of order and attention to details usually had a calming effect on Eugene, who was overwhelmed by life's chaos. This latest incident, though, was proving tough. Until she could recover or replace everything in that briefcase, he'd be a mess. She sat on the couch, a writing pad on her knee, as he paced.

"What else?" she asked.

"Those tickets!" he said, smacking his forehead. He was referring to the Lufthansa flight a German radio station had arranged so that Eugene could meet with their on-air talent for an idea exchange. "They were first class, goddamn it."

"I know," she said evenly.

Eugene Ray was a prominent New York radio personality, usually referred to as a *shock jock*, though he despised the term.

"Relax," Quinn said to him. "I'll call the airline, work something out."

"You're going to work something out with the Germans? Who are you—Mussolini?" He sank into the couch next to her and put his head in his hands. "Fuck. I think my Xanax was in there."

Eugene wasn't allowed to curse on the air, and made up for it at home.

"I just refilled it," she said, patting his knee. "You need one?" She rose.

"No," he said sarcastically, "I'll just sit here quietly and have a stroke from anxiety."

"People don't have strokes from anxiety," she said, walking toward the bathroom.

"They do if their blood pressure gets too high!" he called after her.

She got a pill from the bottle in the medicine cabinet and brought it to him. "You have *low* blood pressure."

"The universe is conspiring to change that."

"The universe didn't leave your briefcase in a cab."

"You're trying to kill me, right?"

"Don't be silly. I'm not even in your will yet."

The phone rang and Quinn answered it. The man on the other end said he was from Star Maintenance Taxis, and that one of his cabs just pulled back into the garage with a briefcase inside. He was wondering if he had reached the owner.

"Who is that?" Eugene asked. "Did someone find it? Is everything inside?"

Quinn nodded to him while she took down the address from the fleet owner, and assured him she would be right there. Then she reminded Eugene he was meeting his agent for dinner in an hour, kissed him good-bye, and took a subway to an industrial part of Queens she had never seen.

It was just after rush hour, and as she walked from the subway stop to the address she was given, Quinn noticed that once she turned the corner past the el tracks, the wide sidewalks were nearly deserted. The businesses, which seemed to be mostly body shops or odd little factories, were closed or closing, their metal garage doors pulled shut and padlocked.

Quinn appreciated that the fleet owner offered to stay and wait for

her, but she understood it was probably Eugene's celebrity status that
made him go out of his way. If he had opened the briefcase to discover
it belonged to an anonymous businessman instead of one of New York's
famous personalities, he might not have phoned so quickly, and almost
definitely wouldn't have made the call himself.

It was such an unglamorous part of town that Quinn expected Lewis
Braverman to be the kind of man her mother would refer to as a schlub—
overweight and badly dressed, with questionable hygiene. So she was
shocked when she rang the security bell and a trim, good-looking man
opened the door. He was young—about her age—and had a messy mop
of dark hair and black-brown eyes that looked from her to the horizon
in a way that suggested he was trying hard not to seem distracted. He
looked back at her face.

"Lewis?" She felt off-kilter, even a little annoyed, as if this guy had no
right to be so attractive.

"Quinn?" He looked as if he were experiencing similar awkwardness.

She smiled and extended her hand. "Thanks so much for calling . . .
and for waiting for me."

He hesitated before responding, and then didn't speak, but simply
shrugged, as if it were nothing. It was such a small, humble gesture that
her annoyance dissolved. His eye contact remained direct and warm, and
she figured he was the type of guy who was a little quiet until he got to
know you. She found it endearing. Guys with too much charm made her
suspicious.

He looked past her again at the sky and she turned to see what he was
looking at. Thin gray clouds lined the horizon.

"You think it's going to rain?" she asked.

"Not today," he said, and invited her in. She followed him up a narrow flight of stairs.

"You're nothing like I pictured you," she said, hoping to make the
conversation flow a little easier.

They reached the offices upstairs, which were also a surprise. The late-day sun streamed in through large windows, lighting a warm and modern space.

He turned to face her. "You're almost exactly as I pictured you," he said.

She was surprised by the admission and waited for him to elaborate, but he was done. Quinn felt a little disappointed, as it would have been a small, sweet ego boost to hear this toothsome guy pay her a compliment. *I could tell you were pretty by the sound of your voice,* he might have said. Just as well he hadn't, though. She didn't want to be tempted to flirt with him. Flirting was just out of the question.

Wasn't it?

"When you called and said you ran a taxi fleet, my subconscious immediately plugged in an image of—" She paused, trying to remember the name of the actor who played Louie, the dispatcher, on the TV show *Taxi.*

"Danny DeVito?" he offered.

She laughed. "That's it!"

He smiled at her then, and something happened. It was as if they each sensed and acknowledged a connection simultaneously. Quinn experienced it as a small electrical charge emanating from her heart outward. Later, she would try to convince herself it was nothing more than a mutual physical attraction. But a sexual current is blood hot, and while this thing may have been bubbling at its core, it was surrounded in a bright white fiber-optic glow. It felt . . . happy.

Lewis led her from the bullpen to his private office, where she saw Eugene's briefcase flat on his desk.

"I hope you don't mind that I looked through some of the papers," he said. "Had to find a phone number to call."

"Not at all," she said.

"You work for him?"

It was the moment of truth, the opportunity for her to say, *No, he's my boyfriend.* Then Lewis Braverman would say, *I see,* and that would be that. Instead, she flushed and pretended she thought he was asking what she did for a living. "No, I uh . . . I'm a special-events coordinator for Baston's Books. It's on the West Side?"

She said the last part as a question, which Lewis Braverman seemed to think was funny. "I know Baston's," he said. "I do get out of Queens once in a while."

"I didn't mean—"

He waved off an apology, smiling to let her know he'd been teasing. He picked up Eugene's briefcase but held it out of her reach, a hostage. "Are you in a hurry to get back?"

She paused and swallowed. She wasn't. She wasn't in a hurry at all. Eugene was having dinner with his agent and she had been planning to nuke a Lean Cuisine.

"Well . . ." she began, trying to buy time to think of a response.

"Ever seen a real taxi garage?"

It was the perfect thing for him to say. If he had asked her out to dinner, she'd have to say no. But a tour of the garage was perfectly innocent.

"Is it that different from the TV show?" she asked.

"The TV show doesn't smell like body odor and gasoline."

"When you put it like that, how could a girl resist?"

IN BED THAT NIGHT, when Eugene pressed her about her evening, she admitted that she had "grabbed a bite" with the taxi fleet owner. She hadn't told him that she and Lewis had hit if off so well that going out for dinner after touring the garage felt less like a decision than the continuation of a conversation that wouldn't be stopped. Nevertheless, Eugene went on the offense immediately, as she knew he would. He was always paranoid that she would leave him, and in fact every time a big-name

male author appeared at her store he would cross-examine her. She and
Eugene had met when he did a signing of his memoir at Baston's, and
he was always certain some Hollywood version of a dashing author—a
John Irving type, complete with good hair and a healthy build—would
swoop in and run off with her. She was always able to roll her eyes and
tell him to shut up and stop being stupid. This time, however, she bit at
her cuticle and tried to change the subject.

"How old is he?" Eugene said.

"You didn't tell me what happened with Andrew," she said, referring
to his agent. "What about that offer?" There had been some discussion
of a cable network interested in giving Eugene his own talk show, and
while his agent had cautioned that these talks don't usually pan out, there
was enough momentum for it to warrant a serious meeting.

"I bet he's young. Is he young?" Eugene was fifteen years older than
Quinn and, depending upon which particular neurosis he was indulging
at any given moment, was sure it was either the reason she was with him
or the reason she would leave him.

She looked at Eugene's profile. His lower lip naturally protruded just
a bit so that it was hard to tell if he was pouting. It didn't matter, though.
Quinn found it sexy. She loved that fleshy lip. She pulled off her nightgown and kissed him there.

They made love, and Eugene, always tender and caring, was almost
obsequious in his attentions. She knew he was trying hard to prove
himself to her, to be the best possible lover, and it made her feel guilty.
Eugene loved her so desperately. It was, of course, part of the whole
appeal of the relationship. Other women might feel smothered by that
level of adoration, but to Quinn it felt like sinking into a feather bed,
comfortable and protected. The fact that Eugene needed her so urgently
made the whole package feel complete. She did her job by taking care of
him. He repaid her with worship.

The next morning she had decided she would put Lewis Braverman out of her mind completely, but when he showed up for the Tom Perrotta reading at her bookstore that night, a buzz of joy lit through her.

HER MOTHER WAS still alive back then, and the next day, Quinn called to ask how the preparations for her gallery show were going. Quinn had no intention of bringing up the whole business with Lewis, as her mother had become close to Eugene. He was the only person who teased Nan about her bipolar disorder, and she adored him for it. Eugene appreciated that there was someone else in Quinn's life who had a personality bigger than his. Their banter had a life of its own.

"What'd you think of the Pamela Anderson segment today?" Eugene had once asked Nan. He knew she listened to his show religiously.

"That Mark Schaeffer made you sound like an idiot," she said, referring to an outspoken guest on the show.

"Are you kidding? I wiped the floor with him."

"Keep telling yourself that, Eugene."

"You know, with you it's hard to know where mental illness ends and just being a plain pain in the ass begins."

Nan laughed and laughed. She loved Eugene for remarks like that. So no, Quinn wasn't going to bring up the fact that she had met a guy who had, in the words her brother might have used, "rocked her world."

"Just wanted to see how your setup was going," Quinn said over the phone to her mother. "You need any help?"

"What's the matter?" Nan asked.

"What do you mean?"

"I can hear it in your voice. Something's wrong."

Quinn poured herself a cup of coffee and lowered the radio in the kitchen. It was broadcasting Eugene's show, which was on five days a week during morning drive time. She could hear it in the background at her mother's house, too.

"Nothing's wrong," she insisted.

"Fine, so don't tell me."

Quinn sighed. "Okay," she said, taking a seat at the kitchen table. "I met this guy."

"Ah."

"Don't say 'ah' like that."

"Like what?"

"Like you knew this day would come." Sometimes it was comforting to know that her mother understood her so well, but when she acted as if every decision Quinn made was easier to anticipate than getting wet in a rainstorm, it made her crazy.

"I'm not judging you," Nan said.

"I didn't say you were judging me."

"Because even if you're fucking this guy—"

"*Mo-om!*"

"What did I say?"

Quinn blew on her coffee. "Never mind."

Nan wore her bluntness like a badge. Growing up, Quinn assumed all adult women spoke like that and figured she, too, would one day care more about directness than people's feelings. Then puberty hit, and Quinn, like most teens, learned to be acutely embarrassed by her mother. And while she outgrew the mortification, she embraced the notion that she would never be so ungentle with her words.

"So you're not sleeping with him?" Nan asked.

"No."

"But you want to."

"I guess. I don't know."

"What's he like?"

Quinn took a careful sip of her coffee and considered the question. "He's . . . smart, sweet. And get this: he's a weather geek. Meteorology is his *hobby*. He has equipment on his roof."

"You always had a weakness for nerdy guys," Nan said. "What does he do?"

"He has his own business."

"Successful?"

"I guess. He's not showy about it. And he's intense, but not in the same way as Eugene. More . . . introspective."

"And not neurotic, I'll bet."

"How did you know?"

"What else?" Nan asked. "What's his family like?"

"Not really sure. I know his parents were divorced when he was small. He was the man of the house by the time he was five."

"I see."

"What do you see?"

Quinn listened to her mother breathing and knew she was considering how to phrase her response for maximum impact.

Nan cleared her throat and spoke. "Kiddo, who does this man remind you of?"

Quinn hesitated. What was her mother getting at? "I have no idea."

"Let's see . . . who do you know that's smart, sweet, a little nerdy, and took care of their mother from a very young age?"

Quinn peered into the coffee cup, examining her own reflection in the liquid. "You make it sound like we're carbon copies," she said, "like I'm some kind of narcissist for liking him."

"Not a narcissist. It's natural to be attracted to people we have a lot in common with."

"You were always so sure I was attracted to needy men."

"People can like both chocolate *and* vanilla. But when given a choice, there's always a natural preference."

"Meaning what? You think I'm destined to wind up with a neurotic guy?"

"If a man isn't desperately needy, my little caretaker, you have no use for him."

QUINN DECONSTRUCTED, NO. I

It was Nan's third attempt at this same canvas. She stood back and assessed the work, trying to remember what had sparked the idea to do a series of portraits of her daughter. The concept was that each subsequent painting in the series would depict her at a younger age, giving the viewer more insight into the subject by seeing her go back in time. It was a study in deconstruction. Now Nan questioned her own motives. Was this really about art, or was she simply trying to learn something about her own daughter?

The composition in this first painting was key. Quinn was in a classical portrait position, sitting in a chair and looking out into the distance. In the foreground on the right Nan had painted the back of Eugene's head. The idea was that Quinn was aware of Eugene's presence but not at this moment communicating with him. She was thinking about her future. Was she envisioning children? Travel? Excitement? Or was she worried about how hard it would be to spend the rest of her life tending to his needs? Nan had tried to depict some of that worry around her eyes, along with hope. Now the latter part concerned her. Had she captured the hope, or would the viewer see only worry?

Nan retrieved her thinnest brush and dipped it in the white paint on her palette. She gave each eye a tiny highlight within the pupil. She stood back again. No, the worry in her face still seemed to be the whole story. Maybe if she repainted the mouth . . .

4

"Are you drawing chickens again?" Quinn asked.

She had kept Isaac home from school even though his throat felt better. He sat at the kitchen table with her, coloring on the sketch paper she had given him. It was from an unused pad she had found in her mother's studio after she died.

"I'm drawing ducks," Isaac said. "And a house." The whole drawing was rendered in blues and greens, using the crayons he had pulled from his box of Crayola 64.

"Do the ducks live in the house?" she asked.

"They're visiting."

He sounded so earnest it made Quinn smile. Isaac took the red-orange crayon from the box and used it to draw the ducks' bills and the roof of the house. He put the crayon back in its place, moved the page aside and started on another drawing.

Quinn remembered her mother telling her about how Rembrandt had used red to draw the eye into the center of a painting. Had Isaac just done that instinctively?

She kept the question to herself because she didn't want to make him self-conscious about his process. But she often wondered if he had a vision before he began or if the process was entirely organic.

A short while later, Quinn's next-door neighbor, Georgette, stopped by for a visit. She was a plump, middle-aged woman who dyed her hair burgundy red, wore green eyeliner under her lower lashes, wrote erotic romance novels, and was on her fourth husband. She had a habit of telling Quinn intimate details of her sex life the same way some people talk about their vacations or their pets or what they'd had for dinner—that is, with more detail than anyone else would possibly want to know. For instance, Quinn knew that Georgette's first husband, Ivan, had insisted every lovemaking session start with a blow job, and that he never reciprocated. She knew that her second husband, Clifford, liked her to insert a dildo in his backside before they had sex. (The graphic details of that one left Quinn more than a little nauseated.) Juan, Georgette's third husband, had a stash of porn that he spent every Sunday afternoon with. And Roger, her current spouse, thought she didn't know he took Viagra. Of course, Georgette had her own secret, which was that she was carrying on a cyber affair with a thirty-one-year-old landscape architect in Miami.

The flip side of this openness was that she expected Quinn to share with equal abandon. Quinn, of course, wasn't as comfortable as her neighbor in exposing such intimacies. But Georgette had a way of drawing even the most guarded information from her. It was a kind of magic charm she had. Quinn didn't know whether it was her neighbor's non-judgmental aura, or simply the way people responded to Georgette's obsessive curiosity. She only knew that nearly everyone who came in contact with Georgette was susceptible to her psychological truth serum.

Today Georgette came bearing a freshly baked banana bread. "I noticed the little guy didn't get on the bus this morning," she said. "Just wanted to make sure everything was okay."

Quinn folded her arms. "Georgette," she began, trying to think of a way to remind her friend that she needed to mind her own business.

"I know, I know," she said, pushing her way past Quinn into the house. "I'm your Gladys Kravitz. Where's my little honeybun?"

"Kitchen," Quinn said, following her. "Who's Gladys Kravitz?"

"Didn't you ever watch *Bewitched*? The nosy neighbor always wanted to know Sam and Darrin's business." She knelt down by Isaac. "How do you feel, honeybun? Auntie Georgette made you banana bread. Would you like some?"

"You're supposed to ask the mother first," Quinn said.

"Oh! I'm sorry. Is he allergic?"

Quinn sighed. "Good thing you're so adorable, Georgette. Give him a slice if he wants it. I'll put up coffee."

"Of course he wants it. Don't you, Isaac?" She held it under his nose. "Smells good, doesn't it?"

"Like banana shampoo," he said.

"Tastier, I hope. Who are you drawing? Is that you?"

"Harry, my friend from school."

"Cute. Is he married?"

Isaac laughed and Georgette mussed his hair. "So is he sick or what?" she said to Quinn. "He looks okay to me."

Quinn explained that Isaac had complained of a sore throat during the night, but seemed better this morning.

Georgette rummaged through Quinn's utensil drawer, pulled out a bread knife, and cut into the loaf. "How are *you* feeling?" she asked.

Quinn stopped dropping scoops of coffee grounds into her French press and realized she had lost count. "Damn it!"

"What's the matter?"

"Nothing," Quinn said, hoping Georgette wouldn't push it.

Georgette put her hand on her friend's back. "Are you okay?"

Quinn shrugged, unable to speak. She didn't want to tell Georgette about the baby—not yet, anyway—and she certainly didn't want to break down. *You don't have to tell her*, Quinn coached herself. *It's none of her business.*

"Oh, God. Is it the baby? Is something wrong?"

That was it. The river rose with a rumble deep in Quinn's throat and the dam burst. She covered her face.

Georgette ushered Isaac into the den, where she turned on the television for him before coming back into the kitchen. "What is it?" she said, taking a seat at the table. "Did something happen at your appointment yesterday?"

Quinn nodded.

"Do you want to talk about it?"

A salty drop found its way to Quinn's lips. She caught it with her tongue. "They think something's wrong with my baby," she whispered, and closed her eyes. Hearing herself say it out loud made it more real than she could bear. And then, in a flood, she let it all out, spilling everything about what she'd learned from the doctors. Georgette handed her a tissue; Quinn blotted her eyes and wiped her nose.

"What does Lewis say?"

"Nothing. That's what makes it so hard. He doesn't say anything."

"That's the way men are. They can put their emotions on hold and go about like nothing's wrong. He'll open up eventually."

"There's so much we need to talk about and he just . . . he won't let me."

Georgette patted her hand. "I know."

"I miss her," Quinn said, and her friend nodded. They'd had enough conversations about Quinn's mother for Georgette to understand the shorthand.

"Do you want to go today? I can stay with Isaac."

When Quinn needed to talk to her mother, she drove to her parents' house and spoke to Nan's paintings. She thought, perhaps, she could glean some wisdom, as if her dead mother could help solve her problems. Sometimes, though, she went hoping to understand more about her mother's death. Intellectually, Quinn understood bipolar disorder, and knew that when her mother fell into a depression it was a chemical imbalance and not a personal affront. But suicide? That was the part Quinn didn't get. Why couldn't she get help? Didn't she love them enough to move past it? No matter what anyone said, and no matter what Quinn understood from all the books and articles she'd read, her mother had left her.

What these visits really did for Quinn was unleash her grief. There, alone in the studio with no one but the paintings to hear her, Quinn could miss her mother with all the messy emotional drama she couldn't otherwise face. It was excruciating, but afterward, she felt lighter.

Quinn glanced toward the den where Isaac sat quietly, and wondered if he felt well enough for her to leave him with Georgette for an hour or so. She knew he loved being with their colorful neighbor, but she didn't want to abandon him if he was under the weather.

"He's fine," Georgette said, reading her thoughts.

"You sure you don't mind?"

"How else would I get a chance to snoop through your personal things?"

IT WAS BARELY OCTOBER, and Quinn's father, a retired attorney, had already packed up and moved to Florida for the fall-winter season. Since he had met Jillian there three years ago, he was leaving New York earlier and earlier in the season. She was a divorced jewelry designer who lived in West Palm Beach year round. At first, Quinn couldn't believe her father had chosen someone so opposite from her mother. Nan had dark, wild hair; a full figure; and dressed in bohemian clothes so long before it became chic that she used to draw hard stares in the supermarket. Jillian, on the other hand, was a reed-thin fashionista, with spiky white-blond hair and perfect manicures. Eventually, Quinn came to understand that her father was attracted to Jillian because she was an artist of sorts, and had a strong personality—the very things that had drawn him to Nan.

It was just as well that Quinn was taking the opportunity to stop by today, since she liked to visit the empty house at least once a week to make sure everything was in order.

The house was on the North Shore of Long Island, several winding miles west of where Quinn and Lewis lived. Her parents had bought it before the community became fashionable. When she was growing up there with her parents and brother, Hayden, it was just a big, old Tudor that needed constant repairs, and not a coveted piece of Gold Coast real estate. Quinn loved the place, and understood that it was a part of her, and what made her know she could only ever live in an old house. New homes always felt so sterile, so lifeless.

Quinn threw her handbag on the hall table and did a lap around the first floor to make sure everything looked okay. She had heard there were a few burglaries in the area over the past several weeks, and though she doubted anyone could break in without tripping the alarm, she needed to see for herself. If there was anything that could push Quinn's buttons, it was the idea of being robbed. She just couldn't find any way to excuse the selfishness that went into taking something that didn't belong to you.

Once a professional thief in Manhattan had clipped an expensive gold bracelet off her wrist, though she didn't realize it until later. It was during dinner at an Italian restaurant with Eugene that she discovered the jewelry missing and understood what had happened. She had given directions to a young man at the corner of Fifty-ninth Street and Lexington Avenue. At the time, she didn't think much of the fact that he didn't move a step even after she pointed him in the direction of the subway station he had asked about. But replaying the scene in her mind, she realized he'd been holding a magazine in such a way that it covered his right hand. He must have been concealing a clipper. By the time she walked away, no doubt her bracelet was already on the sidewalk, and all he had to do was pick it up and be on his way.

Eugene had told her it was insanity, but she insisted on going back to the corner to look for the thief.

"What are you planning to do if you find him, Batgirl? You left your utility belt at home."

"I'll call the police."

"He won't be there anyway."

"How do you know? Maybe he's working the corner."

"Fine," Eugene said, signaling the waiter. "But I'm not leaving before I get my tiramisu. Nothing worse than a vigilante with a cranky sidekick."

Of course, when they got to the scene of the crime, the thief was nowhere in sight. But Quinn still looked for his face every time she passed that corner.

Quinn made sure the house was in order by checking all the rooms. The master bedroom had long ago been cleared of all her mother's things, but she worried what the criminals might do if they broke in and didn't find jewelry, as she had heard that their modus operandi was to break in through a back door, go directly to the master bedroom where every woman kept her jewelry box, and dash out with it before the police had a chance to respond to the alarm.

Quinn decided that on her next visit she would bring a dummy jewelry box, fill it with pebbles, lock it, and leave it on the dresser. She smiled at the thought.

She went downstairs and into her mother's art studio, an expansive room her father had built onto the back of the house so that Nan would have a sunny place to work. The room was bright with the kind of late-morning light Quinn's mother would have described as bland. It was neither the high white light of summer nor the crisp shadowy light of winter, but a hybrid, lacking in drama. Outside, the woods tried to make up for it, with a smattering of autumn colors making their debut on a few random treetops.

The painting Quinn usually talked to was the one her mother had been working on when she died. It was still resting on the easel, covered with a white sheet that Quinn had recently laundered. She did small things to keep the room from falling into disrepair, but it was, for the most part, just as her mother had left it. Quinn didn't think of it as a shrine, exactly, just a place where her mother's energy lingered. Quinn inhaled. All she got was a faint whiff of Windex. She could smell none of her mother's cologne. Even the paint fumes were gone. It had just been too long.

After the suicide, Quinn's father couldn't bear dealing with the studio and the calls from art dealers interested in buying Nan's paintings, so he left Quinn in charge. In the aftermath of her mother's death, it had been easy to brush off the callers, telling them no decisions to sell were being made "at the current time." But that was seven years ago, and Quinn was still procrastinating. She felt as if she were waiting for something to happen, something that would change and make it feel right to sort through the paintings and decide which ones they could actually part with.

Every so often Quinn got a call from Ellis Everett, the art dealer who had managed Nan's gallery showings, saying he had an interested buyer he wanted to bring to the studio. Again and again, Quinn blew him off. Ellis warned that she should, at the very least, be sure all the paintings were framed and mounted for preservation. The stretchers, he said, would eventually warp if she just left them leaning against the walls. He was right, of course, and Quinn knew she had to do something about them very soon. Seven years was just too long to go on ignoring that stack of unframed canvases.

Quinn pulled the cover off the easel and stared at the unfinished painting she'd been talking to all these years. It was a landscape in thickly layered acrylics, with a small hill in the foreground and a lush forest of green trees behind it. If one looked hard enough, one could see a figure amid the greenery. It was this tiny, dark image that Quinn spoke to as if it were her mother.

Today, though, it looked like just paint on a canvas. She simply couldn't muster an emotional connection to Nan by focusing on it. Quinn wandered around the perimeter of the studio, stopping at the stack of unframed canvases that held the one painting she couldn't bear to look at.

All the paintings in this group were family portraits. Hayden, her brother, stared out at her from the top canvas. Nan loved color and had painted him in warm sage and cool turquoise, with tiny pink accents pulling the eye to the ruby stud in his earlobe. She had captured something essential about Hayden in the eyes, which looked as if they were trying to charm the viewer. *Love me*, they said. *Just love me.*

Quinn didn't have to move the portrait of Hayden to know what was behind it. First there was a portrait of her father in a van Gogh–like palette of golden wheat colors. Parts of his face were old and parts were young, and some people saw it as some kind of statement about Nan's bipolar disorder. But Quinn disagreed. She thought her mother was trying to show that when she looked at him she saw the young man he was and the mature man he became.

Behind the portrait of her father was the one Quinn couldn't face. It was supposed to be a portrait of Quinn, but Nan had chosen to include the two of them—mother and daughter—in the painting. They were portrayed on opposite sides of a door. Nan was on a stool, facing the viewer head on. Quinn was in profile, her hand on the door, her head down.

"What do you see?" Nan had asked Quinn after she finished it.

"You're locking me out," Quinn had said, angry that her mother would paint such a thing. Days later Nan took her own life, and Quinn understood that the painting was a suicide note. Nan was envisioning herself on the other side. And even though she couldn't bear to look at it, Quinn knew it was the one painting she would never sell. It represented an intimate message from mother to daughter. It was meant for Quinn alone.

Quinn walked back to the painting on the easel and covered it with the sheet. Today she wouldn't talk to her mother. She couldn't. She left the studio and shut the door, stopping to mimic her portrait self by pressing her palm against it.

She wanted to sense her mother's presence, to get some reassurance that everything would be okay. But the house felt cold and empty.

5

In the car ride on the way to her appointment for a targeted sonogram, Quinn silently prayed the whole thing had been a mistake and that this more sophisticated test would prove it. But the icy climate of the exam room, where she couldn't make out a word of the carefully mumbled whispers among the medical staff, told her all she needed to know. By the time Quinn had put her clothes back on and sat across the desk from the specialist called in to review the results of the ultrasound, she had already lost hope.

Dr. Robert LeBrun, a pediatric geneticist, was sixtyish, gray haired, and imposingly large, even seated. As he spoke, he kept his meaty fingers entwined on his desk.

His appearance was in sharp contrast to that of Quinn's obstetrician, Dr. Sally Bernard, a petite African American woman who sat to Quinn's right. She was about Quinn's age, and the two women had a relationship that bordered on personal. Dr. Bernard was a devoted reader, and so they made a habit of discussing books during Quinn's appointments. (Quinn found this an especially useful distraction during internal exams.) Apparently, they'd had enough casual conversations for Dr. Bernard—*Sally*—to feel comfortable confiding in Quinn, who understood that her ob-gyn was not required to be at this meeting. Yet there she was, despite being in the midst of a messy divorce involving three young children, including one still in diapers. With Lewis holding her left hand and Sally holding her right, Quinn tried to imagine she could draw strength from the completed circuit.

"I understand this is a lot to take in," Dr. LeBrun kept saying, and Quinn would nod solemnly, confused by the concern in his eyes. Why was everyone so worried about *her*? It was the baby they should have been upset about. The baby.

He went on to say something about there being no additional associated malformations, as if that were a piece of good news she could hang her hat on. He also said that the condition wasn't genetic, and that it wasn't caused by anything she had or hadn't done. These, she supposed, were meant to be words of comfort but they were like feathers swatting at swords, and did nothing to protect her from such piercing words as "significant cosmetic abnormalities" and "cognitive and possibly life-threatening issues."

Dr. LeBrun explained that it was too early to tell if the sac protruding through the opening in the baby's skull contained brain tissue or "just membrane." Apparently, this was a key factor in the baby's prognosis, though Quinn had drifted to such a disassociated place that it was hard to follow his point.

"If you decide to continue with the pregnancy," he said, "we'll do a follow-up three-dimensional ultrasound at twenty weeks, as well as an MRI."

He unclasped his hands as he talked about termination options and how long they would have to make a decision. The computer screen beside him was turned to face Quinn and Lewis, and frozen on the monitor was an image of their baby girl's skull in shades of gray. A small, jagged line appeared between her eye sockets, extending upward. It looked so insignificant, the kind of thing Quinn never would have noticed if it hadn't been pointed out.

Occasionally Dr. Bernard interjected, asking Quinn and Lewis if they had any questions. Lewis asked for clarity on a few points, but Quinn kept floating further away until the words just bounced off the walls of the room, with no place to go.

Later, in the car on the way home, Quinn put her hand on her abdomen, trying to connect with her baby, as if this tiny fetus could tell her what the future held. One by one, Quinn played out each medical scenario, testing to see which one felt most likely. Her daughter could be born alive, with a correctible abnormality. She could have surgery that would leave her with a normal appearance and no brain damage. Or the surgery could be only partially successful, leaving the child with any combination of blindness, impairment, or disfigurement. Or she could die within her first days of life, after she'd already nursed at Quinn's breast, her tiny fist wrapped around her mother's finger. She could even die in utero, before she and Lewis got a chance to name her.

Naomi, Quinn thought, as she gently stroked her belly. It was the name she and Lewis had agreed on before she even found out what it meant. Now she couldn't remember if she had ever told him that she'd discovered a definition.

"Do you know what Naomi means?" she asked.

Lewis remained quiet.

"It means 'my delight,'" Quinn said. Delight. She felt the word dissolve on her tongue like cotton candy.

Lewis looked at her and then back at the road. "Are you okay?"

"I don't want to have an abortion," she said into her chest.

Lewis focused on the road. "I don't think we need to talk about that now," he said.

"What do you mean?"

"They said we have time to decide that. We should at least wait for the results of the amnio, don't you think?"

"And then what?"

"I don't know," he said. "We'll hear what they say."

"Do you think they'll tell us something different? Dr. LeBrun even said he expects the amnio to be inconclusive."

Her husband didn't respond.

"Lewis?"

"I need time to think about this, okay? This is a lot. This is a lot to take in."

"Why does everybody keep saying that?"

"What else am I supposed to say?" he asked. "Should I pretend nothing's wrong?"

"That's not what I meant. I just want to know what you're thinking. I want to know how you feel about all this."

"I feel like I can't absorb this now, okay? I need some time, Quinn. I don't process everything in a millisecond like you do."

Is that what she normally did? Processed everything in a millisecond? She didn't feel like that now. Didn't feel like she was processing a thing. Some of the terms the doctor used were still floating around her consciousness like flotsam at sea. What was it he had said about surgical options? Something about "craniotomy" and "microplates"? Lewis had asked questions about the risks, and he said that many of these, such as hydrocephalus, were manageable.

"But brain damage," Lewis had said. "What about brain damage?"

"We'll have a better idea of that when we do the follow-up MRI," the doctor had said.

"But you won't know for sure?"

"Probably not."

That was the point at which Quinn excused herself to the ladies' room. She wanted only to splash cold water on her face, to try to wake herself up, pull herself into the present. But something happened in the bathroom that made her heart race with fear, and slammed her back into place with more force than she could handle.

After being bombarded with an overload of medical information, she had entered the ladies' room in a daze and approached the sink without much thought. Eyes closed, Quinn splashed cold water on her face and reached for the faucet to turn it off. That's when she sensed it. Before she made contact with the chrome knobs, she felt a mild sensation of solid air beneath her hands. It was almost like pushing against wind—nothing but a force, a mass of atmosphere giving resistance. She opened her eyes and saw it: a crack in the porcelain where it met the drain. This time, Quinn didn't jump back. Instead, she brought her fingertips up to the jagged line. The layer of air between her skin and the solid surface remained constant, forcing the crack to widen. Quinn brought her face closer to see what was happening, but she saw nothing more than expanding darkness. She closed her hand into a fist and continued pushing. The fissure became a hole, and the harder she pressed, the deeper it became, until her hand had disappeared up to her elbow. She stuck her other hand inside and pressed her palms together. Quinn closed her eyes and sensed Eugene's energy, feeling as if the scent of his aftershave were lingering around her nostrils. He seemed so close by that his nervousness was almost palpable, but so was something else—excitement. Quinn didn't know what Eugene was happy about, but she sensed it wasn't career related. No, this had to do with his personal life—with *their* personal life. Quinn tilted her head, wondering if she should dive in to find out. Just then the ladies' room door opened and an old woman entered. Quinn withdrew her hands and stood there, trembling, as she realized what she had very nearly done.

Now, in the car, Quinn tried to envision life a day, week, or year beyond the birth of this baby, but it was impossible. She looked out the window. It was a lot to take in.

6

THAT NIGHT, WHEN LEWIS GOT HOME FROM WORK, HE STILL wasn't ready to talk. He'd had a rough day. One of his drivers was in the hospital after a bad accident, and it left Lewis shaken. After dinner, he went straight upstairs to check the data on his weather station, a digital box that connected to a barometer, an altimeter, a rain gauge, and other equipment on the roof of the house. He sometimes told Quinn that accurate weather forecasts were important for his business, as it helped to know the road conditions his drivers would face in the coming hours. But she had always sensed it calmed him to know exactly what the heavens were about to deliver.

The next morning was more of the same. Lewis simply wasn't ready or willing to talk. It wasn't the first time he had shut down, heaven knows, but Quinn was usually able to accept his reticence with patience. It was his way of gaining some control when life got stormy. He couldn't will the rain clouds from the horizon, but he could control how he would react to them.

Quinn watched from the window in Isaac's bedroom as her husband walked toward his car. Georgette must have been watching from her own window as she trotted over to chat with him. Quinn turned her attention back to her son.

"You have to pick up your pajamas, Isaac."

"But the hamper is full," he said.

The hamper. Of course. Quinn had been ignoring the laundry altogether, as she couldn't face going down into that basement. But the clothes were piling up, and they were getting harder and harder to avoid.

Later, after Isaac left for school, Quinn dumped the dirty clothes into a laundry basket and carried it down to the first floor, where she paused. The thought of what had happened in the hospital bathroom after the sonogram made facing that ironing board harder than ever.

If she entered the basement today, would she go into a similar trance? Would the lure of escape be too much to bear? She looked back at the pile of dirty clothes in the basket. Maybe she should just take them to a Laundromat and be done with it.

Ridiculous, she told herself. I'll run downstairs, throw the clothes in the washer, and run back up. It's not like I have no control.

Quinn picked up the cordless phone and dialed her mother-in-law, whom she owed a call. She kept it tucked under her chin as she lifted the basket and went into the basement. If she stayed on the phone while doing the laundry, she reasoned, it would keep her from being tempted to open the ironing board.

"Sweetheart!" her mother-in-law said. "How are you? I just spoke to Lewis."

"You did?"

"Poor thing. He's beside himself."

"He told you about the sonograms?"

"Of course." Her tone implied that she was offended Quinn even asked, but that was her way. Lewis's mother had a huge heart, but was so insecure she perceived nearly every statement as a challenge she had to defend against. Tiptoeing around her insecurities sometimes left Quinn exhausted.

"I'm glad he told you. I'm sure you were a great comfort to him."

"All I did was listen, really. That's what you have to do with Lewis."

Arlene loved giving Quinn the Lecture on How to Talk to Lewis. Quinn switched the phone to her other ear. "Does Don know?" After being divorced from Lewis's father for almost twenty years, Arlene had remarried. Don was an affable guy—a mattress salesman with a painfully corny sense of humor.

"It's not like it's a *secret*, darling."

"I didn't—" Quinn sighed. "Never mind. How did Lewis sound? Was he very upset?" She opened the washer and started dropping in clothes.

"I've never heard him like that. He could barely speak."

"He was crying?"

"Heavens, yes."

Quinn measured the liquid detergent and poured it around the agitator onto the dirty clothes. "What did he say?"

"Not too much. Just told me how scared he was."

She closed the washer door and turned it on, confused and surprised by what her mother-in-law had told her. Lewis had been unable to talk to her, and yet opened up to his mother to the point where he cried and told her he was scared? She glanced over at the built-in ironing board, her heart racing.

"Quinn? Are you still there?"

"I'm here, Arlene. Sorry." She swallowed hard and walked up the stairs. "What were you saying?"

"I just want you to know I'm here if you need to talk."

After getting off the phone, Quinn tried to convince herself it really wasn't any big deal that Lewis had opened up to his mother and not to her. Perhaps he just didn't want to alarm Quinn with his own worry.

That made sense, didn't it? Lewis was always trying to protect her. But later, when his sister called to say she had been talking to Lewis all morning about how upset he was, Quinn couldn't take it anymore. She told her sister-in-law she had to go and dialed her husband's office.

"What's the matter?" he said.

"I don't understand why you can talk to everyone but me," Quinn said.

"Was I supposed to keep all this a secret? I thought my family had a right to know."

"I just don't want you to close me out."

Lewis promised he wasn't closing her out, but said he needed to hurry off the phone for an important appointment. Quinn hesitated before saying good-bye. Something about his tone tripped her suspicions. He was either hiding something or telling an outright lie. But he insisted he was rushed, so she let him go without pressing it.

"OH, HONEY," Georgette said as she threw her arms around Quinn. "I'm so sorry you didn't get better news from the doctors yesterday." She had, of course, dropped by unannounced.

"So you know," Quinn said.

"I spoke to Lewis earlier."

"Of course you did. C'mon in and tell me what he said. Apparently it's the only way I'm going to find out what my husband is thinking."

The two went into the kitchen, where Georgette helped herself by making a cup of tea using a mug that Quinn didn't usually offer her guests. It had been a present from Eugene, who gave it to her the day they met at Baston's Books.

It was a vivid memory for Quinn. Eugene had arrived at the store with his publicist, who approached Quinn to discuss the logistics of the event while Eugene was waylaid by fans. The crowd surrounding him was comprised of mostly women, which she understood. Though he was a far cry from handsome, he had a certain curmudgeonly charisma. Eugene had made a career of his crankiness, and each woman liked to think she was special enough to be the one who could break through and become the one shining beacon in his dark existence . . . if only he would get to know her. Being aware of this didn't make Quinn any less susceptible to his churlish charms. In fact, she had to fight the urge to push her way through the crowd and make her own specialness known.

But she had her chance after the event, when they had a few quiet moments to chat. He pulled out the coffee mug, which was a promotional item imprinted with the cover of his memoir, *Eugenics*. It showed a photograph of Eugene looking down at his crotch, surprised. It was a joke photo—the top half was Eugene's body, and the bottom half was the lower region of a Ken doll. The idea was that his reproductive organs had been removed, hence the title.

"Bet you don't have one of these," Eugene said as he showed it to her.

"No, but I was tempted to pick one up the other day at Tiffany's."

Eugene actually laughed at that, and Quinn was struck by how his face transformed when he smiled. His eyes disappeared into tiny slits, and the word that occurred to Quinn was *mirth*. When this man felt it, *you* felt it. Sure he was a sourpuss by nature, but underneath it was a reservoir of joy he guarded like a miser. When he decided to share it, you felt privileged indeed.

Eugene pulled a Sharpie from his pocket. He turned the mug upside down and wrote on the bottom, *To Quinn, who's my cup of tea.—Eugene Ray*.

Score.

Quinn looked up and watched as Georgette dipped her teabag into the mug and then fished it out with a spoon.

"I was so surprised," Georgette said as she wrapped the string around the teabag and squeezed out the moisture. "I didn't know you two were thinking about terminating."

"Is that what Lewis said?"

"He said it was an option."

Quinn wiped down the counter, which was still sticky from the peanut-butter-and-jelly sandwich she had packed for Isaac's lunch. "I see."

"Did I say the wrong thing? You know, honeybun, you don't have to do anything you don't—"

"It's not that," Quinn said. And it wasn't. She could accept whatever it was Lewis was feeling. But the thought that he could open up to everyone but her was too agonizing. Lewis was the one person in this world who loved her more than he needed her, and the idea of seeing him drift away was too much to bear.

QUINN DECONSTRUCTED, NO. 2

———+———

This would be another portrait that included Eugene. But here, it was the early days of their relationship, when Quinn was electrified by the idea of being the most important person in the life of a very important man. The composition was altered from the first, but only slightly. Eugene's head was higher in the frame and closer to the center. Quinn's eyes were focused directly on him and her expression was amused. Nan was careful in arranging her daughter's features, as it was important to convey something more complicated than happiness. She wanted Quinn to look self-satisfied.

Nan took a step back. The expression was just right, so why did she still feel that something was missing?

"Talk to me," she said to the painting.

She knew it couldn't answer back—not literally, anyway—but Nan felt something she couldn't put her finger on. It was almost as if there were another portrait on the other side of the canvas, and if she looked hard enough, she would be able to see it. The feeling confused her, as she thought she understood her daughter so well. Why, then, did she sense some mystery locked in a box she had no access to?

I'm not going in, Quinn thought as she oiled the hinges on the ancient ironing board, unless I know for sure I can get back. I'll just stick my head in, take a look, see what it's like. If it's a one-way journey I'll stay here, but at least I'll know. Just in case.

She put down the can of WD-40 and once again grabbed the top of the ironing board. This time she pulled it open three inches and closed it, testing the hinge. She did that a few times to let the oil work its way into the mechanism.

Okay, she thought. Now. Quinn closed her eyes and pulled the ironing board all the way down. She stood there a moment with her lids shut tight, feeling the energy from the other side, sensing her life with Eugene pulsing close by. Then she opened her eyes and looked.

Like the crack in the porcelain sink, the opening appeared as an ordinary fissure—a silvery jagged line against the rough concrete. This one was vertical, and almost three feet long. Quinn put her hand toward it, feeling that familiar resistance.

Quinn rose up onto her knees and ran both hands together down the length of the crack. She did it a second time, spreading her fingers like butterfly wings so that the fissure would be big enough to stick her head into.

She tested the ironing board then, pressing on it to determine if it would be able to hold her weight. It seemed that it would, but she pushed a chair beneath it, just in case. Then she climbed from the chair to the ironing board, and faced the fissure on all fours. She picked up her right hand and ran it down the length of the crack, feeling solid air press against her palm. She watched as the opening widened slightly. She tried it again, pushing her hand right into the wall, and the concrete disappeared, as if dissolved by the mass of air.

Quinn looked into the opening, her heart pounding. Though she could see nothing but blackness, she sensed Eugene's presence close by. She felt movement—a bustling kind of energy, as if Eugene were getting dressed and ready to go someplace. Quinn looked deep into the middle of the darkness and saw a small bit of light. It was nothing more than a pinprick, but her thumping heart began to race. Something was there.

The experience in the hospital bathroom wasn't the first time she had touched the other side. It had happened once, almost by accident, when she was a child. Years before that, though, she knew it existed. She always knew. It was just something she sensed. It hadn't frightened her until she asked her mother about it, when she was no more than four.

"Where is the other Quinn, Mommy?"

"What other Quinn?" her mother had said.

"The one who died."

Her mother got quiet for a very long time and Quinn thought she wasn't going to answer. Finally she said, "I don't know." Her voice sounded soft.

"But she's with her mommy?"

"I suppose so."

"I want to see them."

"We can't."

"But they're so close. Closer than Lima and Bean," Quinn said, referring to the nicknames Nan had given to Lindsay and Ben, the twins next door.

"How close?" her mother said.

Quinn pointed to a spot on the floor near the wall, where she had felt a connection to the baby self who had died with her mother. Nan looked frightened then and pulled Quinn close.

"Don't ever try to go there, Quinn. It would be dangerous. You have to stay with me. You understand?"

She heeded her mother's warning and eventually convinced herself none of it had even happened. The memory faded and all but vanished. Then, one day, when she was playing with Hayden in the backyard, it all became clear to her again—clearer than it had ever been. And from then on she understood that every big decision she made had an equal and opposite reality.

Quinn brought her face toward the fissure in her basement wall and pushed her head right inside the hole. She had to see, once and for all. The pinhole of light seemed to recede. She poked her head in farther but couldn't get any closer. It was moving away from her.

I should get a flashlight, she thought, and tried to back up. But she couldn't. Quinn was being pulled inside. She tried to fight it, tried to brace herself against the solid walls of the foundation, but the force was too strong, and suddenly her entire body was sucked inside the darkness. Terror seized her, but only for a second, and then it vanished like vapor. A calmness overtook her, and she floated gently as she was pulled along in the darkness. It was like swimming without effort, the air around her cozy and quiet. Quinn closed her eyes. The tranquillity was intoxicating, and she wanted the feeling to last. She lost track of time, lost any real sense of conscious thought. Slowly, an awareness entered her. She realized she was in warm water now, no longer in darkness.

With a jolt she was Quinn again. And she was underwater, in a very real place with three dimensions and an ordinariness that took her by surprise.

She sat up and looked around. She was in a warm bathtub, and everything about the room was familiar. The striped shower curtain, the sink, the toothbrushes. That was her blow dryer on the shelf above the commode, Eugene's Rogaine on the counter. All the consciousness of this life was as clear to her as her life with Lewis and Isaac. This was *her* bathroom, the one she shared with Eugene in the Manhattan high-rise they had moved into three years before. Eugene was on the other side of the door, dressing to go out. He was being interviewed about the award he had just been nominated for. Minutes earlier she hadn't known any of this. But now it was as if she had lived this life all along. She closed her eyes and pictured Isaac and Lewis. Yes, it was all still there. She was as present in one life as she was in the other. Quinn was straddling both worlds.

There was a sharp rap on the door.

"Are you going to be in there all day?" Eugene asked.

"I'll be right out," she heard herself say.

Quinn stepped out of the tub and put her hand on her stomach. No baby. No pregnancy. It was just her and Eugene. She looked back at the tub, her lifeline home.

"Did you call Isabel?" he yelled through the door.

"Not yet," she said. This too was clear to her. Isabel was their travel agent. They were going to Fiji next month on vacation, and Eugene had a list of requirements about the accommodations. Quinn was supposed to go over this checklist with Isabel.

She wrapped herself in the plush green robe that hung on a brass hook, then opened the bathroom door and stared at her bedroom and the man standing in the middle of it. It was Eugene, looking older than he had when they lived together, but the same in all other ways. His nervousness surrounded him like an impenetrable aura.

"Is this okay for the Plaza?" he asked, showing Quinn his outfit. He wore jeans and a blazer over a checked shirt. He was meeting a reporter from *People* for lunch. In this life, he had taken the cable television job and his star was rising.

The attraction she had once felt for him was still there, like muscle memory. His lower lip, red and just a little plump, protruded a tiny, sexy bit. She tied her robe tighter and tried to assess his appearance objectively.

"You look a little rumpled," she said.

"The shirt?"

She nodded.

Quinn studied him as he took off the blazer and threw it on the bed. His thin hair was thinner now, and more salt than pepper. But his posture was good and he moved well—his gym membership was paying off.

"The black?" he asked, opening his closet.

She shook her head. "The tan cotton sweater."

As he took it from the shelf in his closet and changed into it, Quinn glanced around the room. The landscape her mother had been working on when she died was hanging on the wall over the king-size bed. It looked bigger in this room, richer. Even the tiny figure seemed more distinct.

Eugene put his sport jacket back on and presented himself to Quinn. "Better?" he asked.

"Better," she said.

"I have to run." He kissed her on the mouth. His lips were dry and cool. "You won't forget to call Isabel?"

She followed him out of the bedroom into the living room. "I won't forget."

He opened the door to leave. "And the bed? You'll make sure it's firm? I couldn't sleep last time on that mush."

"Yes, I'll make sure. But don't worry. It's a luxury hotel."

"Right. I won't worry. Because, you know, I can always turn that off when you say so."

"It'll be fine."

He paused at the door and turned back to her, opening his palms to indicate he wanted one last assessment of his clothing.

"You look good," she said. "Hot. Susan Dennis won't be able to keep her hands off you. You'll wind up running off with her and leaving me all alone."

"You wish."

"See you later," she said.

"Bye, babe." He grabbed his keys from the table by the door, stuffed them into his pocket, and turned to leave. "I forgot to tell you," he said, turning back around. "Your mother called." Then he shut the door behind him.

Her mother?

Quinn sat on the couch. Her mother was alive? She looked down at the phone on the side table, trying to wrap her mind around that. Could she really pick it up and dial her parents' number in Long Island and talk to her mother? Her scalp prickled.

Quinn rose and paced the room. I shouldn't do this, she thought. I should go back into that bathroom and find a way back. I'm not this person. I'm not a single woman living in New York with her famous boyfriend. I'm not someone who can go to Fiji next month and stay in a luxury hotel with heated towel racks. I'm Quinn. I'm married to Lewis. I'm Isaac's mom. I'm pregnant with a damaged baby.

And my mother is dead.

Quinn picked up the phone and put it down again, her hands trembling. She went into the kitchen and looked around. The place should have been strange to her, but from the moment she emerged from that bathwater it was all hers.

She opened the cabinet and saw the mug imprinted with the cover of Eugene's book. She turned it over and examined the underside. Most of the inscription had worn off, but the tops of the letters were still there. It was the very same cup she had in her cabinet at home—the one Eugene had given her the day they met.

Quinn filled it with water and put it in the microwave. She'd have some herbal tea, get her wits about her, figure out what to do.

She ran her hand along the smooth counter. Everything about the place was so familiar, so ordinary, and yet. Yet this wasn't where she lived. This wasn't where her life was.

The microwave beeped and she took out the steaming cup. She opened the cabinet where she knew she kept the tea and then shut it, realizing that she could have a glass of wine, since she wasn't pregnant. She pulled a bottle from the wine rack and stopped herself. No, she thought. I can't do this. I have to get home. She went back to the bathroom, where she kneeled beside the tub and ran her fingers over the porcelain of the bottom, looking for the fissure.

It has to be here, she thought. It has to.

The phone rang and Quinn stopped what she was doing. Ignore it, she told herself. But on the second ring she rose and went into the bedroom, where there was an old phone on the nightstand next to the bed. It was a fifty-year-old collectible she and Eugene had bought in the Berkshires last fall. He had gotten a kick out of the fact that this heavy black relic— the kind of phone he remembered from his early childhood—was now an antique. And so they bought it, assured by the store owner that it worked. Of course, it had a heavy old dial and no caller ID, so they didn't use it much. But Eugene enjoyed the nostalgia of it.

It rang a third time and Quinn just stared. On the fourth ring she picked it up.

"Hello?" She had expected her own voice to sound strange, but it didn't. A bit nervous, maybe, but that was all. It was just her, Quinn, picking up the phone in her bedroom.

"Hi, kiddo," said the voice on the other end.

Quinn pulled her robe tighter against the sudden chill that ran through her. She swallowed against a lump in her throat before she could speak.

"Mom?"

8

"ARE YOU OKAY? YOU SOUND UPSET."

Quinn realized tears were spilling down her face. She wiped them with the back of her hand. "I'm . . . I'm okay."

"What's the matter?"

"Nothing. I'm just . . . catching a cold or something." Quinn covered her mouth so that her mother wouldn't hear her weeping. God, she was talking to her mother. Her *mother*!

"Of course you are. You hardly get any sleep. If you don't stop burning the candle at both ends . . ." Nan paused. "Are you crying?"

"Mommy." It was primal. Juvenile. She couldn't help it.

"You *are* crying. What is it?"

Quinn paused to regroup. She glanced around the room, trying to think fast. "Just . . . something dumb on TV." Quinn sniffed, attempting to recover.

"TV? Oh, for heaven's sake. Really, Quinn. If you want to cry, read a book or something."

"I know," Quinn said, smiling now through her tears. Her mother's disdain for television was practically legendary, and it comforted her to know she hadn't changed. She picked up a tissue and blew her nose. "Guilty pleasure."

"You're better off with chocolate. Or sex. But listen, Dad and I are going to be in the city on Monday to attend a gallery show, and I was wondering if you and Eugene were free for dinner. We can make it an early birthday celebration, since you'll be turning thirty-six in Fiji."

That's right, Quinn thought. The Fiji trip was a birthday present from Eugene. It was as clear as every birthday present he had bought her the past ten years in this life, each one more elaborate than the last. He did everything he could think of to keep her from leaving him. Everything except propose, that is. Eugene was freaked out by the thought of marriage.

"Dinner," Quinn said, "sure."

"Great. We'll meet at your apartment and then head over to that place on the corner. I'll call Hayden and see if he's free, too."

Quinn imagined standing in the living room of this apartment and seeing her mother in the flesh. She had to sit down on the bed to catch her breath.

"Quinn?"

"Yes. Okay, next Monday. I'll see you next Monday."

"Perfect. Bye, cookie."

"Wait!"

"What is it?"

Quinn pressed the heavy receiver into her face. She didn't want to let go. "Nothing," she said. "I'll talk to you later."

"You sure you're okay?"

"I'm sure."

"Okay," her mother said. "Love you."

Quinn swallowed. Fresh tears rolled down her cheeks. "Love you, too."

She hung up the phone and sat there, too stunned to go back into the bathroom and search for the portal. Or maybe the part of her that wanted to stay in this life and look into her mother's eyes again was short-circuiting the part that needed to get back to her husband and son.

Quinn found herself supine on the bed, staring up at the ceiling as she tried to recall her last good conversation with Nan in her "Lewis life," which was how she now thought about it. All she could remember was the final talk she'd had with her mother in her studio, and the stupid fight they'd had a few weeks before, on Thanksgiving.

Quinn and Lewis were newly married and excited to make the feast at their place. They lived in a renovated prewar apartment in Queens, and though it was spacious compared to the tiny Manhattan box Quinn had lived in after she moved out of Eugene's place, it had just enough room to fit the two families around the table. Quinn was tense about the get-together because she knew her mother wasn't too fond of Arlene, Lewis's mom, and made no effort to hide her feelings.

But all was going well, and when Arlene's husband asked Quinn what was new at the bookstore, she didn't think her response would be incendiary. She said that the latest event—a reading by an acclaimed novelist— had drawn an embarrassingly small crowd.

"Unfortunately, people just aren't reading much fiction these days," Quinn explained.

"Makes sense to me," Arlene said as she reached for the stuffing. She put half a spoonful on her plate.

"How so?" Nan asked, and Quinn tensed. This was just the kind of remark her mother could sink her teeth into.

Arlene took a deep breath. "I never did understand the whole appeal of novels." She straightened her earrings and then her bracelets. "Just open the newspaper any day. There are so many interesting things going on in *real* life to read about."

Just let it go, Mom, Quinn thought. But one glance in Nan's direction told her there wasn't a chance. Her mother was glaring at Arlene like a bull ready to charge.

"Arlene," she said, and paused, waiting for eye contact from Lewis's mother. "It's called *art*."

"You think I don't know what art is?" Arlene said. "Lewis, tell her how often I took you to the Metropolitan Museum when you were growing up."

"I'm sure you spent hours looking at all the pretty Impressionists," Nan said.

"What is that supposed to mean?" Arlene asked.

"Mom, stop," Quinn said.

Nan put up her hands. "Okay, okay. I'm done."

Arlene folded her arms. "Well, I'm not. I'd like to know exactly what you meant. You think I'm some sort of Philistine?"

Nan cut into her turkey. "You said it, I didn't."

Arlene looked as if she were about to get up and storm out, but her husband jumped in with a joke to defuse the situation. "Phyllis Dean, Phyllis Diller," he said. "Who cares?"

For once, Quinn was grateful for one of Don's corny puns. It broke the tension just enough for the conversation to move in another direction, though the mood remained strained throughout the meal. Later, when Arlene and Don had left and Quinn found herself alone in the kitchen with her mother, she was still furious.

"Did you really have to lay into Arlene like that?"

"She won't even remember it in the morning. Woman has the IQ of a rhododendron."

Quinn picked up the bowl of mashed sweet potatoes and started spooning the contents into a plastic container. "She'll remember. She's not stupid."

"Okay, right. She's brilliant, just incredibly shallow. Where am I putting the cranberry sauce?"

Quinn grabbed the small dish from her mother. "There's no law against being shallow! Not everyone shares your intensity, Mom. And yet they go about their lives and raise families and have every right to be treated with common decency."

"That woman just rubs me the wrong way. Always has."

"Of course—she's Lewis's mother. She'd rub you the wrong way no matter what."

"There you go again. I don't know why you always insist I have something against Lewis."

"Name one thing you've done to be supportive of my relationship with him." She folded her arms and leaned against the counter.

"I walked down the aisle at your wedding."

"Well. I didn't realize it was such a big favor. Thank you, Mom. Thank you for not boycotting my wedding ceremony. Big of you."

"What do you want from me?"

"I want you to admit that it drives you crazy seeing me in a normal, stable relationship."

"That's ridiculous."

"Is it? Remember when you said you didn't think I should leave Eugene for Lewis?"

"I never said I didn't think you *should*. I said I didn't think you *could*."

"Your confidence is inspiring."

"I think I should go."

"I think you should, too."

Two weeks later, when Quinn finally relented and called her parents' house, her father answered and told her Nan was still sleeping. Quinn worried that their fight had pushed her mother into a depression. She tried to remember how Nan had sounded at Thanksgiving. Was she talking fast? Had she seemed grandiose? If she had been in the midst of a manic episode, it was quite possible she had crash-landed into a depression. It wouldn't have been the first time.

"She's fine," her father said. "At least I think so. You know how she gets when she's holed up in that studio."

"What is she painting?"

He paused. "Why don't you come over and see?"

And so she did. But when she got to her mother's studio, she didn't think her mother was fine at all, despite what her father had said. Nan seemed lethargic and melancholy. She didn't usually paint when she was depressed, but Quinn was still concerned. She dispensed with rehashing the fight they'd had, and asked her mother if everything was okay.

"I'm just tired," she said.

"Are you taking your meds?"

"Of course."

Quinn squinted at her mother, trying to figure out if she was telling the truth.

"Isn't a person allowed to be tired?" she asked. "I was up painting most of the night. Started a new piece."

"Can I see?"

"Not yet. But I finished that portrait of you last week. It's there." She pointed to a canvas that was perched on her counter and covered with a sheet.

Quinn approached it hesitantly.

"Go on," her mother said. "Take a look."

Quinn pulled off the sheet and was so surprised it took her a few minutes to understand what she was looking at. She had expected a portrait similar to Hayden's or her father's. But instead of a close-up interpretation of Quinn's face, it seemed to be a statement about her relationship with her mother. The image disturbed her so much that she made short shrift of the visit and left without saying anything complimentary about the painting. It was the last time they spoke, and Quinn couldn't remember if she'd even said good-bye.

Eugene's heavy black phone rang again and jarred her. She looked at the clock by the bed. Isaac. Soon, his bus would pull up at the corner and he'd step down onto the curb. What if she wasn't there?

Quinn went into the bathroom again and studied the tub, looking for a tiny fissure. But the porcelain was smooth from end to end. She examined the perimeter, where the grout met the fixture, but everything was sealed tight. Quinn stood and stared down, surveying the entire bathtub.

There has to be a way back, she thought. There has to be.

She kneeled again and closed her eyes, holding her hands above the bathtub. Maybe things were different on this side. Maybe the fissure was invisible, and she'd be able to feel the resistance of air but not actually see a crack. She waved her hands down the entire length of the tub and up the sides. But there was nothing—no wind at all. In fact, if anything, she felt something quite opposite—a gentle vacuum. It was coming from the drain. Was that just the natural effect of the pipes?

Quinn pressed all around the drain, and even inspected the faucet, but everything remained solid.

She thought of Isaac getting off the school bus. If she was even a second late he would panic. At school he was fine, and at home he wasn't any clingier than most six-year-olds. But outside the protection of the house he seemed terrified of losing sight of her. Quinn sometimes wondered if Isaac sensed his mother could vanish like vapor, or if it was just normal separation anxiety. Of course, if he really knew the truth, he would be more worried at home than at such places as the bus stop or the playground, where she had to be in his line of sight at all times.

She didn't understand just how terrified he was until the day they actually got separated for a few moments. Lewis, Quinn, and Isaac had gone out for dinner at a big, boisterous family restaurant. The waitress led them through three different rooms to their table in the back of the cavernous establishment, and when Quinn turned around, Isaac was nowhere in sight.

"Where is he?" Lewis said.

Quinn looked around. "I don't know," she said. "Isaac? Isaac!" She bent to see if he was hiding under a table.

"I'll backtrack," Lewis said, but before he had gone a few steps, they heard a child's scream so piercing the place went silent and every head turned. Quinn and Lewis ran toward the sound, where they found Isaac standing, rigid with fear. He stopped when he saw his mother and collapsed in her arms.

"Sweetheart," she said.

It took only moments to figure out what had happened. The restaurant had a large chalkboard affixed to the wall in the waiting area—a diversion for kids while their families waited to be seated. Isaac had been trailing his mother and father to the table when he got distracted by the board. He picked up a piece of chalk and got so absorbed in what he was drawing that he forgot he was supposed to be following his parents.

Isaac took a jagged breath. "I thought you disappeared."

Today, Quinn imagined him standing alone on the corner, his little heart pounding in his chest when he didn't see her.

Or would he? Quinn wondered if there was a chance she might continue to exist in both lives. If she spent a day or a month or a year in this life, could she step back into the other life at any time and simply absorb all the memories as she had done when she crossed over to this "Eugene life"?

Her intuition told her it wasn't so, that once she dared cross the portal there was no "substitute" Quinn living her life with Lewis and Isaac. And, of course, she couldn't risk finding out. She wouldn't do to Isaac what her own mother had done to her. She had to return to him. She had to.

Don't panic, she told herself. Just think. Think of how you got here. Maybe it's just a matter of reversing the steps. But how? Did it make sense to get back into the bath?

Quinn turned on the faucets, figuring it was worth a try. "Hurry," she whispered, as she watched the bath fill. At last she took off the bathrobe and hung it back on the brass hook, then lowered herself into the warm water. She lay down, closed her eyes, and submerged herself completely. Quinn tried to relax in the water, let her mind go. After a few moments she felt something like a push, pressing her into darkness. She fought the panic that made her feel as if she were being drowned, and let the force move her down into the space between two worlds, where she floated through a mass that was neither solid nor liquid. This time there was no sensation of peace, but a fear that she might not emerge. She felt vulnerable and conscious of her nakedness. Quinn wrapped her arms around herself in protection as she was pressed forward. The environment went from warm to tepid to cold, and she became aware of a musty, earthy smell. Then her head hit something solid, and Quinn knew it was the concrete wall of her basement. She opened her eyes and saw the ironing board in the light in front of her. Thank God, she thought. She crawled out onto it, scratching her right side on the rough cement, as the fissure was now a solid, physical thing, just wide enough for her to fit through. And then there she was—wet, naked, and bleeding a little bit, but back in her house. Her clothes were in a pile on the floor under the ironing board, as if she had dropped them there before her journey.

She stood and looked down at her body, noting the swell in her abdomen. She touched her breasts, examining them for tenderness. Yes, she was still pregnant. Quinn put her clothes back on and went out to meet her son at the bus stop.

9

As Quinn moved through the rest of her day shell-shocked from the emotional grenade of hearing her mother's voice, she knew there was only one person who would believe what had happened and know how she felt—her brother, Hayden.

And so early Saturday afternoon, after Lewis had taken Isaac to his soccer game, Quinn got in her Volvo and headed to a restaurant in the Park Slope neighborhood of Brooklyn, where she and Hayden had agreed to meet.

The Maplewood Cafe had sidewalk seating, which was filling quickly with people eager to take advantage of the unusually warm fall weather. Quinn sat at a table with a view down the street, and settled in to wait for her brother, who she knew would be late. Even though she was the one who had to drive an hour to get to this place and all he had to do was tumble out of his brownstone and walk two blocks, she couldn't get mad at him. No one could. Hayden's sweet nature brought out the best in almost everyone. He could show up late or forget to come at all. He could miss birthdays, not return calls, overlook important dates— and none of it mattered. His heart was as big as a bear and as tender as a puppy, and he was beloved. Year after year, the students at the New York City high school where he taught social studies voted him their favorite teacher.

Quinn sat sipping sparkling water with lemon as she watched down the street for her brother, thinking about how she would tell him her astounding story. At last she saw his large frame approaching, a huge smile shrinking his crystal blue eyes to tiny slits.

"Sorry," he said. "The phone rang just as I was leaving."

She laughed. "Right. Otherwise you would have been on time."

He kissed her on the cheek. "God, it's gorgeous out." He sat down and examined her face. "You sure you're okay?"

She shrugged. Over the phone, she had told him all about the sono- gram and how little information the doctors had been able to provide about the baby's prognosis. "Tell me about you. How's Cordell?"

Cordell had been at the center of Hayden's life for years. He was an aspiring actor, a beautiful, mocha-skinned god. Quinn had something like a love-hate relationship with him. Sometimes she appreciated his goofy sense of humor and offbeat charm. Other times she found him obnoxious. But what troubled her most was that she felt he wasn't giving enough to Hayden, and that he used his career ambitions as an excuse for selfishness. As far as Quinn could tell, Cordell gave little thought to Hayden as he shuttled back and forth between the East and West Coasts, depending on where there was work. When he was here, he lived with her brother. Supposedly Cordell had his own apartment in Los Angeles, but Hayden had never seen it, and Quinn wondered whether it really existed or if he had another boyfriend in Hollywood. She suspected that deep down Hayden knew he was being used. But he was as devoted as an addict. Quinn wished he would move on—he deserved so much better, after all—but it was hopeless.

"He was supposed to come in on the red-eye this morning but he got held up. He's meeting with a casting agent today."

She reached over and straightened his collar. "On Saturday?"

"There's no such thing as weekends in L.A. That's what he says, anyway." Hayden smiled to show Quinn that none of this really hurt him, but his eyes broke her heart.

"Oh, Hayd."

"I'm this close to breaking up with him," he said, holding his fingers a millimeter apart.

It was a long-standing joke between them, and Quinn laughed. "I won't hold my breath."

"Seriously, Quinn. Cross your fingers for us. Last week he auditioned for a big part on a soap opera, and if it comes through he'll have a career right here."

Quinn smiled and gave her brother's wrist an affectionate squeeze. She had heard this kind of thing before. These big jobs just never seemed to materialize. Besides, she wasn't sure Cordell was the type to settle down, even if he did have a steady job.

"I'll cross my fingers he gets it," Quinn said, "and that it makes you both happy."

"Diplomatically spoken," Hayden said. His sister's feelings about Cordell weren't exactly a secret.

"You know where I'm coming from," she said. "I love you. I want you to have what Lewis and I have."

"No offense," Hayden said. "You two are my favorite breeders. But I don't *want* what you have."

They'd had conversations like this before, and Quinn just couldn't accept it. Hayden insisted the kind of over-the-top security Quinn needed in a relationship would make him feel smothered. She thought he was

trying to justify the volatility of his life with Cordell. Hayden's response
was that she was projecting her neediness onto him. It was a conversation
that never got anywhere.

The waitress handed them menus and said she'd be back soon to take
their orders. Hayden leaned in and asked Quinn what her big news was.
She closed her eyes for a moment and pictured the heavy black telephone
in the bedroom of the Manhattan high-rise she shared with Eugene. The
memory of her mother's voice was so vivid she shuddered.

"Maybe you need a drink first," she said.

"Just spit it out."

On the drive over, Quinn had decided the best way to tell Hayden
was to be direct. Now that she was actually face-to-face with him, it was
hard to find the words. She took a deep breath and licked her lips. Hayden
stared, waiting.

"I spoke to Mom." She said it loud and clear, letting him know she
was serious.

"I don't suppose she answered back," he said.

He thought it was a joke. Quinn didn't smile. She brought her face
closer to her brother's and laid her hand on his arm. *"I spoke to Mom,"*
she repeated, enunciating each word as if it were a single sentence. "I had
a conversation with her."

Hayden blinked.

"A *real* conversation," she added.

"What are you talking about? Mom died over—" He stopped and
stared straight into Quinn's eyes, a realization taking hold. When she saw
it, she nodded, letting him know that what he was thinking was exactly
right. It took him a few seconds to find his voice.

"A portal?"

She nodded again. Hayden's hand covered his mouth while he took
it in. His eyes began to water and his face turned red as his blood pressure rose.

"You okay?" she asked.

He put up his hand to let her know he needed a minute before he could speak. Quinn sat back and let him process.

Hayden was there the first and only time Quinn got close enough to actually touch the other side, to feel the physical reality of her other life. In fact, if it weren't for him, she would have doubted the whole thing had actually happened. They were kids, playing where they shouldn't. It was during the construction on their house, when the art studio was being added to the back. The contractors had dug out a foundation and laid the concrete. Next to it was the big mound of earth they had excavated but not yet carted away. Quinn and Hayden were forbidden from going into the backyard during all this, so of course it was the first thing they did when their mother, who was in a depression at the time, went into her bedroom and locked the door.

Quinn and her younger brother ran up and down the mound of dirt, laughing as they skidded down the side. They were careful not to get too close to the side adjacent to the hole, but at one point Quinn climbed to the peak and looked down into the concrete foundation. Hayden joined her.

"I think I can jump," she said.

"You'll get hurt."

Looking back, Quinn couldn't remember what she was thinking. Maybe she wanted to get hurt. Maybe it was the only way to get her mother's attention. Or perhaps she sensed something extraordinary at the bottom of the pit, beckoning her. She recalled only that as she was falling, time seemed suspended for a moment, and she had the feeling that it wasn't too late to change her mind, that she could slip back just a millisecond and have made the other decision. Then she hit the ground hard, and heard her leg crack before she crumpled and thumped her head.

As she lay there, hurt and bleeding, Quinn became aware of something strange beneath her fingers that distracted her from the pain. It seemed like a small hole the exact same size as her hand. She moved her arm away, and the opening transformed into a simple fissure in the concrete. She remembered sensing as a small child that another Quinn existed somewhere very close but hidden. There was something down here, some kind of opening to the other Quinn. Had it drawn her toward it? She reached out again to feel the crack, and the solid matter gave way beneath her touch. She stuck her arm all the way down into it and knew she was touching another version of her own life—the version in which she had made the decision not to jump. Quinn was aware of Hayden at the top of the mound of earth, screaming and then running into the house, but she didn't pay attention. She was thinking about what it would be like to let herself go right through the crack. Would she be back up at the top of the mountain with Hayden, the unbearable pain in her leg nonexistent?

She must have passed out at that point, because the next thing she remembered was being laid carefully in the backseat of the car by her mother.

"I touched the other side, Mom," Quinn said.

"Shh," Nan said. "You're okay. I'm here."

"I didn't go in," she said, thinking her mother might be angry. "I just touched it."

Nan's expression dropped in a way that was unfamiliar to Quinn. It wasn't sadness or anger. Her mother looked . . . scared. But then she took a breath and pursed her lips, an expression Quinn recognized as a summoning of strength.

"You hit your head, cookie," her mother said, and then her tone changed as she addressed Hayden. "Didn't I tell you two not to play out there? She could have broken her neck."

Quinn's father joined them at the hospital, but she didn't get to talk to him until after they got home and she was resting in bed with her fractured ankle elevated on a pillow. The side of her head was bandaged, hiding the spot where they had shaved a patch of hair to give her more than twenty stitches.

"How are you feeling?" her father asked, sitting carefully on the side of her bed.

"I found something down there," she said.

"Down where?"

"In the new basement. There was a hole that led to the other Quinn, the one who didn't jump. I stuck my arm through."

He touched her face. His hand smelled like soap. "That was a dream," he said. "There's no other Quinn. Only you, sweetheart."

Hayden appeared at the door with a pack of colored markers, asking if he could draw on her cast. Quinn's father kissed her gently on the cheek and left. Hayden took his place on Quinn's bed.

"It wasn't a dream," her brother said, pulling the cap off a black marker.

Quinn propped herself up on her elbows and watched as he outlined a butterfly. "How do you know?"

"I saw," he said. "I saw your arm disappear. I thought . . . I thought maybe it fell off. I was so scared I ran around the hill looking for it." He paused to give his butterfly two careful antennae, the exact same length. He put the cap back on the marker and stared into his sister's face. "Then I looked again and saw you pull it right out of the cement. I was screaming my head off but you didn't look up. How did you do that? How did you make your arm disappear?"

"I don't know," Quinn said, feeling almost guilty, as if she'd betrayed his trust by not having an answer.

Hayden opened a yellow marker and began to color in the wings of his drawing. "Was there really another world down there?" he asked as he worked. "Another Quinn?"

She picked up the black marker he had used and pulled off the cap to sniff it. It was licorice scented. She put the cap back on.

"Yes," she said.

"How come I don't have another life? How come it's only you?"

She fluffed her pillow and dropped her head onto it, staring straight up at the ceiling. It was exactly what she herself wondered.

A few months later Hayden came across the word *portal* in a chapter book and brought it to Quinn. It was a silly science fiction story, but just knowing that such a word existed gave Quinn a way to think about what had happened. She had found a portal.

The waitress came to take Quinn's and Hayden's orders, and they scanned their menus quickly, making fast decisions so that they could resume their conversation.

Quinn told her brother everything that had happened—from the journey through to how it felt to have a whole other life suddenly, and how much harder it was to get back than to slip through. Throughout the account, she barely paused to take a breath, but when she finally finished and waited for Hayden's reaction, he was busy studying his place setting.

The wind carried a dry leaf to their table and it alighted in front of Hayden. He turned it over to examine the veiny underside, and Quinn could tell that he was trying to compose himself so that he could speak without crying.

"What about Mom?" he finally said, looking straight at her eyes. "Tell me about Mom."

Quinn took a tissue from her purse and blew her nose. This was hard. It was as if she were given the ability to bring their dead mother back to life for them both.

"That's the weirdest part of the whole thing," she said. "Mom sounded so . . . normal." Quinn closed her eyes and remembered her mother's funeral. She remembered putting her hand on her father's shoulder when he wept, and how that made him sob even louder. She remembered the unyielding resistance she'd felt when she tried to take his hand at the end of the service. It wasn't that he didn't *want* to leave. He simply couldn't. He belonged with her.

Both memories were real—Quinn's mother's voice on the phone

yesterday and her funeral seven years ago. She glanced down the street, wondering what it would be like if she had never received that terrible phone call that her mother was dead. She tried to imagine Nan meeting them here today for lunch. Her mother might be walking down the street right now, unconscious of her loping gait as her artist's eyes roamed the surroundings, taking in shapes and light. Then she would see her two adult children sitting together and her face would transform.

"I don't feel like she's gone," Quinn said. "When I think about that phone call from Dad . . . about shoveling earth on her coffin . . . it almost seems like a dream." She picked up the dry brown leaf and closed her fist around it until it crackled. "I spoke to her on the phone yesterday, Hayden. How do I find a way to deal with this?"

He reached out and touched her closed fist. "Poor Quinn. You're going to have to start grieving all over again."

She shook her head. "I want to think of her as alive."

"But she's dead."

"I heard her *voice*."

"You've seen her tombstone."

"I have her back, Hayd. How can I let go of that?"

He frowned. "This isn't healthy."

"Do you know what she asked me? She asked if I wanted to go out for dinner for my birthday." Quinn felt herself lightening and smiled. She wanted her brother to understand how wonderful this was. "I can celebrate another birthday with her!"

"You're not thinking of going back, are you?"

"I have to."

"Don't do it, Quinn," he said.

"Why not?"

"You think you're going to get something out of this and you're not. You mourned for her once and it was nearly unbearable. Do you want to go through that again? Do you want to lose her *twice*?"

"I miss her so much."

"I do, too," he said.

"It's different for me."

"Quinn . . ."

She opened her fist. The leaf was now a handful of tiny brown flakes. She blew them away. "I need to understand why she did it," Quinn said, wiping her hands.

"You know why she did it," Hayden said. "She did it because she was sick. Trust me on this."

Hayden spoke with authority. Quinn was the one who had gotten their mother's dark hair and green eyes, but it was her brother who had inherited Nan's bipolar disorder—a fact that had been discovered in college when a manic episode of staggering achievement was followed by a period of tortured confusion that left him unable to read or study. As far as Quinn knew, Hayden neither cursed nor resented his illness. Rather, he saw himself as one of the fortunate few who grew up with such a close view of the disease that he never forgot the importance of staying on his medication.

The waitress arrived with their meals. When she left, Quinn picked up her fork and mixed her salad. "There's more to it than that," she said softly.

"No, there isn't."

"How can you be so sure?"

"You didn't do anything wrong," her brother insisted. "Mom didn't kill herself because you had some stupid fight at Thanksgiving."

No, she thought. She killed herself because I married Lewis.

QUINN DECONSTRUCTED, NO. 3

———

Nan worked on the position of Quinn's foot. She was sketching on the canvas, trying to get the composition just right before laying down any paint. Quinn would appear in the same green chair as in the other paintings, but here she had one leg curled under her and a book in her lap.

Nan was working from a sketch she had completed earlier, transferring it to the larger scope of the canvas. Stupid, Nan thought, as she began to weep. There was simply no reason the turn of her daughter's foot should open the floodgates of love, and yet there it was. Something about the innocence of the position, the unself-conscious openness of this private moment, tapped the most tender place in her heart.

This was going to be difficult. But Nan was determined to finish. She needed to capture Quinn at this particular crossroad in her development, before Eugene had entered her life, and the idea of being an adult was still steeped in the romance of endless possibilities. Not that Quinn was ever excessively naive. But there was something about that moment in a young adult's life where hope hued every opportunity. The pages of the book, Nan decided, would be rose-colored.

10

"You look tired," Quinn said to Isaac. She sat on the closed toilet lid watching him attempt to rinse the shampoo out of his hair in the bathtub. Even as she said it, though, she wondered if she really meant it, or if she was trying to rush him into bed so that she could go downstairs and slip through the portal.

"There's still a lot of suds," she said, pointing to the area around her own hairline to show him where. "Can I help you?"

Isaac smoothed his small hands over his forehead. "I can do it," he said.

It was hard for Quinn to sit by and not complete the task for him, but she knew how important it was to let her son be independent. He dipped his head deeper into the water and sat up.

"I'm done," he announced, and the tiny bit of lather left on his temple made Quinn ache with tenderness.

Isaac got out of the tub, and she wrapped his shivering body in a bath towel, surreptitiously dabbing at the leftover suds. She hugged him and he laid his wet head on her shoulder, drenching her shirt. She held him tighter.

"What do you want to read?" she asked, glancing at her watch. Quinn figured she had just enough time for one book before she went downstairs and slipped through.

"*Good Night Bertram Bear,*" he said.

It was one of his comfort books, and he didn't usually request it unless he was sick.

"You feeling okay?" she asked.

Isaac shrugged. She pressed her lips to his forehead to test for fever but he still felt cool from the water.

They went to his room, where she read him his story, distracted and anxious about getting downstairs. In a matter of minutes, she would get to look into her mother's eyes again, hear her voice, smell her perfume.

At last she kissed him good night and went to the computer room, where Lewis was online, checking his weather statistics.

"I'm going downstairs for a while," she announced. "I have a lot of ironing to catch up on. Can you keep an eye on Isaac? His cold might be getting worse."

"Fever?"

"I don't think so," she said, and paused. What was that sound coming from Isaac's room? She rushed back just in time to see her son vomit onto the bedding. Lewis hurried in behind her.

"I'll get a washcloth," he said. Together, they cleaned off Isaac and changed the sheets. Quinn worked as fast as she could so that she wouldn't miss her chance to see her mother.

When at last they were done and Isaac was back in a clean bed, she gathered up the soiled linens and told Lewis she would probably be doing laundry for quite a while.

"Can you read to me again?" Isaac asked her.

Quinn sighed and looked at Lewis. "Can you?"

"Of course."

"I want Mommy," Isaac said.

Lewis put his hand on her shoulder. "I can do the wash," he offered.

"No!" she said quickly, and then checked herself. She looked back at her son and softened her voice. "Let Daddy read to you now. Daddy hasn't read to you in so long."

Isaac's lower lip went out and Quinn nearly succumbed. But Lewis piped in, saying that he would read any book Isaac wanted, maybe even two or three. And so she said good night and hurried to the basement.

Quinn quickly threw the soiled bedding and detergent into the washer and started the machine. Then she opened the ironing board and stared at the fissure that would deliver her to her mother. She thought of Isaac upstairs in his bed, snuggled next to Lewis, and realized they hadn't given him a sip of water to wash down the vomit. Would her husband think of that? And what if the boy spiked a fever soon? Would Lewis give him the liquid Motrin he needed to be comfortable?

Lewis can handle this, she tried to tell herself as she climbed onto the ironing board. But then she thought about Isaac's lower lip and his tiny voice.

I want Mommy.

Me, too, she thought, and wondered how many times she'd said that to her own father as her mother lay in bed, incapacitated by depression.

"Mommy is sick," he'd say. "We have to be quiet and let her get well."

And she would. She would be quiet and good. Careful and helpful. Anything that might get her mother out of bed. When it didn't work, she thought she just wasn't trying hard enough. And so she'd be quieter, kinder, gentler, better. But it never helped. It was like trying to feed an empty stomach with air, and the deep, desperate hunger never vanished.

I want Mommy, Isaac had said.

Quinn closed her eyes for a moment. Then she climbed off the ironing board, folded it up against the wall, and went back to her son.

——————

THE NEXT DAY, after reassurances from the doctor that Isaac didn't have anything worse than a cold—and had probably thrown up because of post-nasal drip—Quinn drove him home from the pediatrician's office, trying to feel more grateful that her son wasn't sick than miserable over missing her mother. My boy is healthy, Quinn told herself, her free hand resting on her belly. Nothing is more important.

"This is a little darker than sky blue," Isaac said from the backseat.

She glanced at him in the mirror and saw that he was holding up his new toy. It was a rubbery hedgehog about the size of a golf ball, and he'd chosen it from the bin of tiny treasures the pediatrician let the children pick from after each visit. Quinn knew that a lot of mothers used the promise of a treat to get their frightened children to go along willingly to their doctors' appointments, and thought it wouldn't be a bad idea for adult doctors to do the same thing. She wondered what kind of treat might have helped get Eugene to his doctor visits. He had to think his life was in imminent danger before seeking medical help. Even sex wasn't a strong enough motivator to get him to the doctor.

From the beginning of their relationship, Eugene's erections were inconsistent, and as time went on, they became less frequent. Viagra burst onto the scene in those days, and one couldn't open a newspaper or magazine without seeing an article about it. Quinn rehearsed at least a dozen imaginary conversations in her head, but couldn't think of the right way to approach Eugene about the topic, especially since she had already spent so much energy trying to convince him it didn't really matter.

Fortunately, he was the one who brought it up. They were in bed, and he had lost his erection before they had a chance to make love.

"It's okay," she said.

He put his hands behind his head. "I wish I could get a prescription for Viagra. That would solve everything."

"Why can't you?"

"Are you kidding? You expect me to talk to a doctor about impotence? What would I say?"

"How about, 'Would you write me a prescription for Viagra?' "

"And then he'll ask if I'm having trouble getting it up."

"So?"

"So? So it's humiliating."

"You'll feel embarrassed for thirty seconds, Eugene. And then you'll have a scrip for Viagra."

"The media would have a field day with that."

"The media won't know or care."

"You think they're not salivating to find out who's on Viagra?" he said.

"Please. I'm sure half the men in Hollywood take it."

Eugene picked up the covers and looked down at his crotch, as if expecting to see something. He sighed. "Yeah, but they have special doctors in L.A. who write you prescriptions under aliases."

"It's not going to wind up in *Variety*, for God's sake."

"I can see the banner headline," Eugene said. "DOC MOCKS SHOCK JOCK'S COCK."

Quinn laughed. "That won't happen!"

"And the follow-up article: FANS PRAY DJ RAY NOT GAY."

"You should save this for your show."

"Yeah, right."

They were both quiet for a moment as Quinn tried to think of a way to convince him to see his doctor about this. It would, after all, make them both happier. She liked making love to him, and she missed those moments when his passion was so intense that he couldn't wait to be inside her. Even the thought of his desperate desire made her shiver.

He put his hand on her shoulder. "You're going to have to help me."

"I can try," she said, sitting up and lifting the covers from Eugene.

"Not that. I mean, you're going to have to get me a prescription."

"How am I supposed to do that?"

"Have someone else get it and then give me the pills."

"Like who? Your agent? That might not be in his job description."

Eugene looked at her, attempting to telegraph his meaning without saying it. Quinn got it.

"Hayden?" she said. "You want me to ask my brother to score Viagra for you?"

"Why not? Gay men have absolutely no shame about sex."

"I don't think that's exactly true."

"You know what I mean. He probably talks to his doctor about his dick all the time. In fact, his dick probably has its own name and insurance policy."

She laughed. "I don't want to imagine Hayden naming his dick."

"I'm sorry. Was that rude? I take it back. I'm sure he doesn't name his dick."

"Thank you."

"His butt, however, probably has its own credit cards."

"Eugene!"

"Visa. It's everywhere you want to be."

She laughed again, this time so hard there were tears. "Can we move on, please?"

He picked up her hand and kissed it. "Of course. I don't want to gross you out. Besides . . ." He paused and moved her hand to his crotch, where an erection was beginning to stir. "It's your laugh," he said into her neck. "It makes me crazy." He ran his tongue along the ticklish place behind her ear until she giggled.

"That's cheating," she said.

"So's Viagra."

And they did make love that night. But the next time they tried Eugene couldn't get hard, despite her best efforts. And so Quinn approached Hayden, who treated her request with sincere concern, and a week later handed her a refillable prescription for little blue pills.

II

QUINN PARKED HER CAR IN FRONT OF HER PARENTS' HOUSE, cut the engine, and held on to the steering wheel as if she could slow her own heartbeat with the strength of her grip. The last time she visited this house it was empty and she'd hoped to communicate with her mother's spirit through her paintings. Now her mother's car was in the driveway and her heart was in the house . . . beating inside her chest.

It was Wednesday morning, and Isaac had felt well enough to go to school. So after putting him on the bus and, as always, remaining on the corner as it pulled away so that Isaac could watch her through the back window until the driver turned onto the next block, Quinn went into the basement and slipped through the portal to her life in the city. From there she got in her car and drove through the Midtown Tunnel to the Long Island Expressway, following familiar roads all the way to her childhood home.

Now, sitting alone in the car, she didn't know if she could go through with it. How could she possibly do this? How could she face the mother she'd buried seven years ago? Maybe Hayden was right. This was a terrible idea.

She looked at the house and wondered what her mother was doing right this minute. Was she having a cup of coffee and reading the paper? On the phone with a friend? In her studio mixing colors? Doing yoga in her bedroom?

I should just start the car and leave, Quinn thought. She looked back at the house. No. I've come this far. I have to do this.

Quinn approached the front door and rummaged nervously through her purse for the key. She found it, but before she let herself in, she looked at the shiny brass mail slot, situated about three and a half feet from the ground—eye level for a toddler. Once, when they were visiting her father, Isaac stuck his meaty baby hand into the opening and got stuck. Quinn had acted quickly, breaking the hinge to free his little paw. They had never bothered to fix it, but here it was in perfect condition.

Quinn took a deep breath, put her key in the lock, and opened the door.

"Mom?" she called weakly.

No answer.

She left her handbag in the drop spot by the front entry and wandered from the foyer to the kitchen. Empty. A copy of *The New York Times*, open to the crossword, was on the table, a pen lying across it. Quinn glanced at the page. The top half was completed in the familiar block letters of Nan's handwriting.

She went into the dark family room, which had an open view of the sunlit studio behind it, and froze.

There, silhouetted by the sun, was her mother.

Nan was working on a painting and lost in the process, applying long, arching strokes to the right side of the canvas. Her dark, wild hair, pulled back in a clip, was longer than it had been the last time Quinn saw her. Soft music was playing, and Quinn spotted something new—an iPod nestled into a speaker. But everything else was so familiar, it was like . . . Quinn paused to finish that mental sentence. It was like coming home.

Unable to move or speak, she watched her mother work. Why had she never noticed her grace before? Had she always been this profoundly beautiful? Or was this love welling from a place so deep it seemed to come at Quinn from every angle?

Nan put down the brush and took a step back to look at the painting.

"Mom?" Quinn said. Her voice sounded so young to her. Like a child's.

Nan turned around. She smiled and pushed a lock of hair from her face with her wrist. "I didn't hear you come in."

Quinn stepped forward into the studio. Clearly unruffled, Nan picked up a tube of paint and squirted a dab onto her palette.

"Give me a sec," her mother said, as she dipped her brush into the dime of bright yellow paint. Nan didn't usually object to being disturbed while she worked as long as she was allowed to finish whatever artistic thought she was expressing. She mixed the yellow with a smidge of brown until it turned an even mustard shade, then looked back at the painting and added the new color in short, pretty strokes. She stopped to assess what she'd done, added one more small flourish, and put the brush down. Quinn stood by, silently. Nan picked up a rag and wiped her hands, then leaned in to kiss her daughter on the cheek. She smelled of acrylic paint and her favorite scent, Shalimar.

"I was on my way to the mall," Quinn said. She was suddenly nervous her mother would somehow intuit the truth about this visit, and it was something Quinn couldn't possibly reveal. Telling her mother there was another reality in which she'd committed suicide was simply not an option.

"Coffee?" Nan asked.

Quinn exhaled, relieved. Her mother didn't even sense her agitation, and Quinn realized it was a good thing she'd caught Nan in the midst of a creative flow, when her powers of maternal intuition were turned off.

"I don't want to bother you," Quinn said.

"I could use a break."

She stared hard at her mother's face. The flecks of amber in her green eyes made Quinn weak with longing. I need her, she thought, and she fought back tears.

"I'll make the coffee," Quinn said. "Finish what you were doing."

Nan agreed, and Quinn hurried into the kitchen to compose herself. She splashed cold water on her face, coaching herself to get it together, then went through the mechanics of boiling water and counting scoops of ground coffee into her mother's French press.

While she waited for the coffee, she sat at the table and stared at the crossword puzzle. It was such a familiar marker in the daily landscape of her life—those black and white squares with Nan's artistic handwriting marching across and down, and always in blue ink—that in years past it had become practically invisible. Now even its ordinariness felt extraordinary, and it made Quinn's throat swell.

She brought two cups of coffee into the studio—with sugar and milk for herself, black with sugar for her mom—and sat on the white futon sofa while her mother worked.

Quinn had thought she would find herself aching to talk to her mother about the baby, to cry on her shoulder about this thing that was just too big for her to handle alone. Instead, she just wanted to be near her, having a cup of coffee together, breathing the same air.

Quinn watched Nan work on the background of the painting, creating mood. She tried to discern the subject of the painting in the foreground, though it was still only a sketch. It looked to Quinn like a young woman sitting in a chair reading, her head down so that her hair covered her face. Quinn wondered if it was a self-portrait of the artist as a young woman. It did look as if it could have been Nan, though the figure in the sketch seemed to have straight hair, not a full frizzy mop, as her mother did. It occurred to Quinn that it could have been a portrait of her, but she didn't want to ask. Her mother would tell her if she was so inclined.

"What did you need at the mall?" Nan asked, as she continued to work on the horizon.

"Um . . . just underwear for Eugene."

Nan paused and looked over her shoulder at Quinn. She wasn't buying it. "They don't sell underwear in Manhattan?"

Quinn shrugged.

"You don't need an excuse to come visit me."

"I know." It came out as a whisper.

Nan wiped her brush with a rag and dropped it into a can of water. She approached her daughter. "What's the matter?"

"Nothing. I just . . . I missed you."

"We saw each other two nights ago."

Quinn closed her eyes. She remembered it—the dinner she had missed because she wouldn't leave Isaac. The memory was now perfectly clear. The restaurant was dark. She'd had tilapia. Her mother wore a blue peasant blouse and a handmade necklace of hammered brass. Hayden showed up late, without Cordell, and told Quinn he was "this close" to breaking up with him.

"I guess I just needed to get out," Quinn said.

"You know what you need?" Nan asked.

"What?" Quinn said, happy to feed her mother the straight line. She was sure a sexual innuendo was coming.

"Boots," Nan said.

"Boots?"

"New boots. There's a sale at Nordstrom."

Quinn smiled. This was exactly what she needed—a perfectly ordinary day out with her mother. Bliss. She stood. "You know, I probably *could* use new boots."

"Then let's hit the mall. And while we're there maybe we'll stop at Frederick's and pick up some crotchless panties for you. You need to get laid, kiddo."

Quinn laughed, and knew that Nan's vitality would keep her so grounded that she would truly enjoy this outing. Her mother's pull was just too strong for Quinn to float away and feel as if she were experiencing the shopping trip as an outsider looking in.

At the mall, they bought boots at Nordstrom and earrings from a kiosk. As they pored over the racks in the mall bookstore, an infant started to wail, and Quinn instinctively turned to look. The young mother tried to comfort the baby by rocking the stroller back and forth, but Quinn recognized the sound as a hunger cry and it created a knot of concern in her belly.

Nan looked at her daughter. "You okay?"

Quinn nodded.

"There's something different about you today."

"What do you mean?"

The infant continued to cry, and Nan followed her daughter's eyes from the baby and back again. "Are you pregnant?" she asked.

"No!"

"Don't lie. You can tell me to mind my own business, but don't bullshit me."

"Okay," Quinn said. "Mind your own business. But I'm not pregnant."

"You're trying, aren't you?"

"Mind your own business."

"I knew it! You and Eugene are trying to get pregnant. You should fuck every other day all month. I read it in a magazine."

"Mind your own business," Quinn said again, laughing.

Nan grabbed her daughter and embraced her. "I never said this to you before, but if you make me a grandmother I'll die happy. Oh, Quinn, my sweetheart, have a baby. Make me a grandma!"

A grandma, Quinn thought, and remembered those heartbreaking moments—usually around the anniversary of her mother's death— when she would fall apart with longing. She wanted so badly for her mother to know her boy that she would cry and say to Lewis, "She would have loved him so much." And he would stroke her gently and whisper back, "I know."

Later, when they were having lunch in the food court, the woman with the hungry infant passed right by their table. Quinn could see now that it was a little boy, dressed in a tan stretchie with a blue train on the front. He was happy now and had pulled off one of his socks, exposing his fat little foot and kernel toes. Quinn thought she felt her womb contract.

She broke from her reverie and looked at her watch, realizing she had nearly forgotten she had another life to get back to.

"I have to go," she said to her mother.

Nan was still working on her salad. "Right now?"

"Yes."

"I thought we could stop at Betsey Johnson. Did you see that crazy purple thing in the window?"

"I don't have time," Quinn said. "I didn't realize how late it was." She stood.

"What's the hurry?" Nan asked.

"Mom . . . please. Let's go."

"Can't you tell me what the big rush is?"

"No."

"Is this another 'mind your own business' moment?" Nan asked.

Quinn nodded. Nan stared at her daughter's face for a few seconds, then picked up a napkin and dabbed her mouth. "If I didn't know better," she said, "I'd think you were about to turn into a pumpkin."

BACK IN THE CITY, Quinn filled the bathtub and lowered herself into it, preparing for the trip back to her other life. She took a deep breath, closed her eyes, and submerged, counting backward from ten. Quinn waited to feel the familiar tug, but nothing happened. She came up for air, took a big gulp, and went back down. Nothing. A rising panic formed in her belly. Why wasn't this working? She went down again, holding her breath as long as she could. This time she thought she felt a push, but it wasn't strong enough to take her.

She sat up. *Think*. Quinn sensed that there was something she needed to change, something about the condition of the water wasn't quite right. Was it too cool? Too warm?

She was already getting uncomfortably cold in the sitting water, but wondered if that push she'd felt was the result of the dropping temperature. Perhaps it just wasn't quite cool enough. She turned on the cold water tap, shivering as the tub chilled even more. She shut off the water, took another gulp of air, folded her arms across her chest, and submerged. Almost immediately, she sensed it, and in another moment she was sucked into the dark journey back.

Like last time, she sensed a musty smell just before seeing the light of her laundry room through a fissure ahead. Was it her imagination, or had the opening gotten smaller? Quinn squeezed through, trying hard not to scratch herself again, but it was impossible. There was simply no way to get through without sustaining a wound. It didn't matter, though. She had made it. She was back.

QUINN'S OBSTETRICIAN WAS PART OF A BIG OB-GYN PRACTICE, so the waiting room was always crowded with women. Most of them were pregnant, making Quinn's heart feel heavier than her womb. The contrast between her despair and the genial bliss of the others was overwhelming. The women smiled at one another, some softly chatted. It was a cheerful sisterhood Quinn had belonged to just a few short weeks before. But now she felt isolated. She was living everyone's worst nightmare.

A woman carrying a diaper bag and holding an infant car carrier entered and checked in at the desk, then took a seat next to Quinn. The baby nestled inside the high-tech basket was swaddled in a flannel receiving blanket with pink stripes. She looked about four weeks old, which meant that this was her mother's postpartum checkup. At the end of the visit the doctor would examine the woman's episiotomy, if she'd had one, and tell her she was ready to have intercourse again. Quinn remembered that examination after Isaac's birth, and the fear she'd felt about how painful sex might be. Now it seemed such a quaint concern.

The baby fussed and the woman put down her magazine, unbuckled the infant's strap, and lifted her from the carrier. With one hand, she opened her blouse and put the baby to her breast. Quinn was close enough to hear the newborn suck, swallow, suck, swallow in a rhythm so steady it was almost a purr.

Quinn fought the swell of self-pity that rose within like a tide and crashed in angry peaks. But at whom could she direct her fury? It wasn't as if she could throw a tantrum that would convince the doctor to reverse her diagnosis.

After nursing the baby, the woman laid the tiny girl on her shoulder and rubbed her back, trying to coax out a burp. It was exactly what mothers did. They took care of their babies. If they were hungry, they fed them. Gassy, they burped them. Dirty, they changed them. Sick, they made them well.

Except Quinn might never be able to make her baby well. How could she possibly deal with that? A mother was supposed to fix things, to make everything right. It was a drive Quinn had felt even before becoming a mother. Now it was a force so powerful she couldn't imagine being helpless in the face of her child's suffering. How was it possible that Quinn didn't have the resources to fix what was wrong with her daughter?

When she interviewed for her job at Baston's Books, the human resources person had asked Quinn a number of standard questions designed to uncover personality traits. When she asked, "What is your biggest regret?" Quinn answered that she didn't believe in regrets, explaining that she always learned from her mistakes. It was the correct response, the one outlined in all the books that coached on proper interview techniques, and Quinn really believed it.

Now, though, she had to ask herself whether she regretted leaving Eugene. Had she made a mistake? Was that the life she was supposed to have? Had choosing Lewis been some misguided decision she had made simply to prove her mother wrong? Maybe her baby's deformity was the universe balking at her refusal to accept her true destiny.

Quinn stopped herself. No, she thought. That can't be. Destiny is a fairy tale. The world is ruled by free will.

And anyway, even if she was tempted to believe in fate, she could just as easily believe that she was meant to meet Lewis on that day, and to let him kiss her on the night he showed up at her bookstore.

He had been lurking around the perimeter of the store as the reading wrapped up and the line of people waiting for Tom Perrotta's signature finally wound down. Lewis asked Quinn if she wanted to go for a walk and she agreed. It was a beautiful night.

They walked toward Central Park and talked about their families, their childhoods, their taste in books. She told him about her aunt's lake house in the Berkshires and how little television she was allowed to watch as a kid. He told her about sleep-away camp and the terrible birthday cakes he had to endure because his mother had more love than skill. The whole time, she knew he was going to kiss her at the end of the night and that she was going to let him. The thought made her heart pound wildly in her chest, and she couldn't tell whether it was nervousness at the idea of betraying Eugene, or simply the excitement of desire. She wished he would reach for her hand.

They were still two blocks from the park when a delectable aroma stopped them. They were in front of a Chinese restaurant.

"You hungry?" he asked.

"Starved."

They continued talking over appetizers of dumplings, spring rolls, and cold sesame noodles, politely splitting everything. There was half a spring roll left on the table when she went into her purse to retrieve an old Chinese fortune she had saved because it was so damned funny. When she looked up, she discovered that Lewis had placed the last appetizer on her plate without saying a word.

He asked to see the fortune and Quinn handed it to him while she stared at the food in front of her, nearly choking with gratitude. To anyone else it wouldn't have meant much, but putting the last half of a spring roll on other people's plates was the type of thing she had been doing all her life. No one had ever done it for her. Not once.

"Spread your wings and fry like a bird," Lewis read. He laughed.

After dinner, he walked her back to her apartment building, and she knew he was going to kiss her right there on the street, where anyone could see. At that moment, she simply didn't care. She needed the kiss.

He leaned in and pressed his lips softly on hers and then pulled away. A test kiss. She wanted more. He kissed her again, this time deeper, and their bodies moved together. The pulsating she felt was like a current that started between her legs and rushed through her whole being. He pulled her closer with one hand, while the other found her rib cage. She could feel that he wanted to inch it higher, and wished he would. Touch me, she thought. Please. God.

But he didn't. The kiss ended, and they held on to each other, not speaking. She felt lost.

He stroked her hair and released her.

"The ball's in your court now," he said into her eyes, and she nodded. If she wanted to see him again, she'd have to make the call.

It took her a torturous week of going back and forth. She had to call him. She couldn't call him. She was in love with Eugene. And he needed her so desperately. But she kept hearing her mother's words telling her she was destined to be with a man who was an emotional siphon, and it infuriated her. Damn it, she deserved someone who wanted to make her happy!

So at last she made the call. And the romance moved quickly. Two weeks later she put a deposit on a tiny studio apartment in Gramercy Park and started moving in. At first, the idea of leaving Eugene was as oppressive as the August heat. *How could you do this to me?* he asked over and over again, and she wept at the weight of her guilt. *You know I can't take the TV job if you're not in my life, Quinn. I can't do it without you. Don't leave!*

But she did. And as the burden lifted, there were more and more moments when Quinn felt light-headed with freedom.

Still, periods of doubt remained. Would Eugene be okay without her? And what about the lifestyle? She told herself she wasn't starstruck, but on the rare occasions when Eugene accepted invitations, Quinn had found herself elbow to elbow with major celebrities, and it was a thrill. Wouldn't she miss that?

Worst of all, Quinn never stopped wondering if her mother was right. Maybe she just didn't have the temperament to be with a kind and giving man. Sure she was touched by tender moments like the spring roll incident, but there were just as many similar events when her heart wouldn't yield to his generosity.

One night, she and Lewis had dinner at Pete's Tavern, a place Quinn loved for its historic flavor. It was a Manhattan landmark, well known for having been the favorite haunt of America's most famous short-story writer, O. Henry.

The couple settled into their cozy, black-painted booth, and when the waiter came to take their orders, Quinn asked for the stuffed filet of sole. It was her favorite fish and she knew they did a good job with it there. Lewis ordered the same thing.

A few minutes later, the waiter came back and told them there was only one piece of sole left, and suggested one of them have the salmon.

"I will," Quinn said. "That's fine."

"No," insisted Lewis. "I wasn't in the mood for sole anyway."

"I really prefer the salmon," she lied.

"Two salmons?" the waiter asked. The place was noisy and his English was limited, so he was following as best he could.

Lewis and Quinn locked eyes. Neither could find the words to back down from their magnanimous position, so the waiter told them he'd be right back with their salmon.

Quinn cursed her own nature as she chewed on the high-flavored fish she didn't much care for. Why couldn't she have simply accepted Lewis's offer? Would it have been so terrible to welcome his generosity? Wasn't that why she had left Eugene for him—so that she could be with a man who could *give*?

"How's your salmon?" Lewis said.

"It's okay."

"Why didn't you take the last sole?" he asked.

"Why didn't you?"

"I wanted you to be happy."

She paused, taking that in as she glanced around the ancient walls. The building was so rich with history it seemed to have its own spirit. She ran her fingers over the rough brick beside them, as if the past were a physical thing she could touch.

"You know what's ironic?" she said. "O. Henry wrote 'The Gift of the Magi,' in this very tavern, and we're just like the couple in that story. She sold her hair to buy him a chain for his watch. He sold his watch to buy her combs. They both wind up with nothing."

Lewis shook his head. "That's not the way it ends," he said.

"It's not?"

"They don't wind up with nothing. O. Henry makes a point of how rich they are because what they have is more valuable than possessions."

Quinn nodded, trying to remember the actual story. Damn if he wasn't right. Okay, she thought, no matter how hard it is I'm going to try. I'm going to try to appreciate the generosity that comes with his love.

"Of course," he added, "that's only because they weren't stuck with dry salmon and wrinkly potatoes."

She laughed and he signaled the waiter.

"What are you doing?" she asked.

"I'm going to see if they still have that sole."

Despite her vow, Lewis's magnanimous nature continued to be a problem for Quinn except in one crucial area of their lives—the bedroom.

Early on, Quinn discovered that Lewis had the ability to turn on her animal brain in a way that made it impossible for her to reject his benevolence. The first time they made love was in his Forest Hills apartment. He had made her dinner, and it was clear they both knew it was the night they would consummate the relationship. She tingled with excitement throughout the meal, eager for it to be over so that they could get to the bedroom where she would show her appreciation. But once they started, his attentions short-circuited her determination to prove her love. He was slow and deliberate, and each touch made her greedier for more. By the time he went down on her, there wasn't a thought in her head besides the basest desire to feel him inside, filling her up.

"Please," she cried. "Now."

"Wait," he said, and continued until she bucked, reaching for nonexistent bedposts.

He traveled back to her face and kissed her on the mouth, pinning her arms while he entered her. She wrapped her legs around his waist to pull him deeper inside, and when she came, shuddering, it was a release that expelled every last defense, leaving her susceptible to even the tiniest microbes of his affection. Quinn relaxed against him, spent. He ran the back of his finger down her cheek and she kissed his hand.

QUINN DECONSTRUCTED, NO. 4

Nan wasn't sure the series was achieving anything particularly worthy, and yet Ellis Everett, her friend and art dealer, thought it was her best work yet. He had, in fact, called the paintings "sublime."

Maybe Nan would feel that when she had painted the final canvas. Perhaps then she would have the answer she was seeking with this series.

Figuring out how to paint Quinn during her college years was particularly difficult, as Nan so rarely saw her during that period. Her daughter was away, living in a dorm, and barely spoke to her parents during school breaks. Nan considered painting an empty green chair for this portrait—perhaps putting it in Quinn's bedroom. But that seemed too gimmicky. And a bit of a cop-out.

Had Quinn been happy in college? Yes. Almost defiantly so, as if she needed to prove to her parents how she could flourish when she wasn't under their roof. That, Nan decided, was how she would try to capture Quinn at this stage, with anger bubbling beneath the surface of her joy.

She started to sketch Quinn's young face, experimenting with expressions. There was something so troubling about the anger. Nan felt that it was directed straight at her. She wanted to ask: What have I done? Why are you so furious with me?

If only you understood the power of my love for you, Nan thought, you'd forgive me.

13

QUINN DIDN'T LEARN ANYTHING NEW FROM HER VISIT WITH the obstetrician. Her blood pressure was normal. She had gained three pounds. The fetal heartbeat was strong. Except for the fact that brain tissue might be protruding through a fissure in her baby's skull, it was an unremarkable visit.

She sat in front of her computer, determined to stop avoiding the truth and face her daughter's condition. She typed the word *encephalocele* into a search engine. The information that came up was exactly what the doctors had told her. Encephalocele, or *cranium bifidum*, was a neural tube defect characterized by a protrusion of the brain and/or the membranes that cover it through an opening in the skull. There was a long list of symptoms that could accompany it, including hydrocephalus (cerebrospinal fluid in the brain), developmental delays, blindness, paralysis, mental and growth retardation, seizures, and more. Everything she read seemed so grim. Then she came upon a page from the National Institute of Neurological Disorders and Stroke, which had one sentence that caught her attention: "Some affected children may have normal intelligence."

Some. What did that mean? Quinn scoured the information, trying to find a percentage to fix to the word. She wanted something to hold on to, some tiny bit of hope.

She came upon another article filled with statistics. It said that an encephalocele reduced the chance of a live birth to only 21 percent. Could that be true? Did she really have an 80 percent chance of losing the baby? Why hadn't the doctors told her this? Quinn read on. Of the 21 percent who made it to term, 50 percent did not survive. What did that mean? Did not survive a year? A day? An hour? Was Naomi as good as dead? Quinn grabbed a tissue and blew her nose.

Then she remembered something else the doctor had said—most encephaloceles occur in the back of the skull, a much more perilous region. Quinn held to the hope that this meant those percentages didn't necessarily apply to her baby, whose fissure was in a less dangerous area.

Quinn read and read, finding more questions than answers. One particular sentence stopped her: "A good prognosis is indicated for a patient who has an anterior encephalocele containing no brain tissue and who has no associated anomalies."

Anterior. That meant the front, where her baby's was. No associated anomalies. That was exactly what they had told her after the targeted sonogram. The big question was the brain tissue. If the sac protruding through the fissure in Naomi's skull consisted of membrane and not actual brain tissue, she could be okay. And it was the one thing they hadn't been able to tell her. Her MRI, which they said she couldn't have for another six weeks, would surely reveal what they needed to know. She would have to find a way to hold on until then, to live with the uncertainty.

It occurred to Quinn that the cosmetic issues of her baby's condition—which had so horrified her when she first saw pictures on the Internet—weren't even on the radar at this point. Not that she didn't

care if her daughter's face was malformed or required extensive recon-
structive surgery. It was just that right now the concern about brain damage occupied all the room she had for anxiety. There was time to wring
her hands about the rest.

Quinn sat back, exhausted. She glanced at the clock. Isaac would be
home in an hour. Did that leave her enough time for a short trip to the
other side? Could she escape the pressures of this life just for a few minutes? She tried to convince herself that the respite would do her good,
make her a better mother for Isaac. But if she wasn't on the corner when
Isaac's bus pulled up he would be devastated. And last time she'd had
trouble getting back—this time it could take even longer. No, she simply
couldn't take the chance when the timing was this tight.

Still, Quinn couldn't help wondering what Eugene was doing right now
on the other side. Then another thought occurred to her: What was Eugene
doing right now in *this* life? She knew he had turned down the cable television job, and that he lost his radio show about a year later, when his ratings
began to slip. Where had he wound up? She assumed he was back on the air
in another market, but had not followed his career. It was too depressing.

Now she needed to know. Quinn typed his name into a search engine and
discovered that Eugene was still an on-air personality, doing a morning-
drive-time show in upstate New York. It was a pretty small market, and
she imagined that he considered himself a miserable failure. The tug of
guilt she felt mixed with anger. Surely he could have taken the cable television job after she left him. It was as if he wanted to fail to prove how
devastated she had left him.

Quinn found a current image of Eugene at his studio, wearing head-
phones as he interviewed some local figure. *This isn't my fault,* she wanted
to say to the picture. *I can't fix everything. I can't!*

The phone rang, and Quinn was glad to hear her brother's voice. He
sounded ebullient.

"Cordell got the job!" he said.

"The job?" Quinn had traveled so deep into her own troubles it was jarring to realize joy could be so close at hand.

"The soap opera," he explained. "Taped right here in New York. He'll be playing the tennis pro every housewife wants to boink. Or something like that. It's his huge break."

Her brother was happy. Quinn's heart softened. "What great news!"

"Now we can really make a life together, Quinn. Maybe we'll finally get married. Cordell and I talked about that the last time we went to the Berkshires. We can have a real wedding in Massachusetts now. Did you know that? Same-sex marriages are legal—we don't even need proof of residency."

She listened carefully to his voice. Sometimes it was hard to tell the difference between a manic episode and just run-of-the-mill joy. But this sounded genuine, and Hayden deserved to be happy. Maybe this career break would really be the thing to center Cordell. Maybe this was her brother's happily-ever-after.

"A wedding in the Berkshires would be magnificent, Hayden."

"There's a five-star resort just a few miles from Aunt Bunny's place, and I understand they're gay friendly. I'm going to call and see if they have a date for us in the summer, when everything's in bloom. Wouldn't that be beautiful?"

Summer. To Hayden, it was just a bright spot in the future. To Quinn, it was ominously opaque. What would her life be like? Would she be happily burdened with diaper bags and nursing bras and spit-up cloths? Or would her daily routine include trips to the hospital, praying for her baby to survive surgery? Or worse, would Naomi be no more than a sharp pain of a memory . . . the baby who didn't live.

"Yes," she said to her brother, "that would be beautiful."

THAT NIGHT QUINN had trouble sleeping. The idea of Hayden's possible wedding made the future too real to avoid. Over and over, Quinn played out every possible outcome for Naomi, as if she could actually figure out what might happen just by thinking about it enough. In the morning, when her alarm went off, she hit the snooze button and tried to get a few more minutes' rest.

"Did you have a bad night?" Lewis asked.

"Terrible."

"Come here."

Quinn rolled over into her husband's arms and he stroked her back. She relaxed into him and breathed in his scent.

"Why don't you stay in bed," he said. "I'll give Isaac breakfast."

"I won't be able to sleep anyway."

He pulled her closer and she burrowed into his neck. His morning erection pressed against her pelvis, and her body responded with an unconscious squeeze toward him. He reached over and picked up the clock to look at it.

"If we're quick . . ." she said.

He smiled and kissed her on the mouth.

Quinn needed to make love to Lewis. She needed to lose herself in the heat of his touch, and to see her own body through the desire in his eyes. She pulled off her nightgown and he rolled on top of her. His thumb found her nipple, his other hand traveled between her legs. Her hips rose toward his fingers, which lightly touched her clitoris. Her body was greedy with want. Don't stop, she thought. God, please.

Isaac's small fist knocked on their door. "Mommy?"

"Shit," she whispered to Lewis.

"Mommy?" Isaac said again.

"I'll be right there!"

"Rain check," Lewis said, kissing her on the top of the head.

"Shit," she repeated.

———

LATER, AS QUINN stood on the corner watching Isaac's bus drive away, Georgette appeared at her side and asked if she could come in for a cup of coffee. It had been a few days since they'd chatted.

"Of course," Quinn said. "I just made a fresh pot."

"Excellent. I need to keep my mind off Esteban this morning. His webcam is broken."

Esteban, Quinn knew, was the Miami landscape architect with whom Georgette was having a cyber affair.

"Webcam?" Quinn said, as she led Georgette into her house. "I thought you just typed dirty messages to each other."

"Please. That's kindergarten stuff."

"Dear God, I hope not." The coffee was still hot, so she poured a cup for her friend and one for herself. Dr. Bernard had told Quinn there was nothing wrong with having coffee, as long as she didn't have more than two a day. She stuck to that, grateful she was still able to get her fix.

Quinn noticed Georgette was holding her cell phone. "Are you expecting him to call?"

"Don't worry, I'm not planning on having phone sex in your kitchen. He can go twenty-four hours without me."

"I didn't realize it was a daily activity."

"It's part of my routine," Georgette said. "Roger leaves for the office and I get nasty online with Esteban. And then I get to work writing steamy sex scenes for my readers."

"Such a structured life," Quinn said.

"I love it when you're ironic." Georgette took a sip of her coffee. "Tell me what's new with you. I rang your bell the other day but you didn't answer."

"Yesterday?" Quinn said. "I was at the doctor."

"Day before. Your car was here."

Wednesday. It was the day she had crossed over to visit with her mother.

Quinn rubbed her eyes, picturing her neighbor ringing her doorbell and getting no answer. It was just as Quinn had suspected. She existed concurrently in both lives only if she didn't slip through the portal. Once she crossed over, she was removing herself from this life.

"I must have been in the shower," she said to Georgette.

"I thought maybe you had your own cyber thing going on with someone," Georgette said.

Quinn laughed. "No offense, Georgette, but I would never cheat on my husband."

"Cheating? Who said anything about cheating?"

"You don't think cybersex is cheating?"

"As long as there's no touching involved, it's innocent."

"There's no touching?"

"Let me clarify," Georgette said. "There's no touching *each other*. Self-touching, on the other hand, is pretty much the whole point. And don't get me started on sex toys."

Quinn nearly spit out her coffee. "Too much information!" she said.

Georgette laughed. "What did you think? That we just typed dirty words to each other? When I said we got nasty together, I thought you understood."

"I guess I just didn't want to think about it."

"That's the difference between you and me," said Georgette. "I think about it all the time."

"Do you and Roger still—"

"Of course. Probably more than you and Lewis."

"How would you know how often Lewis and I do it?" Quinn said. She didn't want to talk specifics, but she also didn't want Georgette to get the wrong idea. Unlike a lot of other married couples, she and Lewis still had sizzle. She felt a certain pride in that.

"Just guessing. Parents usually have less energy."

"Energy isn't the problem."

"Opportunity, then?"

Quinn nodded. "Not always easy with a six-year-old in the house."

"You two need some time alone. That's one nice thing about being an empty-nester. Roger and I have no one to disturb us."

"And you don't feel guilty about your cyber friend?"

"Why should I? My porno sessions with Esteban get me all fired up for the real thing. It makes my sex with Roger that much better."

"But there's another man in your life," Quinn said, rising. She opened the pantry and looked inside. "It's a huge secret to keep."

Georgette shrugged. "Everyone has secrets. Even you, I'll bet."

Quinn turned to face her friend, who stared at her, unblinking. Her face was so open, so nonjudgmental that Quinn was almost tempted to invite her to the basement and show her the portal to the other life. It would be so liberating. But she wouldn't. She simply couldn't tell anyone she had two lives she could switch between. Even gentle Hayden was alarmed by it. If anyone else found out, they might try to stop her.

"I'm pretty much an open book," Quinn said, pouring some wheat crackers onto a plate.

LATER THAT DAY, when Quinn went into the basement to do laundry, she promised herself she wouldn't slip through. She was tempted to, but the conversation with Georgette had her thinking about the duplicity involved. It was indeed like cheating. She was a married woman, and yet there was another man in her life. Hell, there was another *life* in her life. She wasn't just cheating on Lewis. She was cheating on Isaac. She was cheating on Naomi. She was cheating on the suburbs, her Volvo, and her membership in the PTA.

Quinn opened the washing machine, spun the temperature dial to hot, and turned it on. As water rushed in, she poured in detergent and Clorox. Then she watched as the water level rose and the bleach diluted.

Quinn thought she heard something above the rush of the water, and closed the lid to get a better listen. Nothing.

She opened the washer again and began dropping in gym socks, undershirts, towels, and other whites. At last she closed the machine and paused to listen again. There was something, wasn't there? She sensed that the sound was coming from the fissure.

Quinn pulled down the ancient ironing board and stared at the crack. She realized then that she hadn't actually heard a sound but felt something powerful going on with Eugene on the other side. He was emotional. No, hysterical. Something had frightened him and he was begging for her help.

Quinn waited for the feeling to pass. Surely the alternate Quinn was there with him, helping. Eugene would calm down any minute.

But he didn't. And while Quinn wanted to ignore the pleas from the other side and go upstairs to straighten the house and make her daily phone calls, she felt riveted to the spot. Eugene needed her. Not only that, but something terribly exciting was happening. It called to her.

14

"Are you ever coming out of there?"

Quinn sat up in the bathtub of her Manhattan apartment and heard Eugene pounding on the door. She had decided there was no harm in investigating what was happening in her Eugene life. She wasn't really having an affair, after all. She would just learn what the trouble was and see if she could help. Then she'd go right back.

"I'm taking a bath," she said. "I'll be out in a minute."

"Please, don't rush on my account. I'm only having the most major crisis in my career."

Quinn got out of the tub, wrapped herself in a terry-cloth robe, and opened the door.

"What is it?" she asked. "What's wrong?"

Eugene was in the middle of their bedroom, pacing. His hair was messy, his eyes were wild.

"That was Andrew on the phone," he said, referring to his agent. "I'm being seriously considered for the late-night slot on network television. Network, Quinn!"

Eugene's TV talk show was on cable. Network television had always seemed like a dream just outside his reach.

"That's fantastic," she said.

"Network! Fuck me!"

"Eugene, this is *good* news. You should be thrilled."

He whirled around to face her, as if she couldn't possibly understand his point if she wasn't looking straight into his eyes. "It's lose-lose. If I don't get it, I'm the laughingstock of the industry. Everyone will know I'm the schmuck who was passed over. And if I do get it and my ratings suck, it's total public humiliation."

This was just like Eugene. He always processed good news as apocalyptic. He just couldn't accept that something wonderful could happen to him.

"Take a deep breath and consider one more possibility," she said. "You could actually get it and do well."

"That doesn't make me feel better."

"Why not?"

"I don't have what it takes to succeed in network TV. I'm not mainstream enough."

"That's why they want you. Late night is edgy. You're perfect."

He didn't respond. Quinn folded her arms and watched Eugene pace. He was in a frenzy and locked shut against letting in a single ray of light.

"When will you know for sure?" she asked.

"Not for a few weeks—after we get back from Fiji. How am I supposed to enjoy this vacation now? I'll be worried the whole time."

"You'll be worried the first day. Then you'll unwind. The beach does that to you, remember? Once we're out of the city, all this stress melts away. We'll just enjoy the sun and the ocean. We'll have slow meals and long walks. It'll be wonderful. Sit down."

He did as she said, and Quinn began rubbing his neck and shoulders. As she kneaded the knots in his muscles, she considered how familiar it felt to be massaging him like this. At the same time, she was glad it was the kind of touching that lacked intimacy. She didn't want to risk feeling the stirrings of desire. Complete strangers could work on the kinks in your neck without any of the sexual connection of lovers. It was almost clinical.

As she worked, Quinn pictured what she knew about the exotic beauty of the Fiji Islands. She imagined the warm sun and the blue Pacific, palm trees and lush hillsides, waterfalls and rain forests. She started to wonder if the relaxed pace and soothing scenery were just what she needed as well. The idea of paradise was almost unbearably tempting.

Quinn rubbed her thumbs into the sides of his neck as she looked out the window at their view of Central Park. Eugene had accomplished so much and yet rarely seemed proud. Deep down, he had to know he was talented and that few people achieved what he had. All this anxiety, she thought, was the result of some foolish idea that if he admitted to believing in himself he would lose it all. Cynicism was his talisman, the charm that would ward off evil.

"You're allowed to feel happy about this," she said. "Nothing bad will happen."

He pulled away from her and stood. "Give me a fucking break."

"Eugene—"

"Don't psychoanalyze me, okay? Even my therapist admits that I'm too fucked up for that."

"I'm just trying to calm you down."

"Then don't tell me this is good news!" he said, getting angrier. "This is a potential disaster. You should know that by now, Quinn!"

"Don't yell at me!" It wasn't the first time she'd said that to Eugene. But it felt different now. It felt . . . justified. She didn't deserve to be yelled at. She wondered then if being married to Lewis all these years had actually broken down her defenses and convinced her she deserved to be treated with kindness.

Eugene stopped pacing and looked at her. His face softened. "I'm sorry," he said. "I don't mean to take this out on you."

"I know."

He hugged her. "I don't know what I'd do without you," he whispered.

She relaxed into the familiarity of his body. He was taller than Lewis, but still thinner, despite his personal trainer. And his embrace was entirely different. It was tighter, more desperate. She remembered the passion of making love with him, how the greedy heat in his eyes aroused her. She pushed him away.

"I wish I could help you," she said, "but I can't. I can't make you happy. You're just too stubborn about your misery."

"You keep me from falling apart."

"Is that enough?"

"It's almost enough." He kissed her neck, untied her robe, and opened it.

For a moment, she hesitated. It was so familiar, so tempting. And her body was still on high alert, as it had been only a few hours since she and Lewis had groped each other in breathless passion, only to be interrupted by Isaac. Her nerve endings were awake and hungry. She wanted to be touched.

Eugene ran his hand down her smooth back and grabbed her behind. She was about to push herself into him when she recalled her conversation with Georgette. *I would never cheat on my husband,* she had said.

Quinn pulled away. "Damn it, Eugene!" She closed her robe and tied it tight.

"What? What's wrong?"

"I . . . nothing."

He took a step toward her. "Come here," he said, even though they were barely an inch apart.

"I didn't finish my bath."

He tugged at her robe again, smiling. "I'll take you dirty."

"Stop!"

His eyes narrowed. "You're hot when you're hard to get," he said, and slipped his hand inside her robe again. He grabbed her naked breast.

She pushed him away. "I mean it, Eugene."

"I have a hard-on and I didn't even take anything."

Quinn ran into the bathroom, slammed the door, and locked it. Eugene jiggled the handle.

"Let me in," he said.

"Go away."

"I'll wash your back."

The tub was still filled and Quinn tested the temperature with her fingers. It had gone chilly, which she knew was critical for her journey. She lowered herself into it and closed her eyes, praying she'd be pulled back quickly. It was cold. So cold. And she could still hear Eugene pounding on the door. Finally she felt herself being pushed into that other space, and the last thing she heard before the journey went silent was his muffled voice.

"I need you, Quinn!"

WHEN SHE EMERGED back in her basement, naked, shivering, and scraped down both sides of her torso, the phone was ringing and someone was alternately knocking on the front door and pressing the bell. She froze for a moment, not sure what to do first. She picked up her clothes and dressed as fast as she could, then answered the phone.

"Is this Quinn Braverman?" said the caller.

"Yes."

"I'm calling from Cowitt Alarms. You're listed as the emergency contact for the Gilbert residence at Sixteen Laurel Drive."

Oh, God. Her parents' address. The pounding on her front door continued. She tucked the phone under her chin and ran up the stairs as she continued the conversation.

"Is there a problem?" she asked.

"There was a security breach on the premises. The back door. We notified the precinct, and the police are already at the location."

"Is the house okay? Was anything taken?" She looked through the peephole on her front door. It was Georgette.

"I don't have that information, ma'am. The police will want you to inspect the premises and file a report."

Quinn's heart raced. She pictured two men breaking in, taking something that belonged to her father. Or maybe even her mother. She knew they were professionals and would probably get away with it, which infuriated her.

Georgette knocked again. Quinn swung open the door and held up a finger to let her friend know she needed a minute.

"Tell the police I'll be right there," she said to the caller, and got off the phone.

"Police?" Georgette said.

Quinn quickly explained the situation to Georgette, hoping her friend would understand it wasn't a good time for a visit.

"I have to get over there right away," Quinn said.

"You know there's not much you can do, right?"

Georgette was correct, of course, but the thought made her want to scream. There had to be *something* she could do.

"They need me to file a report," Quinn said.

"Is everything else okay? I came back because I left my cell phone here, and I was knocking for so long."

Uh-oh, Quinn thought. How could she possibly explain her disappearance?

"Oh, I see," Georgette said, pointing to Quinn's wet hair. "You were in the shower. Sorry."

Quinn felt as if she had dodged a bullet. Yet another reason why she had to stop doing this.

"Is there anything I can do?" Georgette said as she went into the kitchen to retrieve her cell phone. "You want me to get the little guy off the bus?"

"No, thanks, I'll be back in time. Besides, he would freak if he didn't find me waiting there."

"But he loves me like a grandma."

The two of them stepped out onto the front porch. Quinn closed the door behind her and locked it. "I know," she said, and it was true. Isaac was very comfortable with Georgette, who often babysat for him. "But he still has this issue about seeing me at the bus stop when he gets home. I have to be there for him. Always."

A POLICE OFFICER standing outside Quinn's childhood home explained to her that the lock on the back door had been broken, though they couldn't tell if anything had been taken. "We've been seeing a lot of break-ins in this area," he said. "Usually they just take jewelry and get out fast."

"So you didn't catch anyone?"

"I'm afraid not."

Quinn and the officer went inside so that she could try to determine what was missing. When they reached the master bedroom, it was clear the thieves had ransacked the room, as drawers were pulled open and emptied. Quinn shuddered at the thought of strangers going through these personal things, trying to choose what might be worth stealing.

She took a deep breath. "I'll have to call my father," Quinn said. "I don't know if he had anything valuable in here."

She looked in the other upstairs rooms, which also showed signs of a quick search. Downstairs, everything seemed in good order. All the electronics—the stereo, the computer, the television, which was so rarely used—were still there. Quinn reached the studio and stopped. The landscape her mother had been working on when she died was still on the easel, covered. Stacks of framed paintings leaned against the walls, and her mother's brushes were on the table where she had left them. Still, something in the room felt different. Then Quinn realized what it was, and a chill prickled her flesh. The series of family portraits—the last collection Nan had completed, including the only one that showed the two of them together—was missing. The thieves must have grabbed them because they were easier to carry, being the only unframed canvases. Quinn looked around the studio again and again. Those paintings couldn't be gone. They just couldn't.

She closed her eyes and tried to envisage the painting of her and Nan, together but apart. She hadn't even bothered to look at it the last time she was there.

"What is it?" the officer asked. "What's missing?"

"My mother," Quinn said. "I've lost her again."

That evening, Quinn left Isaac and Georgette tucked comfortably into the den, watching Nickelodeon and drinking hot chocolate, while she and Lewis went back to her parents' house to clean up. Hayden and Cordell met them there to pitch in.

The four adults worked together in the master bedroom. Lewis was busy trying to get the drawers back on their runners while the others sorted and folded the massive piles of clothing that had been dumped onto the floor.

"We should do Dad a favor and throw some of these away," Hayden said, holding up a multicolored cotton sweater that looked like it was from the 1980s.

Cordell held up another that was almost identical. "How many of these does he have?"

"That was his Cosby show era," Quinn said, laughing.

Cordell looked at her. "I thought TV was forbidden in this house."

"Not forbidden," Hayden explained, "discouraged. Dad loved his sports . . . and his Cosby."

"No kidding," Cordell said, holding up another sweater. "He must have dozens. What was he thinking?"

"I bet Mom was going through a manic phase," Hayden said, "spending like mad. She probably brought home bags and bags of these."

"You know what's sweet about that?" Quinn said. "He kept them."

Quinn treasured her father for his sentimentality, especially since it was a quality her mother lacked. If someone was going to squirrel away the art projects, report cards, and other mementos from Hayden and Quinn's childhood, it was always their father.

"Is your dad a pack rat like you?" Cordell asked.

Quinn bristled. She didn't like Cordell calling Hayden names. "I don't think either of them are pack rats," she said.

Cordell rolled his eyes. "Are you kidding? Thank God Hayden has cute legs, because he's got a drawer full of bicycle shorts he hasn't worn since the Clinton administration."

"I guess it's all relative," Hayden said. "Compared to you, I'm a pack rat. You don't save a single thing—just like our mom. She threw away *everything*."

"Not everything," Lewis said, and the others turned to him. "I was wondering why this one drawer wouldn't close, and I realized something was in the way." He held up a package wrapped in creased white paper and tied with thick yellow yarn. Quinn's name was artistically painted across the top in Nan's handwriting. "It must have fallen out of the back of the drawer," he said.

"What is this?" Quinn said, taking the beat-up package.

Lewis shrugged.

"Open it," Hayden said.

The others watched as Quinn untied the yarn and opened the small bundle. Inside was a tiny pink baby outfit with matching hat and booties. The cartoonish teddy bear emblem on the front of the stretchie gave it a dated look. Quinn was confused.

"I've seen this before," she said.

Hayden nodded. "And I think I know where." He dashed out of the room and came back a few minutes later with a photo album open to a page showing their parents, Nan and Phil, bringing a newborn Quinn home from the hospital. They were posing inside the front door, holding up a sleeping infant wearing the same pink outfit with the cartoon bear on the front.

"I don't get it," Quinn said.

"She was saving it for you," Lewis said.

"But why? She never saved anything."

"She brought you home from the hospital in it," Lewis said. "It's special."

Quinn turned to her brother. "Does this seem like something Mom would do?"

"No, but it's her handwriting. And the wrapping is pure Mom."

Quinn put her hand on her belly. "Maybe I'm reading too much into this, but . . ." She paused, considering how to phrase it without sounding silly. How could she explain that she felt there was some kind of message in this gift—almost as if her mother had known she would one day need this connection?

"I don't know," she continued, "but maybe this means she's still here in some way." That felt right to Quinn. She liked to think she didn't have to cross over to be close to her mother. Her spirit, perhaps, was always here.

Cordell stuck his arm under a pile of clothes and poked his hand out, as if it were rising from the dead. "Ooh! A message from beyond!"

Hayden ignored him and addressed his sister. "I think you can attach as much significance as you want."

Quinn brought the little garment to her nose and sniffed. She imagined a tiny warm body inside. "I'm going to bring her home from the hospital in this." She glanced at Lewis to check his reaction and he met her eyes. The message that passed between them was hope and fear. Hope that they might actually bring Naomi home from the hospital. Fear that her mother may have left them their baby's burial outfit.

"She'll be the youngest-ever participant in *What Not to Wear*," Cordell said, laughing.

Hayden turned to him. "Inappropriate." He looked back at his sister. "I'm sorry, when things get emotional he starts making bad jokes."

Cordell folded his arms. "Don't apologize for me," he said to Hayden. "I'm not one of your students. I'm a grown man."

"You're right," Hayden said. "I'm sorry."

"*You're* sorry?" Quinn said, well aware that it wasn't her place to butt in. She simply couldn't keep herself from defending her younger brother. Cordell should not be treating him like this. He should be kind, gentle, grateful. "Don't let him turn this around, Hayden. You're not the one who's acting like a creep."

"No offense, Quinn," Cordell said, "but this doesn't really concern you."

"It *does* concern me, because he's my brother and I don't like the way you treat him."

"Don't you think the way *he* feels about it is more important than the way *you* feel about it?"

"All I'm saying is that he deserves better."

"Better than me, you mean?"

The idea that Cordell found that inconceivable drove Quinn to the breaking point. "You can't even imagine that, right? Who could be better than you? God's gift to the gay community!"

"Spare me the homophobia," Cordell said.

Quinn sneered, disgusted. "Just because I think you have an ego the size of Prospect Park doesn't mean I'm homophobic."

"Okay, okay," Hayden said, "I think this is going too far."

Lewis agreed. "I guess we're all tired," he said.

"I'm not tired," Quinn insisted. "I'm pissed."

"I know you're going through a hell of a lot," Cordell said, his hand on his chest as if he could actually feel her pain in his own heart, "but that doesn't give you an excuse to treat others badly."

Quinn's jaw dropped. The nerve of him to be so condescending! She wanted to explode, to tell him to get the hell out of the house and never come back. But poor Hayden. He'd be crushed if she and Cordell were on the outs.

Lewis, clearly sensing her agitation, put his arm around her. "I think it's time to call it a night."

"There's still a lot of work to do," Quinn said.

Hayden approached and hugged her. "Are you okay?" he asked.

"I'm fine." She rubbed her forehead, sensing the beginning of a headache. "Maybe not. I don't know, but I think it would be best if you guys went home."

"She's throwing us out," Cordell said.

Hayden kissed her on the forehead. "I'll call you tomorrow."

Quinn nodded, and then Hayden left with his boyfriend, who couldn't resist making a joke as they went downstairs toward the front door.

"At least we don't have to fold any more of those butt-ugly sweaters."

There was a pause before Hayden replied. "Shut up, Cordell."

15

THE SHEER WHITE NEGLIGEE QUINN SLIPPED INTO HAD AL-
ways made her feel sexy. Now, however, with her swollen breasts and
darkened nipples straining against the diaphanous fabric, she felt almost
embarrassed by her sensuality. She considered taking it off and changing
into one of her regular cotton sleep shirts, but stopped herself. It was
okay to be hyper-sexy. Lewis would be turned on, and she was aching
to sleep with him. It was more than just pregnancy hormones run amok.
After that morning's *Isaac interruptus*, as Lewis called it, she was ready
for action.

She walked from the bathroom to the bedroom, where her husband
was reading a book about global warming.

"Anything new in the science of climate change?" she asked.

He looked up and his eyes scanned her body. "Temperatures are definitely rising. Get over here."

Lewis put down his book and Quinn got into bed with him. They
kissed, and he brushed a hair from her face.

"You okay?" he asked.

"Yes," she said. Temperatures were rising indeed. She felt such a surge of heat, it was as if she'd swallowed fire.

"I'm sorry about the paintings," he said.

"Me, too," she said, but wasn't really thinking about much besides the pulsating between her legs.

He kissed one corner of her mouth and then the other. "You didn't need that extra stress right now."

"And that Cordell," she said.

He didn't respond.

"He was such a jerk," she said. "Wasn't he?"

Lewis shrugged. "He was just being Cordell."

Quinn pulled back and looked at her husband's face. "You think I was overreacting?"

"It's understandable."

"What do you mean?"

"I mean it's understandable that you're a little more . . . emotional right now."

"You don't think Cordell was being a jerk to my brother?"

"I think he was being himself, and so was Hayden. It works for them, Quinn. It's not really our business."

She thought about that for a moment. "Hayden thinks I project my own emotional needs onto him."

Lewis didn't respond.

"You think that, too?" she pressed.

"I think everyone does that, especially when they're under a lot of stress. You're not made out of stone, hon. There comes a point where your resources run out."

Quinn sat up and positioned her pillow behind her back. "You act like I'm the only one under emotional strain. What about you?"

"I never said I wasn't under emotional strain."

"But you don't talk about it. Not to me, anyway."

"You have enough on your plate."

"But I need to know what you're feeling. You can't keep closing me out. It's not good for us."

He sighed and sat up against the headboard next to her. "What do you want to know?"

"I want to know . . ." Quinn leaned over and switched on a light. "I want to know how you feel about the baby."

He stared off in the distance, his eyes soft and unfocused. It took him a few minutes to answer. "Scared," he finally said.

She waited for him to continue, but he didn't. "More," she said.

"I don't know what else you want me to say."

"I want you to say whatever it is you say to your mother, or your sister, or Georgette. You're holding back. I can feel it. Believe me, whatever it is you have to say isn't as bad as shutting down on me."

He took her hand and stared hard at her face. Quinn thought his eyes looked wounded. "The hardest part of this whole thing," he said, "is that I can't protect you. I can't make everything better."

"You're more worried about me than the baby."

"Of course I am. I love you. The baby is just an abstraction to me, especially since . . ."

"Since what?"

He shook his head.

"Since she might not even get a chance to be born?" she offered.

"Right."

"And I suppose you've thought about abortion."

"Yes, of course," he said.

"But why didn't you tell me?"

He pulled the covers over them. "Remember the Ackleys?" he asked.

Robert and Faye Ackley were a couple who had lived down the hall from them in their Queens apartment building. The two couples had become friends, and one Saturday night when they had plans to go out for dinner together, Faye knocked on their door saying she had to cancel because she and Robert had separated. Quinn and Lewis invited her in, and listened to her whole sad story. Their problems, according to Faye, started several years back, when she got pregnant with her third child. Robert said they couldn't afford another baby, and had pressured her to get an abortion she didn't want. She thought she could get past it, but it just never went away. She didn't know if she could ever forgive him, and the strain on their marriage just got to be too much.

"We're not the Ackleys," Quinn said.

"I know, but I would never want to put you in that position."

"So you think it's all my decision?"

"Maybe not all, but mostly. Mostly your decision, yes. It has to be."

"But if you got a vote, would you vote to terminate?"

He put his arms out and she leaned in for an embrace. He kissed the top of her head. "Do you really want me to answer that?"

"Yes, but I don't want you to tell me how you feel about protecting me. I want you to tell me how you feel about fathering a child who might be disabled."

"Do you remember that flight to Daytona Beach I told you about?"

She did. During college, Lewis and some friends had flown down to Florida on spring break. They were 30,000 feet in the air when a fire broke out in one of the engines, and the flight attendant asked Lewis to switch seats with the elderly man who was in front of the emergency exit, just in case. She wanted to be sure the passenger by the hatch was someone strong enough to open it.

"Of course I remember. You said it was the scariest thing that ever happened to you."

Lewis nodded. "This is scarier."

ON MONDAY, Quinn and her brother took Isaac and a friend to the Long Island Children's Museum. It was Columbus Day, and though Lewis had to work, the schools were closed and the place was jammed. Isaac and his playmate didn't mind the crowds at all. If anything, the noise and energy excited them. Quinn and Hayden trailed behind, talking, as the boys went from exhibit to exhibit.

"Cordell is back in L.A.," Hayden said to Quinn.

"Seriously? I thought the soap opera was a done deal."

Hayden shrugged. "Another audition came up and he said he didn't want to leave any stone unturned. A movie role is his real goal. Always has been."

"So what does this mean to you two?"

"Depends whether or not he gets it."

Forget him, she wanted to say. *He doesn't deserve you.* But she wasn't going to butt in again. She gave his hand a squeeze.

"Mom, look!" Isaac called.

Quinn watched as her son stood on a small, round platform surrounded by a moat of liquid bubble soap. His friend, Ethan, tugged on a pulley and a giant ring rose above Isaac, dragging a soap film with it until Isaac was encased in a giant cylindrical bubble. He squealed with laughter.

After Ethan took a turn, they both insisted that Uncle Hayden give it a try. He stepped onto the platform and the boys pulled and pulled until the ring was above his head.

Quinn couldn't resist. She stuck her finger into the soap film and popped it.

"You trying to burst my bubble?" Hayden asked, stepping out of the exhibit. He winked at his sister, who laughed.

"If only I could."

The boys continued on, heading upstairs, with Hayden and Quinn following.

"I know you think I'd be better off without him," Hayden said. "But he's all I ever wanted. And I understand that he can be inappropriate and immature and a thousand other negative things. But he can also be spirited and spontaneous and make life so delicious. He's good for me. And I think I'm good for him, too."

"You don't have to sell me, Hayden."

"I'm just trying to work up to a favor," he said.

Isaac and Ethan made a dash for a room filled with percussion instruments from all over the world. They moved from one to the other, banging, clanging, and making as much noise as they could.

"What is it?" Quinn said to her brother, straining to be heard over the cacophony.

"When he gets back, can you talk to him and smooth things over?"

"I was afraid you were going to ask that," she said just as Isaac found the bongo drums.

Hayden couldn't hear her, and Quinn pulled her brother outside the room, where it was quieter.

"Please, Quinn," Hayden said.

She remembered the conversation she and Lewis had had the night before, and imagined Hayden and Cordell having a pillow talk of their own. Her brother had probably asked Cordell to be the one to smooth things over, and he refused.

The door to the percussion room opened and Isaac and Ethan came through and ran to the next exhibit.

"You shouldn't let him bully you," Quinn said, as they followed the boys.

"He's more sensitive than you realize. The way he gets when he's around you and Lewis—that's Cordell showing off. Around me, he's more open, more sensitive."

"Hard to picture."

Hayden frowned. "I know you hate him."

"I don't hate him. I just . . . I love you. I love you and I care about you and I want to see you happy."

"*He* makes me happy, Quinn. I love him." Hayden looked like he was about to cry. "And I'm worried that he'll use any excuse to walk away from this relationship."

"If that's the case—"

"Don't," he interrupted. "Please. Don't tell me if that's the case, then I shouldn't be in this relationship to begin with. I'm not like you, Quinn."

"What does that mean?"

"It means I don't live my life in fear that the person I love most is going to disappear."

"Is that how you see me?" Quinn asked.

She heard a child's voice crying, "Mom! Mom!" and realized it was Isaac. "I'm right here!" she shouted, and thought about his irrational fear of losing her. Maybe it had nothing to do with sensing that she could disappear into a portal. Maybe he had simply learned it from her.

THE NEXT DAY, Quinn's obstetrician called to tell her the results of her amniocenteses had come in, and that they were "unremarkable." For a split second, Quinn held her breath, thinking it might be good news. Was it possible the results would be in conflict with the sonogram report? Could there be some kind of miracle here? Maybe the images had lied and it was all a mistake. But no, her doctor friend went on to explain that the alpha-fetoprotein level was markedly elevated, which is exactly what they had expected, as it was par for the course when there was a neural tube defect.

Quinn took notes as the doctor spoke, though after that she barely listened. What difference did it make that no chromosomal abnormalities were found, and that disorders such as Down's syndrome, spina bifida, and cystic fibrosis had been ruled out? Her baby was still disfigured, still in danger of dying or being terribly brain damaged.

Quinn had little time to process the information. The call had come just as she was about to get Isaac ready for his soccer practice, so she was left rushed. She promised Sally she would call if she had more questions and got off the phone. She quickly helped her son with his cleats and shin guards before getting him into the car. Since Quinn was the designated snack mom that day, she swung by Dunkin' Donuts to pick up a box of Munchkins for the kids, and while she was there she ordered the ten-cup take-out container of hot coffee to help the moms stay warm while the kids ran around the field.

By the time she got home, she had just enough time to put a chicken in the oven, help Isaac with his homework, get him into the bath, fold a load of laundry, and empty the dishwasher before Lewis got home.

"How was your day?" he asked.

The oven timer beeped. Quinn put on a mitt and pulled out the roaster. "Got the amnio results," she said.

"And?"

"I wrote it down." She pointed with her chin.

Lewis picked up the page and read it while Quinn carefully put down the pan and moved the chicken to a cutting board. She fanned the steam away, and though it was still too hot to cut, she retrieved her poultry shears, aimed the bottom blade inside the chicken's gaping cavity, and squeezed the handles, working her way through the center of the bird.

Lewis put down the paper. "Smells good," he said.

She looked at him. "Is that all you have to say?"

"There's no news, Quinn. It's exactly what we expected."

She continued cutting the bird. "Still—"

"Still what?"

"I don't know, Lewis. After our conversation the other night I thought you were going to start being more open with me."

"What do you want me to say? That I'm miserable about it? Okay, I'm miserable about it. How does that help you?"

She put down the shears. "It helps me because I need to know what you're feeling."

He folded his arms. "I don't know how much more open I can be."

"Don't be like that," she said.

"Like what?"

"Like you think it's stupid to say how you feel."

He unfolded his arms and exhaled. "I'll answer any question you want to ask."

Isaac called from upstairs and Quinn sighed, resigned to the fact that the conversation would go nowhere.

"Is he in the bath?" Lewis asked.

Quinn nodded and wiped her hands on a dish towel.

"I'll go," Lewis said. He squeezed her shoulder.

"Make sure he got all the shampoo out."

Later, when the dishes were clean and nothing was left of the chicken but a sickly pile of bones Quinn had thrown into the trash, she watched out the front window as Lewis brought the garbage to the curb. She saw him glance toward Georgette's house, and then jog over there when their neighbor stepped out her front door. Clearly, he had a lot to tell her, as he started to talk immediately and kept going for quite some time. Georgette interjected occasionally, but mostly just nodded. That went on for nearly fifteen minutes. Finally she gave Lewis a warm hug, and he jogged back home.

THE NEXT DAY, Quinn couldn't fight a floating anxiety that seemed to settle on every thought that crossed her mind. Just when she thought she had convinced Lewis it was okay to open up to her, it turned out he was drifting further away. This only exacerbated her panic about the possibility of losing her baby, not to mention her own fear about raising a disabled child. Plus, she was still worried that her brother's love life might push him into a depression.

Still, Quinn refused to cross through the portal to avoid her troubles. The close call with Eugene had taught her that she needed to stay in this life and face her problems. Going into the other life wasn't just an escape. It was cheating.

Quinn decided to quiet her anxiety by taking action. She knew that anything she could do to feel in control would help. So she drove to her parents' house to check on the new back door lock and make sure everything was okay. Perhaps it would be enough to calm her.

When she got there, the place was just as she had left it. The new lock on the back door was secure and the alarm system was working. The paintings, of course, were still missing, and Quinn couldn't help feeling as if a bit of her heart were gone with them.

She looped around the first floor of the house again and again, and kept coming back to the same spot in the family room, in front of a large antique curio cabinet. It was an area that gave her a terrible feeling. Something about it frightened her.

Was it simply the fact that her mother had always warned her not to go near this particular piece of furniture? Maybe that was it. As a child, she had been trained to give it a wide berth. In fact, it was the only thing in the whole house her mother had been so stern about. Now that she thought about it, it seemed odd that her mother had moved this off-limits piece from the living room to this high-traffic area.

She wondered if the furniture might have been an excuse to keep her away from this spot. But if so, what was the real reason? What was her mother protecting her from? Quinn tried to focus on a vague memory that went back to before the curio cabinet had been placed in this room. She couldn't have been more than four years old. Hadn't she sensed something and tried to talk to her mother about it? That must have been why this heavy piece of furniture had been transferred from the living room, where it suited the decor, to this corner of the family room.

Quinn placed her hands on the curio cabinet and closed her eyes. Within moments, she felt it. There was a portal beneath it. But it wasn't the kind of passageway she was used to. This one felt cold. Quinn didn't sense another life pulsing by on the other side. She felt death.

Terrified, she backed away. What the hell was that? And why did she feel like it was related to the baby outfit her mother had left her?

Scared as she was, Quinn needed to find out more, to get closer to the portal. The furniture was too big for her to try to push out of the way without hurting herself, so she lay down on the floor and stuck her fingertips between the short legs of the heavy piece. As she got closer, a chill prickled at the skin on her back, sending an electrical current of fear down her spine. She pulled away and stood up.

Frightened and confused, Quinn began to pace. Why did she feel like her mother had died in this spot? It made no sense, because she knew Nan had overdosed in the upstairs bathroom.

Courage! she told herself, and in a frenzy began unloading all the curios from the cabinet. She needed to finish before losing her nerve. She removed all the hand-painted plates, bits of pottery, blown glass, African art, and porcelain sculptures her mother had collected over the years. She carefully took out the glass shelves from the top of the case and the wooden drawers from the bottom. Considerably lighter, the cabinet was now easy to push out of the way. Quinn planted her feet on the floor, leaned her back against it, and gave a shove. The thing easily slid aside.

Quinn lowered herself to the ground and sat cross-legged, facing a crack between the slats in the hardwood floor. The dim memory of discovering this spot as a child was becoming clearer. But it felt different, and a cold nausea rose within her. The feeling got worse and worse until Quinn could barely move. She felt sick and so very weak. She knew she could fight it, but sleep caressed the edges of her consciousness and seduced her. Her head got too heavy to hold up, so she let it rest against the cool floor and began to drift off.

As she lost the battle for consciousness, Quinn's fingers and toes went numb, and she felt as if she were dying. Or maybe it was her baby.

Her baby? God, no! She forced herself awake and summoned enough power to crawl from the spot. The farther away she got, the stronger she became. When she felt well enough to rise, she stumbled from the house and drove away.

16

THE ROUTE HOME WAS FAMILIAR ENOUGH FOR QUINN TO PUT her brain on autopilot. She was jarred from her driving trance when her cell phone rang.

"You know those tan pants I wore to Allen's fortieth?"

It was Lewis. She had him on speakerphone.

"What?" she asked.

"I was just wondering if they were still at the cleaner's or if they were in my closet."

"Tan pants?"

"Are you okay?" he asked. "You sound terrible."

She tried to speak, to tell him about the terror she had just experienced, but all that came out was a soft wail that escalated so quickly to full-fledged sobbing that she had to pull over.

"Honey, what is it?"

She couldn't speak.

"Quinn? Do you need me to come home?"

"No. I'm okay, I . . . I was at my parents' house. I just got a terrible feeling there. About my mom, about . . ." She swallowed, reminding herself why she never told Lewis about the portals. And maybe he didn't need to be protected from this truth, but she had kept the secret for so long that breaking it now required more energy than she could possibly summon.

"I felt like I was going to die," she said.

"Oh, baby. You're under so much stress."

"I think there might be some strange thing about my mother I never knew before. And I think it has to do with me."

"You know, I only have one meeting this afternoon. I can cancel it and come right home."

"You don't need to," she said.

"Are you sure?"

Was she? Maybe she should accept his help now. But what could he possibly do for her? No, all she needed was some time to decompress.

"I'll be fine," she said. "And you're right—I'm just under a lot of stress. I'll go home and put my feet up."

That was exactly what she did, except that she had only just sat down when the doorbell rang. It was Georgette, bearing another loaf of her banana bread. Quinn made them each a cup of herbal tea, and they sat at the kitchen table.

"You don't look so good," Georgette said.

"I'm tired."

"Is that all?"

"Stressed," Quinn said, stirring her tea. "*Very* stressed."

"Maybe you should stay away from your parents' house for a while."

Quinn looked up, surprised. "How did you know I went there?"

"Hmm?"

Quinn stood. "Did Lewis call you?"

"Don't be mad."

"Why *shouldn't* I be mad? He won't tell me one damned thing and goes running to you to spill his guts."

"It's not like that, Quinn."

"What is it like, then?"

"He's concerned about you."

"Then he should talk to *me*!"

"When he gets home tonight—"

"*Please* don't give me advice on how to make my marriage work! You're not one to talk." Quinn gasped and covered her mouth. "Oh, God. I'm sorry. I didn't mean that."

Georgette waved away the remark and then wrapped her arms around her friend. "It's okay," she said. "Because you're right—I absolutely suck at marriage. But I do know one thing. You and Lewis need some time alone together."

Quinn couldn't imagine what "time alone together" would do for her marriage if Lewis wouldn't speak to her, and by the time he got home her anxiety had been displaced by anger. She was petulant all through dinner, responding to his queries about her state of mind with curt answers like "I'm fine," or "Don't worry about it."

"You sure you're okay?" he asked.

She rolled her eyes. Why couldn't he just let it rest? Didn't he understand she wasn't in the mood to talk?

"Whatever," she said.

"That sounds angry."

"Just leave it alone, Lewis."

"Honey, how can I help you if you don't tell me what's going on?" he asked.

That did it. "I guess you don't like it when I won't talk to you, right?" she said, seething.

"Huh?"

"How the hell do you think *I* feel when you turn to stone around me and yet go running to Georgette to spill your guts?"

"What?"

"I saw you jog over there to talk to her last night. And then today, the first thing you did after we spoke was call Georgette to talk about it!"

"Honey—"

"The other night," she went on, "you made a big fuss over the fact that you're there for me. Well, I'm here for you, too, Lewis, only you seem to be able to talk to anyone but me!"

"Calm down."

"I will *not* calm down!" She was crying now. "You're the most important thing in my life and you're closing me out."

He grabbed her by the shoulders. "Quinn, listen to me. The reason I went to talk to Georgette last night is because I was planning a surprise for you."

"What?" she said. It was as if the wind suddenly changed direction. Or stopped blowing altogether.

"For your birthday," he said. "I thought we needed some time together. Some time to have fun and forget about everything else. So I called your aunt and asked if her lake house was available. And then I asked Georgette if she could babysit for Isaac. I want to take you away this weekend, honey. All the arrangements are made. I was going to tell you tomorrow."

"You did that for me?"

"Yes!"

She collapsed into him. "Oh, Lewis."

"We really need this," he said softly.

"We do."

"So you're okay with this?" he said. "You want to take this trip?"

She did. In fact, it sounded like a lifesaving prescription. The trip was exactly the kind of escape she needed. Instead of slipping through a portal to another life, she could escape right into her husband's arms. But it wouldn't be truly romantic unless they could agree to make it a vacation from stress. This trip could be like a chance to go back in time to before this pregnancy, before they were even parents. And, given how she had been pestering him to open up to her, she almost couldn't believe what she was going to say next.

"Under one condition," she said.

"What's that?"

"We don't talk about the baby. I want this to be all about us."

QUINN DECONSTRUCTED, NO. 5

———+———

Quinn as a high school girl. At first, Nan had considered doing something teenage with her body position, like putting her sideways on the chair with her legs hanging over the arm. Or situating her on the floor with her legs up on the chair, so that she would be upside down to the viewer. But she rejected these as banal. She didn't want the painting to look like a scene from Bye Bye Birdie.

Adolescence was all about pushing away your family and pulling in your friends. But this wasn't a painting about puberty. It was a painting about Quinn. And Nan believed that this was the age where her daughter began to realize that she was truly separate from her mother and would grow up to be an entirely different kind of person. So Nan positioned her in the chair with her knees pulled up to her chest and her arms wrapped around them. She was embracing herself.

Nan felt good about this one. She had a very clear direction and thought it worked so well with the other paintings. But after working on it for several days she looked at the canvas and saw something she hadn't realized was there. Quinn wasn't just embracing her differences. She was self-comforting, being her own mother.

Have I failed you? Nan wondered. All these years she had been telling herself that her children hadn't really suffered ill effects from her disorder. Yes, there were times when depression stole her from them, but they always had their father. And surely learning to deal with a bipolar mother had made them stronger and had taught them compassion.

But now, looking at the daughter she had created on canvas, Nan felt reproached. There was something accusatory in the way Quinn was looking at her.

"What have I done?" Nan asked aloud.

17

WITH THEIR BICYCLES STRAPPED TO THE BACK OF THE CAR, Quinn and Lewis drove north across the Throgs Neck Bridge, heading for the scenic Taconic Parkway. It was an older highway, with narrow lanes and sharp curves, but it was Quinn's favorite way to head toward her aunt Bunny's vacation home in Massachusetts, especially in the fall.

Her choice was rewarded with spectacular bursts of color on all sides. A week ago, half the leaves were still green. A week hence, more than half would be gone, leaving cold, gray branches. But on this crisp Friday morning, the trees offered nature's most richly dappled autumn palette— a backdrop of warm rusts and earthy browns splashed with brilliant reds, shocking golds, and oranges that seemed almost aflame.

The farther north they headed, the more the horizon rose before them in rounded mountains. Quinn's appreciation for the splendor of it all was so tied to her relationship with her mother that she didn't know how to separate the two. For as long as she could remember, her mother made sure that she and Hayden paid attention to the beauty around them. On a day like today she might have said, "Look, children! Do you think any artist could capture this? Could imagine this out of nothingness? Only God. And it's all for us. It's a gift."

Yes, it was a gift. And her mother's gift was teaching them to appreciate it. Quinn wished she could express her feelings about it to Lewis without sounding trite. He took his eyes from the road for just a moment to smile at her. He knew. She didn't have to say a word.

They rode in silence for a few more miles until they came to a scenic overlook and Lewis asked her if she wanted him to pull over. She did.

It was midmorning, and the sun was starting to warm the crispness from the air. It could turn out to be an Indian summer kind of day. They stood, looking out at the vista—nature's canvas of autumn colors brushing the mountainous scoops all the way to the horizon.

Lewis put his arm around her. "I'm glad we came," he said.

"Me, too."

They sat on a wood bench, holding hands, enjoying the view and the breeze. She leaned against him. His skin would absorb the scents of nature and later, when they made love, she would breathe in this moment.

They made their way from the Taconic to Route 7, which meandered north from Connecticut to Massachusetts, dotted with charm and more antiques shops than even the most dedicated collector could possibly visit in a day. Quinn had a couple of favorites she liked to stop into, but the best part was discovering some quaint treasure of a shop she had never been to. They traveled off the main road in search of just such bounty.

"There," she said, pointing.

It wasn't exactly an antiques shop, but a small gallery with a sign that said FINE ART AND COLLECTIBLES. Lewis pulled into the small gravel lot.

The store was cluttered, with paintings covering every inch of wall and lying in stacks on the floor. Quinn imagined people loved going through the piles in hope of finding an unrecognized Winslow Homer or John Singleton Copley hidden among the canvases. But that wasn't

Quinn's quest. The treasure she sought was an American artist of lesser fame but more personal interest. Her mother had spent years living and painting in this area, and her work was still sprinkled in small galleries throughout New England, and in the Berkshires in particular. So it wouldn't be at all unusual to find one of her paintings in a place like this.

The gallery owner was a woman in her seventies, who introduced herself as Eliza Macie. She was erect and fit, with pale blue eyes and fine cheekbones. Good genes, Quinn thought.

"Are most of these local artists?" Quinn asked, hoping to narrow her search to a specific section of the store.

"Everything on the right is local, more or less," Eliza Macie said. "Is there anything in particular you're looking for?"

"Nan Mazursky," Quinn said, giving the woman her mother's maiden name. "Or Nan Mazursky Gilbert."

"I used to have a Nan Mazursky," she said. "Sold it years ago. But these here are community artists who painted in the sixties and seventies, if you want to have a look."

The woman seemed to know her inventory, so Quinn doubted she would find one of her mother's creations among these paintings. Still, she would work her way through the indicated stacks, just in case. Meanwhile, Lewis found a table assortment of weather photographs that captured his attention.

Quinn went through framed paintings of landscapes, still lifes, portraits, and abstracts. Occasionally she stopped at a piece that resembled her mother's style, but never hit pay dirt.

One of the portraits she quickly flipped past caught up with her consciousness a few moments later. Could she have imagined what her brain was telling her she had seen there? She went back to the painting and pulled it out. It was a dark-haired young woman with amber-flecked green eyes painted against a violet background.

"Lewis?" she called. "Can you take a look at this?"

He approached and studied the painting.

"Who does this look like?" Quinn asked.

"You?"

"No, not me. Keep looking."

He folded his arms as he stared. "Your mother?"

She nodded.

"I see it," he said. "It looks like a young Nan."

"And yet . . ." She trailed off, trying to find a way to articulate what it was about the woman in the painting that didn't feel like her mother.

"Right features, wrong personality?" Lewis offered.

"That's it," she said. "There's a coquettishness to her. Like she knows she's cute, or hopes you think so. I don't mean that in a bad way, just an innocent pride in her appearance. But I can't imagine my mother ever had that kind of girlish vanity. Still, it looks like her."

Quinn called the gallery owner over and asked her what she knew about this painting. The woman explained that the artist was a local man who studied and lived in the area his whole life.

"Nan Mazursky was my mother," Quinn said, "and I think this might be a portrait of her."

"It's possible," Eliza Macie said. "I think they both studied under the same local teacher. If you like, I'll see what I can find out about it and give you a call in a day or two."

"We're only in town for the weekend," Lewis said, writing down his cell phone number. "But that would be great."

"Where you folks staying?"

Quinn told her where her aunt's house was, and the gallery owner said she lived just a few blocks away.

"Tell you what I'll do," she said. "I'll take the painting home with me today so you won't have to travel far if you decide to buy it."

Quinn and Lewis thanked her, took a card, and were on their way. After stopping for lunch in Great Barrington, they went straight to Aunt

Bunny's house, as Quinn was eager to take the rowboat out onto the lake while it was still daylight.

It was warm enough to leave their sweaters behind, so, wearing T-shirts and jeans, Quinn and Lewis lowered themselves into the rowboat on the banks of Lake Garfield. Lewis took the oars and Quinn relaxed as he rowed them to a secluded inlet, surrounded on three sides by tall trees dropping leaves into the water. In the distance, the gentlest mountains kissed the horizon. A loud flock of geese flew by, and then there was nothing but the sound of the rustling leaves and the water sloshing softly against the small boat.

Quinn tilted her face back toward the sun, realizing it was the last vitamin D she would get to absorb for many months. The only flaw in this perfect moment was that it wouldn't last. Soon enough, she would have to return to the fear and anxiety. She put her hand on her belly and told herself that no matter what happened, there would be more moments in her life like this. There had to be.

"You feel okay?" Lewis asked.

"I do." She put her hand over her eyes like a visor and squinted at him. It was the best birthday present anyone had ever given her. Even the trip to Fiji, she imagined, couldn't surpass this. Okay, so maybe it was more exotic—and certainly more expensive—but there couldn't possibly be more love behind it. "Thank you," she said.

"I requisitioned this weather."

She smiled. "I don't doubt it."

Quinn watched as Lewis looked around at the trees and then up at the sky, his eyes scanning the horizon for clouds. He was thinking about the weather.

"You know what we should do?" she said. "Get naked and jump in the lake."

He laughed. "I know the air temperature feels like summer, but put your hand in the water."

She did, expecting to tell him that the cool water would feel bracing, invigorating. But the chill reminded her of being submerged in the cold bathwater in the Manhattan apartment, and she changed her mind. No, they would not go swimming in the lake on this trip.

When the sun lowered in the sky, Lewis rowed them back to the bank behind Aunt Bunny's house. They went inside and Quinn put fresh sheets on their bed, so that they could rest awhile before dinner. Once they lay down next to each other, they automatically rolled together. Quinn put her head on her husband's chest and breathed in his scent. She was right—he smelled like earth and leaves. She tilted her head up and kissed him. Within moments, they were pulling off each other's clothes and luxuriating in flesh against flesh. They took their time, letting the excitement build until their bodies wouldn't let them hold back one more second.

When they finished, Quinn and Lewis held on to each other until they both dozed. She slept for only a few minutes, though, and then went into the bathroom and took a long, hot shower. Afterward, she blew her hair dry so that they could go out for dinner.

When she came out of the bathroom the bed was empty and there was a note from Lewis saying he had gone for a walk and would be back in an hour. Quinn was feeling refreshed and energetic, and considered how she would spend the time waiting for him to get back. Then she remembered the promise she had made to herself to scope out the local five-star resort. After Lewis had told her about the arrangements he had made for this trip, Quinn realized it would present a good opportunity to make peace with Hayden and Cordell by gathering information for them on what it might entail to make a wedding at the place. She wasn't going to go so far as to apologize, but she felt comfortable making this gesture. This was the man Hayden had decided to marry, and Quinn would make the best of it.

She wrote a note back to Lewis telling him where she was going, grabbed the car keys, and left.

The entrance to the resort had a splendid roadway canopied by large oak trees. The building itself looked like a romantic brick mansion, with mountains on one side and a manicured golf course on the other.

Quinn parked and went into the main entrance, which was elegantly lit and richly appointed in subtle hues of hunter green and deep browns. She asked the concierge—a young woman in a dark suit—if she could speak to someone about planning a wedding at the resort. The woman telephoned the gentleman in charge of catering, and then told Quinn he would be tied up for a few minutes, but if she would care to have a look around on her own, he would be happy to meet her in the banquet facility they called the Garden Room.

The concierge showed Quinn a map of the grounds, pointing out the different areas with the tip of her pencil. The next day, she explained, there would be a wedding on the premises, so the Oak Room, which doubled as a chapel, was set up for the ceremony.

"You should stop in there and have a look," she said. "It was part of the original estate that was here over three hundred years ago, and it has a lot of charm."

The woman was right. The Oak Room was rustic and romantic, with an ornate coffered ceiling and a wide-plank wood floor, stained dark and lustrous. Antique wood paneling lined the walls, and a modern skylight had been added above the altar so that the bride and groom (or groom and groom, as the case may be) could be bathed in heavenly light.

Chairs were set up on either side of the aisle, each covered with white fabric tied in the back with a gold bow. Quinn was charmed by the effect, and thought Hayden and Cordell would love the place.

A white runner had been placed from the doorway in the back all the way to the altar in the front. Quinn took off her shoes and walked down the aisle, hands clasped in front of her, as if she were holding a bouquet. She took slow steps and imagined an organist in the corner playing the "Wedding March."

She remembered the joy she felt taking that walk on the day of her own wedding, her father by her side. The two of them stopped several feet from the altar, as they had been instructed, and Lewis came down to get her. It was, she knew, a sexist custom for the father to give the bride away to the groom, but she was comforted by the tradition, and felt especially touched by how much it meant to her dad, who quietly wept.

In addition to his tuxedo, Lewis wore the goofiest grin, and it made her laugh when he took her arm. At the altar, Quinn glanced over at her mother, who had already walked down the aisle and was standing under the floral chuppah in a pale blue dress. She expected a grin or a wink from Nan, but instead saw a stony expression, neither joyful nor sentimental. She got the feeling that her mother was angry and just wanted to get through the ceremony. It infuriated Quinn, and she knew that a part of her would never forgive her mother for her attitude that day. Maybe Nan couldn't help how she felt, but surely she could have faked it a little bit for her daughter's sake. It was, after all, the most important day of her life.

Quinn walked slowly down the white runner and vowed that she would not do the same thing to Hayden. If she couldn't be happy for him on the day of his wedding to Cordell, she would smile anyway and wish the couple a long life of health and happiness.

She walked up the two small steps to the platform that served as an altar in this ancient room, and got a strange feeling. Was there a portal in this place? She closed her eyes for a moment. Yes, she could sense it. But she didn't feel that her New York City life with Eugene was pulsing by on the other side. Nor did she experience the dark and deathly chill she had had behind the curio cabinet. This energy was more related to the place. She looked around. Where was it? Quinn wanted to get closer to figure out what was on the other side. It seemed important.

At the back of the altar was a white lattice. She approached it and touched the slats. Something was behind it.

Quinn stepped off the platform and walked around it. There, hidden in back, was an old stone fireplace, scorched black from centuries-old flames. She could see a crack within, and knew that it was the portal. She didn't want to get close enough to pick up any of the ancient soot, so she just held her hands toward it to see if she could sense what was so important about her life on the other side.

She closed her eyes and almost immediately felt something about a wedding. But it wasn't happy. Someone wanted to get married and someone didn't. Was it Hayden and Cordell? That had to be it. Cordell was about to break Hayden's heart, and she could feel the impending pain. It was terrible.

Quinn heard the door to the chapel open.

"Mrs. Braverman?" a man's voice called.

It was the caterer. She stepped around from behind the lattice and tried to smile.

"Sorry," she said. "I was just curious about this old room."

"No problem," he said. "I looked for you in the Garden Room and thought I might find you here. I'm John McCormack, catering director here at Stonewell. Can I give you a tour?"

Quinn was now more interested in finding out what was going on across that portal than seeing the facilities. After all, if Cordell was breaking Hayden's heart in her parallel life, he would probably do the same here. She felt a duty to her brother to at least figure out what was going on.

But she couldn't very well tell this man to get lost so that she could commune with the old fireplace. And so she filled him in, saying that her gay brother was considering getting married here, and that she had heard the resort could accommodate them. John McCormack didn't bat an eye. He said that Stonewell was known for having hosted some of the most beautiful gay and lesbian weddings in New England, and he would be happy to discuss it with her.

Quinn allowed herself to be taken on a tour, and went through the motions of asking all the appropriate questions. She was as polite as she could be, without prolonging the meeting. She wanted to get it over with, in order to sneak back to that fireplace.

"I have a special photo album I'd like to show you," John McCormack said, and led her back to his office to show her beautiful photographs from recent same-sex weddings that had been held at the resort. She thanked him and tried to be on her way, but had to wait while he gave her brochures, menus, and various price lists to take back to her brother.

"I'm just going to take one more walk around the grounds on my own, if that's okay," she said as she shook his hand.

John McCormack said he didn't mind at all, and Quinn made a beeline back to the chapel.

THERE WAS SIMPLY no way to get close enough to the portal to sense what was happening without crawling into the fireplace and getting covered with soot. So Quinn rolled up her jeans and crept forward on her knees until she could place her hands directly on the fissure.

The feeling here was entirely new. Yes, it was a portal like the others, but the life on the other side was farther away. It was as if there were a physical barrier to cross before she could truly understand what she was sensing about the marriage in question.

Quinn argued with herself about whether or not she should go through. Was she merely trying to vindicate herself by proving that her problem with Cordell was based on more than her own emotional issues? Maybe she should stick to her vow to stop crossing over. Besides, Lewis would be returning soon, and she needed to get back to him. Still, finding out what was giving her that prickly feeling seemed important. Would it be so terrible to slip though one last time, especially if she could save her brother a whole lot of grief? Okay, she thought, I'll do it. But only for a few moments and then I'll do whatever it takes to get right back.

She pressed her hands against the crack in the back of the fireplace and it opened, pulling her inside its musty warmth. She felt herself spin like a corkscrew, and her anxiety about the decision to make the journey gave way to a calm that floated her into a meditative space between consciousness and sleep. Like always, when she realized she was in a new place with real dimensions, it felt like awakening from a strange dream. She was in water, but it wasn't the bathtub of her Manhattan high-rise. Quinn opened her eyes and saw hundreds of fingers. Fingers? No, it was sea life—some kind of coral. And what was the movement behind her? She turned and found herself amid a school of bright blue fish. Shocked and disoriented, Quinn opened her mouth and swallowed a terrible gulp of water. Just then, a hand reached from above and grabbed her arm, yanking her from the water into brilliant sunshine.

"Holy crap. You were down there a long time. What the hell were you doing?"

It was Eugene, and he was pulling her into a boat. Quinn coughed up water. He patted her on the back.

"You okay?" he asked. "What happened to your snorkel?"

The air was dry and warm. Quinn looked around. The boat they were on was in the middle of a vast expanse of azure water. The light was strange, disorienting. Was it morning here? She looked for the sun, which wasn't yet overhead. In the far distance, she could see what looked like a lush, mountainous island. In the other direction she saw a sandy shoreline dotted with palm trees.

Good Lord. She was in Fiji.

"Is she okay?" a woman asked. "She looks pale."

Quinn glanced around the boat, which seemed to be filled with American tourists sitting on a shelflike bench that ran from port to starboard on both sides. A slender, dark-skinned man stood at the back by the motor.

"She's fine," Eugene said to the woman. Then he turned to the man at the back. "We're ready."

"Ready for what?" Quinn asked.

The man started the motor.

"We were waiting for you to get back on board," Eugene said, as the boat started to move.

Quinn panicked. "Where are we going?"

"To shore," Eugene said. "Where else?"

Quinn jumped to her feet and glanced over the side of the boat. The portal was right beneath them, but she might never find it again if they went to shore.

"Relax," Eugene said, and she put her bottom down on the hard bench. But as soon as he looked away, she was up again. Jumping ship right this moment could be her only hope of getting back.

She took a deep breath and got ready to dive in. Here goes, she thought, but before she could leap into the water, a burly man sitting on the other side of her grabbed her around the waist and pulled her back.

"Are you nuts?" he shouted over the motor. "You'll get chopped up by the propeller."

She swallowed hard and sat down again. He was right. But if she couldn't jump now, how would she get back? Quinn needed to think fast. Was there a way to mark this spot so that she could find it again? She looked at the mountainous island in the distance and then back at the tallest palm tree on the shore, drawing a mental line between them. She crossed her fingers and hoped that it would be enough to help her find her way.

When they approached land, the boat's captain cut the motor and jumped out, pulling the craft into shallower waters. The tourists stepped out and walked toward the dry sand, heading for the hotel. Eugene draped his arm over Quinn's shoulder and smiled.

Her toes dug into the fine white sand. Under different circumstances, she could be quite taken by the beauty of this place. The water was a clearer blue than anything she had ever seen.

"Isn't this great?" Eugene said.

"Great," Quinn echoed. She needed to fight the impulse to enjoy anything about this. As soon as possible, she would need to ditch Eugene so that she could get back into the water and try to find the portal.

"You were right," he said. "This is just what I needed—a romantic getaway."

"Uh-huh."

"Are you having fun?"

"Sure."

"You want to go for a cold drink?"

"Why don't you go and I'll catch up with you?" she said. "I'd like to take a swim."

"A swim? Don't be ridiculous. You were just in the water for almost two hours."

"Still—"

"C'mon, Quinn. Indulge me. I want to sit and enjoy your company for a while."

Eugene wore khaki swim trunks and she watched as he led her to a bamboo deck overlooking the ocean. All those hours at the gym had transformed him. His slender body was now ropey with defined muscles, and he had actually added bulk to his pecs and arms.

"Here," he said as they reached two empty lounge chairs with an open view of the water. His eyes looked so clear and relaxed that Quinn felt a stirring she did not want to admit. *Don't,* she warned herself. *Don't even think about it.*

As she lowered herself into the lounge, Quinn felt a lovely breeze off the ocean. It was as if everything about this environment was conspiring to seduce her. But she was determined to be strong.

When a lovely young woman with a broad smile asked if they wanted drinks, Quinn ordered an iced coffee. It was, after all, morning in the South Pacific, and she saw no reason to add alcohol to the forces she might need to battle.

"C'mon," Eugene said, "you only live once." Then he turned to the waitress and ordered them two mimosas.

The view was spectacular—exactly the kind of thing photographers tried to capture on postcards but never could, because it was the scope and the grandeur of the beauty that made one's heart open wide. Quinn wiggled her toes against the warm breeze. She took a deep breath and decided it wouldn't be so bad to spend just a few minutes enjoying this paradise.

"It's so beautiful here," she said.

Eugene looked her up and down. "It sure is," he said.

Quinn glanced down at her own body. She was wearing a print two-piece bathing suit, and her belly was tan, flat, and toned. Not the tummy of a woman with a child, let alone a woman pregnant with her second baby. She put her hand on her abdomen.

She sipped her mimosa, thinking she should make some excuse to Eugene—like saying she had to go to the bathroom—and find her way back to the spot she had come from. But the idea of lingering awhile was so appealing she couldn't quite find the words. She decided she would finish her drink and then figure out a plan.

"I love you," Eugene said.

Quinn glanced over at him. It wasn't like Eugene to be demonstrative. Clearly, this romantic vacation was having an effect on him.

She swallowed. "Love you, too."

From where they sat, Quinn could see the boat they had been on. She redrew the mental line she had made earlier from the tall palm tree to the island on the horizon. Would it help? Would she really be able to sense where the portal was? What if she couldn't? What if it was impossible to find a way back?

Oddly, the thought spun only the thinnest thread of panic, buffered by a plush layer of tranquillity. This island was having a hypnotic effect on her, aided and abetted by the champagne in her drink.

She sucked the last of her mimosa through her straw and put down the glass.

"Let's go to our room," Eugene said, reaching for her hand.

"In a bit," she said, stalling.

He sat up in his lounge chair and swung his feet to the ground. "You know, I'm not feeling so great."

"What's the matter?"

"I think I'm seasick from that boat ride."

"And you're just noticing it now?"

"Maybe it was the drink. I think I need to lie down in the room."

"That's a good idea," she said.

He rose and looked down at her. "Aren't you coming with me?"

"I thought you would want some peace and quiet."

"I need you."

Of course you do, she thought, standing. Just as well, anyway. If she could get him to lie down and take a nap, it would be a perfect opportunity to sneak away.

Once they were in the room, however, it was clear Eugene had other plans. As soon as the door was shut, he grabbed Quinn and kissed her hard on the mouth. At this point, she couldn't very well push him away. He pressed his body into hers, and she felt more heat than she wanted to admit.

"I thought you didn't feel well," she said, when they came up for air.

"It was a ruse to get you alone."

Oh no, she thought. I can't. No matter what, I can't get into bed with him. She moved back a step. "I'm not sure I'm in the——"

"Please," he interrupted. "Don't say anything. Just close your eyes for a minute."

This could be trouble, Quinn thought. But she did as he said, and heard him open a drawer and close it. Then he took her hand.

"Open your eyes," he said.

She did, and he was in front of her on one knee. Beyond him was a large window with a view of the Pacific. A dark blue velvet jewelry box rested on his palm in front of her, opened to the most spectacular diamond ring she had ever seen outside of a glass case.

Eugene spoke. "Quinn Gilbert, will you marry me?"

Marry him?

No, she thought. God, no. She looked at his face. He seemed so smitten, so completely in love, it occurred to her that this was what she had sensed on the other side. It wasn't Hayden and Cordell whose love life was a massive train wreck. It was hers and Eugene's.

But why? Why was the Quinn in this life so conflicted about marrying Eugene? Hadn't she been waiting for this moment? Wasn't she still comforted by his adoration?

Maybe not. Maybe his neediness was at last wearing thin. That, she concluded, was why he was finally popping the question. He must have sensed the relationship was winding down, and couldn't bear the thought of losing her.

He stared at her, a tight smile holding its place on his face while he waited for a response.

Both parts of Quinn's heart wanted to say no. The part of her that had stayed with Eugene couldn't commit to a life with him. The fun part of the banter and the lifestyle just wasn't enough to offset the sacrifices she would have to make, tending to his endless needs for the rest of her life. And the part of her that had left him all those years ago had to get back . . . and had to do it soon. The panic she had managed to suppress was now threatening to overwhelm her. How long had she been here? Was it just a few minutes or much longer? She couldn't put her finger on it. Was Lewis back in the room yet? Was he panicking?

But what to do at this moment? Should she tell Eugene no? What good would that do? On the other hand, was it right to lie? Should she say yes for expediency?

"My knees are about to crap out," he said.

"What?"

"I'm waiting for your answer, Quinn. But you'd better hurry, or I'm going to need an orthopedist before we leave this island."

She took a deep breath and looked out the window, studying the expanse of ocean she would need to navigate. She closed her eyes for a moment and pictured Lewis reading her note. He would be looking at the clock, wondering when she would get back. Perhaps he was calling her cell phone right this minute.

"Is it the diamond?" Eugene said. "Is it too showy? I knew it. I was looking at a tasteful solitaire that was half the size, but Andrew talked me into this one. He said that after dragging my feet for ten years I needed to wow you. I can return it, you know. You can pick out any diamond you want. It doesn't even have to be a diamond. There was another ring with a beautiful ruby surrounded by baguettes. Maybe you'd like that better."

"No," she said.

He went pale. "No?"

"I mean no, it's not too showy. It's beautiful." She paused, took a deep breath. "And yes."

"Yes?"

God help me, she thought. But there's no faster way out of here. "Yes," she said. "I'll marry you."

His face lit up. "You will?" He took the ring from the box and slipped it onto her finger. Then he stood and embraced her.

She hugged him back, trying to think of a way to extricate herself so that she could get out of the room and back into the ocean.

"Were you surprised?" he asked, without releasing her.

"Quite."

"I hope you're happy."

"I am."

"I was going to wait and see if I got offered the network job, but then I realized it didn't even matter. And I wanted this to be a birthday you'd remember forever."

"No question about that."

He kissed her deeply. She went along, trying not to let herself get pulled into the fever of desire.

"We should celebrate," he said. His voice was soft. Lascivious.

No, no, no, she thought. Please don't let him be talking about sex.

"Let's order champagne," she said, hoping to divert him.

"I have a better idea." He pulled her toward the bed.

"Maybe we should wait," she said.

"For what?"

"For our wedding night." She was desperate, grasping at straws.

He laughed.

"I'm serious," she said. "I think it will be more special."

"Quinn, we've been sleeping together for over ten years. It would be pretty silly at this point to pretend you're a virgin on our wedding night. Besides, this is the most romantic place we've ever been." He kissed her neck. "And I really, really want to fuck you right now."

Still kissing, they fell onto the massive bed. Quinn considered her limited options. Could she feign illness? Tell him she had to go to the bathroom? And then what?

He pressed his pelvis against her and she felt his erection. Her hips automatically moved forward and her breath quickened. She wanted the chance to slow down and think without the interference of hot blood rushing to her private parts.

He grazed her nipple with his thumb and she cried out. Maybe this wasn't such a bad idea. It was, after all, the quickest way to get out of there, wasn't it? It could be over in minutes. Besides, she reasoned, since this was another life, it wasn't really cheating . . . was it? It was more like adding another memory to her pre-Lewis past.

Eugene put his hand on her crotch and Quinn felt herself go wet. She was dangerously close to the point of no return.

He fumbled with the clasp on her bikini top, which didn't hook like a bra and was giving him trouble.

"I'll get it," she said, and that was it. The decision was made. She would do it. She would have sex with Eugene. In fact, she would give it everything she had in order to get him to finish fast. Then he would fall asleep and she could dash out.

Quinn moaned and arched her back, playing up the ecstasy maybe just a bit more than she actually felt. Her excitement, she knew, would hurry him along.

"I love it when you're hot," he said, grabbing her breasts.

She scrambled out of her bottoms. "I want you!" she cried.

"If I had known a ring would make you this horny, I would have proposed years ago."

"Let's do this," she whispered.

"I think I'll make you beg for it."

He was not going to make this easy. But if he wanted her to beg, she would beg.

"Oh, Eugene," she said. "I need you. Please!"

"*Shh*. Wait."

Wait? When did Eugene acquire patience? She did everything she could to rush things along, but he was intent on taking it slow. When at last they engaged, Quinn thought her problems were over and that it would just be a matter of minutes. But then she remembered that she had scored him a prescription for Viagra all those years ago and he was still taking it. The result was that he could last and last and last.

Finally, after it seemed as if the best years of her life had gone by, he finished and rolled off her, exhausted. Five minutes later he was softly snoring. Quinn ducked out from under his heavy arm, put her bathing suit back on, and slipped out the door.

"I'D LIKE TO RENT A ROWBOAT," she said to the man who sat on a folding chair in front of the boat rental shack just a few yards from where she had docked earlier. He was older than the islander who drove her boat, with a gray beard and shaved head.

"I cannot rent you a boat," he said.

"Why not?"

"You are alone, missus."

"So?"

"Too dangerous. Bring the gentleman and you can take a boat."

"Please," she said. "I'll bring it right back."

"If you want to hire one of my men—"

"I want to go out by myself."

"It is not possible," he said, and pointed to a sign hanging on the shack behind him. It had a list of rules for boat rentals, including "All boats must be manned by two or more people."

She glanced down the beach and saw a single rowboat resting on the sand about twenty yards away. By hook or by crook, she was going to find that portal.

"Okay," she said. "I'll come back later with my . . . fiancé."

She walked off toward the water, pretending to be interested in going for a swim. When the man went back to reading his book, Quinn headed straight to the unattended boat. She pushed it into the water, got inside, and rowed as hard as she could.

A voice called out from the shore. "Missus! Missus! Come back here!"

Quinn ignored him and kept rowing.

She looked left and right, trying to find the mental line she had drawn, but it was impossible for Quinn to tell where she needed to be. The best she could hope for was to try to get close enough to the spot to sense it. She rowed on.

"Missus!"

The man's voice got fainter as she pulled farther away. Quinn glanced back and saw him talking with some other men. She kept moving, and felt she was getting closer, though it was hard to tell if she was actually sensing something or just so anxious that wishful thinking had taken over.

She looked out on the horizon. Should she pull left or right? The water was one clear sheet. She kept her eye on the lush island she had first noticed when she had emerged from the water and used its highest mountain as her north star and made a path.

She heard a motor and looked back. Two of the men were now in a boat, racing toward her. This was bad. She had to find the spot fast.

Quinn closed her eyes for a moment, hoping to block out the distractions long enough to feel where she needed to be. She wasn't quite there. She rowed harder. At last, Quinn felt something definitive. She was getting close!

But so was the motorboat. It was gaining on her. If she could just get a few more yards away before they caught up with her, she could make it.

The boat closed in on her. When it got within a few feet the engine went quiet. One of the men stood and shouted, "Stop, missus!"

Quinn kept rowing.

The man dived into the water and swam toward her boat. Quinn rowed on, but slowly, because she sensed that she might be in the right spot. She stopped and peered over the side into the clear water. She could see straight to the ocean floor but nothing looked like a way through. She felt a jolt as something knocked against her small craft. Quinn turned around and saw the man who had been swimming after her. His arms were latched onto the other side of her boat. It was now or never. She dived in.

She let her feelings guide her as she swam. Something silvery flashed on the ocean floor, and Quinn wondered if that could be her portal. It moved, and she realized she was looking at a fish. Beyond it, though, was a coral garden with fingery protrusions. Was that where she had come through? Then she saw something yellow caught on the coral. It was her snorkel!

Quinn glanced behind her and saw the swimming man moving toward her underwater. She was a strong swimmer and tried to pull out ahead, but he wore flippers and moved even faster. Before she could reach the coral, he grabbed her ankle. She struggled to kick free, but he held fast. Quinn stopped struggling and turned to him. She puffed her cheeks to indicate that she needed air, and pointed to the surface. The man let go of her ankle. Instead of breaking for the surface she headed straight for the spot that called to her.

Quinn remembered learning that there were two types of coral, hard and soft, and the type she was about to plunge into was definitely not soft. But it didn't matter. She had to risk it. She plowed headlong into the scratchy sea life, paying no attention to the scrapes she endured, even as she saw her own blood floating toward the surface.

And then it happened. Quinn felt that familiar tugging and was at last sucked into the darkness, leaving Fiji behind. The journey was cold and rough, nauseating her. But it didn't matter. She was on her way back.

Naked, wet, and bleeding, Quinn emerged through a crack in the stone fireplace. The chapel was now dark and cold, as night had fallen. She felt around for her clothes, which were in a pile by the fissure, just as they had been in her basement. Trembling, she dressed quickly and hurried through the grounds to her car.

"I was so worried about you," Lewis said, when she finally got back to Aunt Bunny's house. He hugged her. "Are you okay?"

"I'm fine."

"What took you so long?"

"I . . . I went to see that resort and got lost on the way back. And then my cell phone died."

"Your hair is wet. And your face is bleeding. What happened?"

Quinn looked into the eyes of her loving, trusting husband and felt herself break in half. *I didn't cheat on him,* she told herself. I didn't. It was another life. Another body. The important thing is that I got back. She covered her face with her hands and started to cry.

"Oh, my God," Lewis said. "Did someone hurt you? Should I call the police?"

"No! I'm fine, really. I was just . . . stupid. I was upset about getting lost and thought a swim would calm me down." It was a story she had invented during the drive from the resort.

"You went for a swim in that cold lake?"

She nodded, hating herself for telling these lies.

"How did you cut your face?"

"It was dark and there were rocks. It was a stupid thing to do."

"Are you sure you're okay?"

"I'm sure."

He pulled her close and hugged her tightly. "I was scared to death. I love you so much, Quinn. Promise me you'll never do that again . . . promise me you'll never disappear."

I should promise, Quinn thought. I should promise to never go through a portal again. But when she closed her lids, she saw the way her mother looked when she visited her the other day. She saw her deep in concentration as she swept her brush over the canvas. She saw the light in her eyes when she turned and noticed her daughter standing behind her. She remembered the smell of her perfume, the touch of her hand.

"Okay," she said to Lewis, but wondered if it was a promise she could keep.

19

AFTER THEY GOT BACK FROM A LATE-NIGHT DINNER AT A cozy New England inn, the couple sat on the floor in front of the fireplace warming their feet. Quinn used Lewis as back support and he used the sofa. He wrapped his arms around her. She watched the fire's graceful dance with the flue, the flames flouncing and swaying, interrupted occasionally by a crackle from the log as it gave way to ash. Quinn relaxed, comforted that this fireplace bore no portal.

She leaned into her husband and rested her hands on her swollen belly, now even more distended after a full meal. This body, she thought, is not the same one that had sex with Eugene. The idea that she had cheated on Lewis was already starting to fade. Since it hadn't happened in this physical reality, was it any different from dreaming she had sex? She considered her next-door neighbor's definition of infidelity, which excluded everything but actual physical contact.

"Did Georgette ever tell you about her, uh . . . extracurricular activities?" she asked Lewis.

"You mean the cybersex?" he said. "She mentioned it in passing."

Quinn smiled. "She talks about sex the way most people talk about the weather."

"Two topics near to my heart."

Quinn paused, considering whether to advance the conversation. Did she really need to hear Lewis say Georgette's transgressions were forgivable? Were the situations even analogous?

"Can I get you anything?" he asked. "A cup of tea?"

"I'm stuffed. But if you want anything . . ."

"I'm fine."

"You sure?" she said. "It wouldn't bother me if you had a glass of wine."

"I know," he said, and kissed the top of her head. "Do you miss it?"

She shrugged. "Maybe a little. Right now it would feel so relaxing."

He moved her hair and began massaging her neck with his thumbs. "Does this help?"

Quinn closed her eyes. "Mm." She rolled her head forward.

"I think Georgette will tell anyone who will listen," he said, continuing their conversation as he kneaded her muscles.

"I wonder if she tells Roger," Quinn said.

"Doubt it."

"She might. She told me flat out she doesn't consider it cheating since they don't actually touch each other's bodies."

Lewis worked his way to the taut place between her neck and shoulders as he considered this. "I'm not sure I'd define cheating that way."

"No? You think cybersex is cheating?"

"It's not as bad as having an actual affair," he continued, "but not quite as benign as looking at porn."

Quinn dropped her head while Lewis worked out a knot in her trapezius muscle. She knew she should probably change the subject. After all, getting Lewis to forgive Georgette's cyber affair had no bearing on their relationship. Still, she couldn't let it rest.

"As sins go," Quinn said, "I think hers is forgivable, don't you?"

"You mean like she gets points for not having physical contact?" he asked.

"Something like that."

"Maybe," Lewis said. He moved his hands to the other side of her neck. "It would depend."

"On what?"

"Let's say you caught me having cybersex," he said, "and I asked for forgiveness. What would you say?"

Quinn considered that for a moment. "I would say I could forgive you as long as you promised not to do it again."

"Exactly."

Quinn took her husband's hands from her shoulders and wrapped them around her. *I promise to never do it again,* she thought, and tried to imagine her guilt as vapor that dissipated into the atmosphere. Perhaps it would get pulled up into the flue and leave through the chimney.

They sat quietly for a few minutes watching the flames flicker and wave in gentle chaos.

"Are you having a happy birthday?" he asked.

"I am now."

"I have a surprise for you," he said. "Wait here."

Lewis went into the kitchen and Quinn heard him opening and closing cabinets and moving things around. Finally he called out, "Okay, close your eyes!"

She did as he said, confident this surprise would be less dramatic than the one with Eugene. When at last he said she could open her eyes, she saw a piece of chocolate mousse cake in front of her with a lit candle in the middle of it. She sat and smiled while Lewis sang her the happy birthday song.

"Make a wish," he said.

Quinn's mood changed from cheerful to reverent. Ever since she was a child, she had taken her wishes very seriously. Not that she actually believed in them, but whenever the occasion for a wish presented itself, her cynicism moved to the back burner, if only for a moment. In fact, in that single crystallized measure of time, Quinn felt it was monumentally important not only to make the right wish, but to get the wording precise.

She wanted to wish for the diagnosis of an encephalocele to be a mistake, but that would be like asking for broccoli to taste like chocolate mousse—desirable, but unrealistic. A wasted wish. It would be better to wish that there was no brain tissue involved, allowing her daughter to have normal development. Or she could ask for Naomi's condition to be 100 percent correctible. Was that also unrealistic? Quinn rolled around more possibilities. She could wish for her daughter to be healthy and strong by the time she turned one, two, or even three. Or maybe she could wish that her daughter would get a chance to blow out a birthday candle on her thirty-sixth birthday, while someone who loved her waited patiently for her to finish making a decision. She closed her eyes.

I wish for Naomi to have a full and wonderful life.

Quinn opened her eyes and blew out the candle. Lewis reached over and used his thumb to wipe the tear that escaped.

"The baby?" he asked.

She sniffed. "We agreed not to talk about that this weekend."

"You don't want to change your mind?"

She shook her head.

"Okay, then," he said. "I have another surprise for you. But first, eat your cake."

"With pleasure!"

Quinn adored chocolate mousse. She stuck her fork into the rich dessert and brought it to her mouth. She closed her lips around it and delighted in the sensuality of the bitter chocolate flavor dancing in creamy pirouettes around coffeelike undertones. It was delicious enough for her to believe wishes could come true. She fed Lewis a bite. He kissed her.

After they finished the piece of cake he reached behind the couch to pull out a large, framed picture.

"I wasn't really just out for a walk earlier," he said. "That Eliza Macie called while you were in the shower and told me she learned that the painting checked out. In fact, she got the whole history from the artist himself. It *is* a portrait of your mother, Quinn." He turned the canvas toward her. "Happy birthday!"

Quinn gasped in surprise. How sweet and tender of Lewis to do this for her! Would she ever stop marveling at his love, and how different it was from Eugene's? While her ex loved her fiercely and desperately and believed he would do anything in the world for her, the truth was that he was too self-involved to consider her feelings. Sure, he would take them into account when she spelled them out in explicit terms, but that wasn't her nature. So the relationship was always about him and his needs. Lewis, on the other hand, thought of her constantly, always seeking new and creative ways to make her happy.

Surely you knew that, she wanted to say to the painting. But of course this light, sunny young woman was not the Nan she knew. It was hard to imagine this girl growing into the woman who could be so grave at her own daughter's wedding. This girl would be happy for her.

Quinn touched the canvas lightly, as if she were reaching for her mother. *What happened to you?* she wanted to ask. *Where did you go?*

Quinn remembered something her mother had taught her about art appreciation. She had told her that when one faced a painting, the question that mattered most was "How does it make you feel?"

She stared at this portrait as she thought about that. Funny, but at this moment she didn't feel angry or resentful toward her mother. She felt grateful. Grateful to know that Nan had once been able to skim the surface of life and enjoy it.

But her gratitude didn't stop there. Anyone who had lost her mother would ache to have any part of her back. But for Quinn, who could actually slip through a crack in the quantum universe and make it a reality, the longing was unbearable. Without even knowing it—but perhaps sensing it—Lewis had tried to patch that tear in her heart by giving her this gift. What had she done to deserve such a soul?

She looked at him, choking with gratitude as she tried to find the words to express her appreciation.

"Do you like it?" he asked.

She could only laugh. "I like it."

AT BREAKFAST the next morning in a local coffee shop, Quinn pored over brochures listing area antique shops, a red pen in her hand. One, in particular, caught her eye. She circled it and turned the page to Lewis.

"Amelia's Vintage Baby," he read. "'Antiques and collectibles for baby and you.'" He looked up at her. "Doesn't this violate our agreement for this weekend?"

"I don't care," she said.

He looked concerned.

"It's not going to upset me," she said. "And, besides, when will we get another chance to see this stuff?"

"I don't know, Quinn. Could be an emotional minefield."

THE SHOP WAS out of the way for them—about an hour's drive from Aunt Bunny's house. It was really just one cramped room that was an adjunct off a larger store selling a wider variety of antiques. It was overly heated, and soon after entering, Quinn pulled off her sweater.

She started by looking at the larger items. There were a few dressers and high chairs. The cradles captured her attention for several minutes. Some of them were quite beautiful, though clearly not as safe as modern equipment. Most were made out of wood, with curved bottoms for rock-ing. Two were hanging cradles made from wrought iron.

Quinn moved on. She fingered a fine, hand-decorated bib from the mid-1800s and a sweet crocheted bonnet from the 1920s. She saw a whole case of silver spoons and baby dishes. White christening gowns covered in clear plastic hung from small silk hangers. A shelf of baby dolls and stuffed animals had a sign in front inviting shoppers to visit the main store for a wider selection. Quinn looked at some dresses and went back to the bonnet. It was a delicate piece in off-white with a ribbon threaded through. She showed it to Lewis.

"Isn't this beautiful?" she said.

"Mm-hm."

She turned over the tag: $250. "Too extravagant," she said, and put it back.

She went from shelf to shelf, examining each little treasure. Every time she came to a cap or bonnet, she paused to look at the price. Each one appealed to her in some way, though none seemed exactly right. And of course the prices were out of reach.

The woman who ran the store sat in a vintage rocker in the corner, knitting something in a color Quinn thought of as Christmas red. "You're looking for a head covering?" she asked, without looking up.

Am I? Quinn wondered. It hadn't occurred to her until that moment that she was so focused on items that went on the baby's head. Was she unconsciously looking for something to protect Naomi's skull?

"Not really," Quinn said, self-conscious. To prove her point, she approached a case of little baby shoes and began inspecting them. Some still had the imprints of infant toes inside, and this touched Quinn in a tender spot close to her womb. She picked up a very tiny pair of cloth shoes that had a tag indicating they were from the early 1900s. Inside, the silk lining looked pristine, almost new. She remembered the famous Hemingway quote, reputed to be the shortest story ever written:

For sale: baby shoes, never used.

She stared at the tiny footwear that fit so easily into her hands, and imagined the woman from Hemingway's story clearing out a nursery that would never be used. By then her body—though left permanently barren—would have recovered from childbirth. But what about her heart? Was it, too, barren? Had it gone as cold and hard as the earth covering her baby's grave?

She turned to Lewis. "Let's go home."

QUINN DECONSTRUCTED, NO. 6

———+———

People weren't yet using the term "tween" when her daughter was ten. But now, as Nan worked on a painting of Quinn at that age, she thought it was the perfect description. Upon approaching double digits, girls floated in a magical place at the cusp of understanding. Quinn, bookish and smart, was especially astute, grasping so much of the world. In that sliver of time between the inno- cence of the tooth-fairy years and the obsessive self-consciousness of the teen years, a girl could be a fierce warrior of truth and singularly committed to understanding the convoluted world of adults.

Nan had placed Quinn in the green chair again, only this time she was sit- ting on a pile of books, ostensibly to make her taller. But Nan hoped the viewer would also sense how important reading and knowledge were to this child.

Quinn was sitting erect, grasping the arms of the chair as if ready to bolt from it. She stared right at the viewer, unabashed, probing for information.

Nan took a step back to assess her progress. The color decisions she had made were subtle. When she painted the chair and the background, she had kept a dab of black paint on her palette, adding the tiniest amount to each color— just enough to mute it without turning anything gray. When she painted Quinn, she kept dabs of yellow and white on her palette, to add light to her subject. The effect worked the way she had intended.

As she stared at the painting, Nan felt she understood her daughter at this age, but was she any closer to the larger goal of this series? What is the essence of this girl and who she becomes?

Nan wiped off her brush and dropped it in a can of water. She had hoped these paintings would help her answer something absolutely vital about her daughter, but now she couldn't even put her finger on the question.

20

THE CLOSER THEY GOT TO HOME, THE MORE ANXIOUS QUINN became about walking through the door and reuniting with Isaac. She had spoken to him and to Georgette several times over the weekend and knew everything was fine, but she needed a fix, needed to pull him close to her and breathe in his scent. Also, she hoped this time apart would ease his anxiety about losing her. She needed him to learn, deep in his heart, that she would always come back.

"Hey," she said, as she dropped her bag on the floor in the hall.

Isaac, who was sitting at the kitchen table with Georgette, drawing with markers, jumped off his chair and ran into her arms. Lewis joined in for a group hug.

"I missed you," Quinn said.

Isaac gave her a tight squeeze and then scrambled from her arms. "I drew a picture of our family," he said.

"Let me see."

Quinn hugged Georgette and thanked her for staying with Isaac, then lookcd at the picture her son was holding. It was an outdoor scene, with the sun in the upper left and a tree with orange leaves on the right. Isaac drew himself in the middle of the composition, between his mother and father. Everyone was smiling.

"What's this?" Quinn said, pointing to a strange shape he had drawn on the other side of her.

"That's the baby."

Quinn blanched. She had not yet told Isaac she was pregnant. She had planned to break the news to him after the amnio, but on learning about the baby's serious condition she had decided to hold off. She glared at Georgette.

"I'm sorry," her neighbor said. "It slipped out."

Slipped out? How does something like that *slip out?* Quinn stared at her son, trying to see into his heart. How was he handling this enormous news? And was he traumatized by hearing it from their neighbor? He appeared unruffled.

"I didn't know if it was a boy or a girl," Isaac said, "so I just made it a scribble."

Lewis glanced at Quinn with a look that said, *It's going to be okay.* Then he said to Isaac, "That's fine. You did a good job."

"If it's a boy," Isaac said, "can we give him a really cool name?"

"Like what?" Lewis asked.

Isaac straightened and smiled, ready to present his father with the world's coolest boy name. Clearly, he had given it a lot of thought.

"Gary," Isaac pronounced.

"Gary," Lewis repeated, the mirth in his eyes belying the serious expression he tried to affect.

Isaac nodded. "Isn't it perfect?"

"You don't think it's maybe just a little *too* cool for a baby?"

"He'll grow into it," the boy said.

The adults laughed, including Quinn, who realized it wasn't so terrible for Isaac to know she was pregnant. After all, they would have to tell him eventually. Meanwhile, she figured she might as well seize the opportunity. She kneeled down in front of her son and took his hands. "It's not a boy, Isaac. It's a girl."

Isaac looked thoughtful as he took that in. "Will she be a good climber?"

Two doors down lived an eight-year-old girl named Audrey who sometimes came over and climbed the big tree in their backyard.

"I don't know," Quinn said. "The doctors tell us she might be sick."

"Then let's get medicine."

"Sometimes people get sick and"—Quinn waited a beat, fighting the urge to cry—"and there isn't any medicine that can make them well."

"Why not?"

She lost the battle against tears. Her eyes burned and watered. "Because the doctors haven't invented it yet. But they're going to try. We all will."

Isaac put his small, warm hand on her cheek. "If she can't climb, I'll teach her to draw."

A FEW NIGHTS LATER, Lewis took Isaac to an Islanders game, and Quinn went to see Hayden, who had invited her over for dinner. She sat at the kitchen table as he cooked, watching him put a large pot of water on a burner and salt it before going back to the chicken fillets and garlic sautéing in a pan. The aroma was intoxicating. Hayden took a sip of red wine. Quinn nursed a glass of sparkling water with lemon.

"You sure you don't need any help?" she asked.

He waved her offer away with his free hand. "Relax."

Quinn heard something from the bedroom, which shared a wall with the kitchen. It sounded like the scrape of chair legs on the floor and she was caught off guard, as she had thought they were alone.

"Cordell's here?" she asked.

"Came in on the red-eye this morning. Surprised me."

"No wonder you look so happy. Is he joining us?"

"In a bit. I told him you and I needed time to talk. Besides, once he goes online I don't see him for hours."

Quinn thought of Georgette's cyber adventures and made a face.

"It's not like that," Hayden said. "He shops. He can spend half the day trolling for treasures on craigslist and eBay. He's like an addict."

Quinn looked around for something to do. She didn't like being idle, and found it frustrating to be treated like a patient. She wasn't sick, she was pregnant. She noticed a head of romaine on the counter.

"I'll wash the lettuce," she said. She found Hayden's colander, put it in the sink, and began tearing leaves from the base and dropping them in. "If Cordell wants treasures," she said as she worked, "he should go antiquing in the Berkshires. You never know what you're going to find."

"Sounds like you and Lewis did some shopping of your own."

"We stopped in an art gallery and I went hunting for a Nan Mazursky original, but I found something better."

Hayden turned the chicken pieces. "Better?"

"A portrait of her, painted by a fellow art student in 1966. Lewis bought it for me as a birthday present. I already hung it in the living room. Can't stop looking at it."

Quinn finished tearing the lettuce and rinsed it under the running faucet. She turned off the water and banged the colander against the bottom of the sink.

"What's it like?" Hayden asked. "It's not op art, is it?" He pulled a big salad bowl from a cabinet and handed it to her. She dumped in the lettuce.

"They were students, and I think they were still studying Impressionists, so it's more Mary Cassatt than Andy Warhol. It's lovely. Mom looks beautiful and young. But young in a way you could never imagine her."

"What do you mean?"

"You have to see it," she said. "There's a lightness to her. It's like the artist captured her before she decided that everything had to be complicated. She looks happy, without the layers of analysis beneath it. She's just . . . a girl. It's sweet."

"You sure it's Mom?"

She laughed. "Hard to believe, right?"

He added some olive oil to the pan and asked her what else was going on. Over the phone, she had alluded to a major ordeal over the weekend.

Quinn took a sip of water and steadied herself. This was going to be so hard to relive, but she couldn't keep holding it in. She needed to tell someone before she burst, and Hayden was the only one she could confide in.

Quinn retrieved a cutting board and began to sort through the vegetables Hayden had left on the counter. Finally, she cleared her throat and cut the greenery off a couple of carrots. "I stopped by that Stonewell Resort," she said. "I wanted to check it out for you and Cordell."

He turned and looked at her. "Seriously?"

"It's beautiful. I got a bunch of brochures for you."

"That really touches me." Hayden put down his fork and gave his sister a hug. "It's going to mean a lot to Cordell, too."

"I was hoping to mend fences."

"Thank you."

"Is everything on track with you two?" she asked.

"Thank God," he said, smiling. His pan sizzled and he went back to it. He checked for doneness and then began moving the pieces of chicken to a plate. "He got a small walk-on in an HBO show, and is going back to Los Angeles next week to shoot it. But then he's coming back here to stay."

"I'm happy for you, Hayd."

"Thanks. We've been talking more about a wedding, so your timing with this stuff"—he paused to indicate the brochures—"is perfect."

"I'm glad," she said, and sipped her water. "There's something else."

"I thought so."

"I was in their chapel," she began, "thinking about how much you guys would love it, when I sensed something . . ." She trailed off, trying to find a way to explain it. She finished chopping the carrots and dropped them into the salad. Finally she just blurted it out. "There was a portal there, Hayden."

She waited for a reaction. He stopped cooking and stared at her.

"You didn't . . ." he said.

"I had to. I could feel something critical happening. I thought it had to do with you and Cordell."

"And?"

She shook her head.

"Mom?" he asked.

Quinn began peeling an onion. "No."

"What, then?"

"Eugene." She sliced into the onion. Her eyes burned. "And me." She cut another slice. "In Fiji."

Hayden gasped. "Get out!"

"There's more."

"More?"

"He proposed."

Hayden's jaw dropped. Suddenly, Quinn thought the story was sounding more entertaining than traumatic. Her brother's reactions tickled her.

"How did he do it?" Hayden asked. "On one knee? With a diamond?"

Quinn smiled. "The size of a peach pit."

Hayden's eyes went wide. "What did you say?"

Quinn started to laugh. "I said . . . *yes!*"

"You didn't! You're killing me here. This is the best story I've ever heard and I can't even tell anyone."

"I'm not done."

"What else could there be?"

"Guess."

Hayden washed his hands in the sink as he considered this. As he dried them on a dish towel, his face lit up.

"Sex?" he said.

She nodded.

"You slut!" he said, laughing.

She laughed, too. "I had to, Hayd. I thought it would be the fastest way for me to get out of there. A real quickie, you know? But I miscalculated. He was like the Energizer bunny—kept going and going."

"Viagra!" Hayden cried, and doubled over laughing. "I knew I should never have gotten him that scrip!"

Hayden and Quinn were holding on to each other, shaking with mirth, when Cordell walked into the room. They both turned to look at him, their faces wet with tears.

"Oh, my God," Cordell said, putting his hand on his heart. "What is it? Has someone crossed over?"

This struck Hayden and Quinn as excruciatingly hilarious, and they collapsed into a longer fit of laughter than they'd had in years.

THE NEXT DAY, Quinn faced a daunting task, and laughter felt as remote as the lunar landscape. It was time for her to call the hospital and schedule her appointment for an MRI. She wondered if she would ever again laugh so hard she could barely make it to the bathroom in time. This test, she knew, was the moment of truth. She might not emerge from it with *all* the answers, but she would certainly have enough to know just how serious Naomi's condition really was.

With the date of the MRI circled in red on her calendar, Quinn found it impossible to stay emotionally even, no matter how hard she tried. The following weeks were a tumultuous ride, as Quinn vacillated between sullen silence and fits of fury. She felt guilty for snapping at her husband and son, but it was beyond her control. She simply could not endure the wait with any kind of grace.

Then at last the day arrived, and Quinn was told to "just relax" as she was pushed inside a humming cylinder. She shivered from nerves, and found the words as hollow as the giant tube.

Quinn didn't consider herself as particularly claustrophobic, but as she lay inside the monstrous machine, listening to the whir of a fan, and imagined her baby's fate being sealed by the images being generated and analyzed, Quinn felt as if she could rip off her own skin if it meant getting out of there.

"How are you doing?" came a disembodied male voice.

"Not so great. How long have I been in here?"

They had told her it might take close to an hour, and she figured she had already been in there at least that long.

"Almost twelve minutes."

Twelve minutes? Tears ran down Quinn's still face. How would she ever endure this? She closed her eyes and tried to take herself on an imaginary journey. She was back in Fiji, this time with Lewis. But, no, the vision wouldn't stick, as she couldn't imagine a time in her life when such a trip might be possible. If Naomi lived, their family would forever be burdened with a disabled child. Such a trip would be possible only if the baby didn't survive, and she didn't want to envision that outcome.

"You still hanging in there?" came the voice some time later.

"Barely."

"We're almost done."

Thank God thank God thank God, she thought. She counted backward from one hundred. She counted forward to one hundred. She counted to five thousand by tens. She sang songs in her head. Recited poems. When the hell were they going to pull her out?

"You have a strange definition of 'almost done,'" she finally said.

"Sorry," said the voice. "The baby moved and we need to take some pictures again."

She closed her eyes. Okay, little girl, she thought. We're in this together. Literally. If you hold still, I'll hold still. Deal?

She imagined the baby as a sentient being understanding her message, and all at once, Naomi felt as real to her as Isaac did. She pictured the smooth skin of her cheek, the curl of her tiny toes, the thin skin of her delicate eyelids. And she would have a smell, Quinn realized, distinctly her own.

"Are you okay?" came the voice again, and Quinn realized that she was making crying sounds deep in her throat.

LATER, AS SHE stood facing the painting of young Nan hanging in her living room, Quinn finally got it. Sometimes we don't just simply grow and change. Sometimes life is so harsh and so dark, a part of us gets excised completely, leaving us permanently altered.

It was the day after her MRI. Lewis was at work and Isaac at school. Quinn needed her mother, and was trying hard to resist the temptation to slip through to the other side. So she got in her car and drove to her parents' home. She wondered if she would ever be able to think of it as simply her dad's house.

As usual, she dropped her handbag on the table in the hallway, and did a lap around the first floor. Everything looked in good order, but something about the family room gave her pause. What was different? She looked at the couch, the rug, the chairs, and then she saw it—the curio cabinet. That was it! The last time she was there, she had left in such a state that she hadn't put the furniture back in place. Now the piece was where it belonged and all the knickknacks were back inside. How odd. Who had been there to straighten up? Wouldn't Hayden or Lewis have told her if they had visited the house? Later, she would ask them. There had to be a simple explanation.

Quinn went into the studio and headed straight for the unfinished landscape resting on the easel. She undraped it and studied the painting.

"I need to tell you something, Mom," she said to the dark figure in the distance. "I wish I could talk to you in person, because . . . I don't know. I really need you." She stopped and thought of her mother in the other life. It would be so easy to go home and cross over. To stand facing her mother in this very room, looking into her eyes.

You should still be here, Quinn thought. You should be alive so I could tell you about your granddaughter.

"Damn you," she said to the painting.

She knew it wasn't her mother's fault that the doctors had discovered brain matter in the sac protruding through Naomi's skull. She knew Nan wouldn't have been able to do a damned thing about the fact that her baby's only hope was surgery, and even that offered no guarantees. But she was furious anyway.

She picked up the painting. "If only you were here!" Her muscles tensed in anger, and she looked for something to smash the picture on. She wanted to crack the wooden stretcher, break holes in the canvas. But as she glanced around the studio something shocking caught her eye, and she dropped the landscape.

The curio cabinet wasn't the only thing that had changed since the last time she was in this house. There, leaning against the wall in the same spot it had been before the break-in, was a stack of unframed paintings. The stolen family portraits! Someone had put them back.

Quinn approached and pulled out each painting to be sure she wasn't imagining things, then hurried to her cell phone. She called Lewis first, and wasn't surprised to learn he didn't know anything about it. Hayden would be working, but she left messages at his school, at home, and on his cell. She had to get to the bottom of this.

That night, when she still hadn't heard from her brother, Quinn tried him again, but he didn't answer. By the next morning she was getting nervous. She phoned the office at the high school where he taught, and was told he had called in sick. Quinn wasted no time. She got in her car and drove to his apartment in Brooklyn.

"Hayden, it's me, Quinn," she said into the intercom.

Nothing.

"I have a key," she said. "If you don't buzz me in I'm just going to let myself in. Please, Hayd."

The buzzer sounded.

Quinn walked up the two flights to Hayden's apartment and he answered the door barefoot, in a grubby T-shirt and pajama bottoms.

"What's the matter?" she said. "What's wrong? Why aren't you answering my calls?"

Hayden pushed the door closed behind her and turned the deadbolt. He shuffled to the couch and dropped himself into it.

"It smells in here," she said, picking up tissues from the floor.

He didn't respond.

"Are you sick or depressed?" she asked.

Her brother turned away.

"Answer me, Hayden!"

"What's the difference?"

Depressed. Her stomach twisted in a knot. "Are you taking your meds?" she asked.

"They're not working."

"Did you call Dr. Price?" Though she had met his psychiatrist only once, she had been hearing his name for years.

He shook his head.

"What happened? Is it Cordell?" Quinn felt a rising fury. If Cordell had done this to Hayden, she would tear him apart.

He didn't respond.

"Answer me, Hayden. Please."

He looked away.

"Fine, you don't have to tell me. But I need to know if you're okay."

Obviously, he wasn't okay, but they both knew that the question was shorthand. She was asking if he was suicidal.

She swallowed hard, waiting for a response. It took several moments before he finally spoke. "No," he whispered.

Quinn gave his shoulder a squeeze and walked into the kitchen. She opened the drawer where Hayden kept his personal phone book and looked up Dr. Price's phone number. She got his service and told them it was an emergency. The doctor called back within minutes. Quinn explained the situation to him and he asked to speak with Hayden, who took the phone into the bedroom.

Quinn straightened the living room while she waited, listening to Hayden's soft murmurs from the other side of the door. When at last he emerged, he handed the phone to Quinn.

"He wants to talk to you," her brother said.

Dr. Price explained to Quinn that Hayden had agreed to check himself into the psychiatric ward at New York University Hospital. He asked her to stay with her brother as he packed his things, and then bring him directly to the facility.

Quinn did as Dr. Price asked. She had lost her mother to suicide. She'd be damned if she was going to lose her brother, too.

21

"WHAT'S THE MATTER?" GEORGETTE ASKED A FEW DAYS LATER. She had stopped by unannounced and Quinn stood by her front door, blocking the entrance.

"It's not a good time," Quinn said.

"Do you want to talk about it?"

She didn't. What good would talking do? Would it make her brother well? Would it help her control all the things in her life that threatened to consume her? Quinn shook her head.

"I'm worried about you," Georgette said.

"I'll talk to you later," Quinn said, and gently shut the door.

She picked up the basket of laundry, telling herself she would not go through the portal, despite her state of mind. She knew, though, that her resolve to resist the temptation had diminished. Between the situation with her brother and the truth about the baby, her whole life felt like an extenuating circumstance.

Downstairs, Quinn set the basket of dirty clothes on the dryer and opened the washing machine. As she dropped in items of clothing, one by one, she could feel the fissure behind her like a human force, calling out to her.

No, she thought, as she tossed in a pair of Isaac's jeans.

No, she thought, as she threw in Lewis's gray T-shirt.

No, she repeated, as she balled up her purple blouse.

She turned to the fissure. *Don't you see what I'm doing?* she wanted to say to her mother. *I'm staying with my family! They need me. Just like I need you.*

She knocked the basket of clothes onto the floor and kicked it. It felt good to unleash her anger, but she needed something more. If her strength had matched her fury, she would have ripped the washer from the plumbing and hurled it away. She would have pulled the cabinets off the walls and smashed them to pieces. She would have kicked holes in the drywall and smashed the lights. She was as infuriated with her own impotence as she was with her mother. She knew it wasn't Nan's fault that her brother was in the hospital and that her baby was damaged. But, damn it, she should be there to help her through! Quinn stood in the center of the room panting and sweating. Was there no outlet for this rage? No outlet for a woman whose mother had made the most selfish decision of all?

There was, of course. There was one perfect outlet, and Quinn knew it.

At last, she pulled open the ancient ironing board and crossed through to the other life.

"Is that . . . me?"

Quinn had emerged in her Manhattan apartment and driven out to her parents' house on Long Island, her anger finding its way to her fists as she gripped the steering wheel. She now stood in her mother's studio. She had let herself into the house and walked directly to the back room, where her mother was at her easel, putting the finishing touches on a painting of a young girl sitting on a pile of books.

"I didn't hear you come in," Nan said.

"How old am I supposed to be? Nine? Ten?"

"Right around there," Nan said. "It's part of a series."

"What kind of series?"

"I call it *Quinn Deconstructed*."

Quinn's jaw tensed. "Is there a point to it? Are you trying to prove to the world what a dedicated mother you were?"

Nan put down her palette. "Someone got up on the wrong side of the bed."

Quinn folded her arms and nodded toward the canvas. "It's good." She meant it more as an accusation than a compliment.

"Thank you."

"You captured me."

"That was the idea."

"I'm just wondering," Quinn said, "how you could know me so well and yet not know what I needed? Or is it that you just didn't care?"

"What are you getting at, kiddo?"

Quinn started to pace around the room. How could she accuse her mother of leaving her by committing suicide when she was right here? Finally, she pointed to the living room.

"What's behind the curio cabinet, Mother?"

Nan's face went pale.

"Ah!" Quinn said. "Did I strike a nerve?"

"Tell me what you're talking about," her mother said.

"I think you know."

"Please, Quinn. You have to tell me."

"No!"

Nan took a deep breath, wiped her hands on a rag. "I thought you forgot about that."

Quinn rubbed her forehead. "What do you mean?"

"Don't you remember? You sensed something there when you were small. It scared me. I thought if I blocked it off . . ."

"And made me stay away . . ."

"Right."

"But I didn't. I got close, Mom. Very, very close."

Nan shut her eyes and covered her heart, as if remembering something that made her weak. She opened her eyes and adjusted her posture, regaining strength. "What was it like?" she said to her daughter. "What did you sense in that spot?"

"You tell me."

Nan pursed her lips in thought. Then she walked to the slop sink and rinsed off her paintbrushes. She splashed water on her face and dried it with a paper towel before turning to her daughter. "It was a dark time in my life," she said. "I didn't see any alternatives."

"What about me?" Quinn said. "Were you thinking about me at all?"

"You weren't born yet."

"I wasn't?"

Nan shook her head.

Quinn walked out of the studio and into the family room, where she placed her hands on the curio cabinet, trying to understand. What was it she felt here? God, it was so cold. There was no life pulsing by on the other side. Her mother was dead. And so was she. Dead, without ever having had the chance to live. At last she understood. She turned to face Nan, who had followed her into the room.

"You were pregnant with me," Quinn said.

Nan's eyes went sad and soft. "Yes."

Quinn started to cry. "You were pregnant with me and tried to kill yourself?"

"I'm sorry."

"How could you?" Didn't you love me? she thought. Didn't you love me as much as I love Naomi?

"There's no way to explain depression to someone who hasn't been there."

"You think I haven't been *depressed*?"

"It's different, Quinn. It's not like being sad. It's . . . blackness. You just go so numb, nothing matters."

Quinn started to feel sick to her stomach and backed away from the curio cabinet. Nan tried to approach her.

"Are you okay?" her mother asked.

Quinn shook her head but held up her hands against her mother's approach. She sat heavily on the couch.

"I'll get you some water," Nan said, and left the room. When she returned, Quinn drank the entire glass before she spoke.

"Was that the last time you were depressed?" Quinn asked.

"No, I . . . Of course not," Nan said. "You know that. You saw me depressed many times."

"But you never attempted suicide again."

"No."

"Why not?"

"Because I was a mother. So even when I was falling into the abyss, I found something to grab on to."

"Exactly!"

Nan's brow tensed. "Quinn, I don't understand."

"You're my mother! You were supposed to be there for me!"

"I did my best."

"Ha!"

"Tell me what I've done," Nan said.

Quinn rose. "Never mind. I have to leave."

"Honey, don't go, please. Tell me what's going on."

"I can't."

"Why not?"

Quinn glanced toward the curio cabinet. "Never mind, Mom," she said. "Forget I ever came here today."

Nan looked at the heavy furniture and back at her daughter. Her face was locked in concentration, as if she were working on a crossword puzzle.

Quinn looked away, avoiding her mother's eyes. Nan was filling in the boxes, and Quinn simply wouldn't help her with any more clues. "I have to go," she said.

She walked toward the front door but her mother beat her there and stood in her way.

"I'm not letting you leave unless you explain all this," Nan said.

"Don't, Mom."

"Why not?"

Quinn looked at her watch. It was almost two o'clock. She did some quick math in her head and understood she had to leave immediately if she wanted to have any chance of being there for Isaac's bus.

"It's late," Quinn said. "If I don't leave now—"

"Finish your sentence."

"I can't."

"You were in the same kind of hurry when we went to the mall," Nan said.

Quinn looked into her mother's eyes—so different from the eyes in the happy portrait that hung in her living room. These eyes were all fire, and they were getting very close to the truth.

"Get out of my way, Mom," Quinn said.

"Not until you explain yourself."

"I'll push you if I have to."

"Is it really that important to leave right this minute?"

"It is." Quinn looked hard at her mother, communicating the importance of her departure. There was a moment of hesitation, and then Nan nodded, sadly, and stepped aside.

Quinn rushed to her car and tore away from the curb, heading for the Long Island Expressway as fast as she could. If she hurried, she might still make it home in time for Isaac's bus. She barely stayed on all four wheels as she navigated the twists and turns to the highway's entrance ramp.

Traffic on the expressway was heavy, but it was moving pretty well. Quinn looked at the clock. She could do this. She could make it.

She maneuvered to the left lane and tried to make up time, speeding until she got close to a car doing under seventy, then fought her way around it. For ten minutes or so it looked promising, but then Quinn saw something ahead that alarmed her. Brake lights. She crossed her fingers and said a silent prayer. *Let it be a momentary slowdown. Please.* But no. This was the Long Island Expressway, and when someone threw a toothpick in the road, traffic backed up for miles.

She made bargains with herself as she inched along. *If traffic lets up now and Manhattan is free of gridlock, I could still do it.* But she knew she was fighting a cruel clock.

When at last she made it through the tunnel and into Manhattan, Quinn raced uptown and tried to find a clear through street to get to the West Side, where she and Eugene lived. But crossing town was Manhattan's gnarliest beast, and Quinn had to abandon the car two blocks from her apartment building. She sprinted through the streets, around nonchalant pedestrians, who thought nothing of a woman weaving through crowds like a running back.

When at last she got to her apartment, she rushed right past Eugene, who was sitting in the living room with Walt St. Pierre—an old friend and former *Saturday Night Live* writer who lived in the building—without saying hello.

"I *told* her to stay away from Taco Bell," she heard Eugene say to his friend as she slammed the bathroom door.

Quinn was dripping sweat as she watched the tub fill with cold water. She undressed and lowered herself in, worrying that she would get hypothermia before being pulled through. But she stayed underwater, shivering and holding her breath, until she felt a jarring tug.

The journey felt like a bus ride on a dirt road, as she was bumped and jolted toward her other life. When at last she saw the slender sliver of light from her basement through a fissure in the concrete, she was nauseated. Worse yet, the opening had diminished even more, and Quinn had to struggle to push her swollen, naked body through the rough cement. At last she made it through, just in time to vomit onto the floor of the laundry room, soiling the pile of clothes she had been wearing before her passage.

She quickly rummaged through the laundry she had dumped from the basket earlier and put on a mismatched shirt and pants, and dashed out the front door barefoot.

Quinn knew she had missed Isaac's bus, but hoped it hadn't been by more than a few minutes, and that he wouldn't be too hysterical. But when she got to the corner, he wasn't there. She glanced up and down the street. There was no sign of the bus. There was no sign of Isaac.

She stood there in a panic. What should she do? Race through the streets looking for him? Go home and phone the school to see if he had stayed on the bus? Dial 911?

"Quinn!" she heard Georgette call.

Goddamn it, she thought. I have no time for that woman now. She ignored her and started to call out. "Isaac! ISAAC!"

"Quinn!" her neighbor called again.

"Not now, Georgette!" she shouted. Her heart was pounding with panic.

"Turn around," her neighbor yelled.

Quinn did as she said, ready to scream at the top of her lungs at her annoying friend. But she stopped. Georgette was standing in front of her house with a small boy at her side.

"Isaac!" Quinn called, and ran to her son. "I'm sorry," she said as she hugged him. "I'm so sorry. I'll never leave you again. I promise."

22

THE NEXT DAY, QUINN WENT TO THE BUS STOP TEN MINUTES early, as if she could make up for yesterday by spending extra time standing on the corner in the cold. Guilt had seeped into her psyche like a noxious gas, and she was trying to dissipate it any way she could. Isaac would be okay. At least, she hoped he would. Meanwhile, he was suffering, and it was her fault.

He had been almost catatonic after she picked him up from Georgette's house the day before, and was still quiet this morning when she sent him to school. Maybe if they did something fun together this afternoon, he would start to come around.

The bus pulled up and she watched him get off, her heart contracting at the sight of his tiny frame overwhelmed by an oversized jacket and big kid's backpack. He was still at such a helpless age. She smiled when he caught sight of her. His relief was palpable, but his expression remained pained.

"Guess what?" she said when he reached her. "There's a special arts-and-crafts program at the library this afternoon. They're making fall window decorations. Do you want to go?"

He shrugged.

"You feel okay?" she asked.

Another shrug. She felt his head. It was cool, as she expected. This wasn't illness, it was defensive retreat. She hugged him. His arms hung limply.

"I think it'll be fun," she said.

"I guess."

She took that as a yes. "Do you want to have a snack before we go?"

"I don't know."

"I got those doughnuts you like," she said, leading him to the house. "The ones with the sugar that make Daddy sneeze."

She thought that might get a laugh, but Isaac remained stoic. They went inside, where she gave him his snack and watched as he ate about half the doughnut and pushed it away.

"Is that all you want?"

"Yeah."

"Finish your milk."

He picked up his glass, drank the last inch of fluid, and put it down hard. She touched the back of his head and smoothed his hair.

"I know you're still mad at me for not being at the bus stop yesterday. Do you want to talk about it?"

He shook his head. "Can we go now?"

"Sure."

At the library, she took him straight to the children's section, and was instructed to bring him across the hall to the large meeting room. Inside, there were at least two dozen children sitting at long tables with piles of arts-and-crafts materials in front of them. Quinn watched her son eye the materials. She sensed something shifting in him as he focused on the colors and textures. Already his creative wheels were in motion.

"Isaac!" someone called.

Quinn looked up and saw a boy from her son's class. "Look, honey," she said. "It's Rasheed."

Isaac grinned, and Quinn realized it was the first time she saw him smile since yesterday morning. He took the seat next to his friend, who picked up two purple foam circles and held them in front of his eyes like glasses. Isaac laughed, and Quinn felt relieved. He was going to be fine—he just needed some time.

A short woman with shiny black hair clapped her hands to get everyone's attention, and announced that the grown-ups should leave and come back in forty-five minutes. Uh-oh, Quinn thought. This is going to be trouble. She looked at Isaac, expecting the wild-eyed panic he always exhibited in these situations, but his face was placid. She put her hand on his shoulder and addressed him gently.

"They want the mommies and daddies to wait outside," she said.

No response.

"You'll be fine, right?"

He shrugged.

"I'm not leaving the library," she said. "I'll be right across the hall in the children's room, finding some books we can read together, okay?"

He picked up the purple rings and held them in front of his eyes as he looked at her.

"You're invisible," he said.

Isaac, she realized, was coping with the trauma of losing her yesterday by finding a way to "control" the situation. If he held the power of making her disappear, he could also make her reappear.

"Those must be magic rings," she said.

"They are."

She kissed the top of his head. "I'll be right across the hall."

Quinn spent the remainder of the day by Isaac's side, and little by little he warmed up. By that night, they were cuddled up together in his bed as she read to him from the library's copy of *Charlotte's Web*. It had been one of her childhood favorites, and she hadn't read it in years.

Reading it as an adult, of course, was a completely different experience, and Quinn found herself choked with emotion from the very first page, struggling to read aloud over a strangling lump in her throat. By the middle of the book she was weeping.

"Why are you crying?" Isaac asked.

Why? Because her sweet son was coming around. Because he was still young enough to nestle in the crook of her arm as she read him a book, but old enough to appreciate this wonderful story that started out as a simple tale of a girl saving a small pig, and evolved into a fable about trust and treachery, love and miracles, and, ultimately, all the heartbreak and wonder in the circle of life. She was crying because a grown-up writer believed that beautiful sentences weren't wasted on children. And because even as an adult, she still struggled to believe she deserved any tenderness at all.

THE NEXT DAY, Quinn and Hayden sat facing each other in upholstered chairs in the visiting room of the New York University Hospital psychiatric ward. Unlike the last time she saw him, his hair was clean and his eyes were bright. Hayden was fully dressed—in jeans and a faded sweatshirt—as the patients on this floor weren't allowed to lounge around in pajamas like sick people. The only difference was the footwear. He was in slippers because laces (and indeed all things that could be fashioned into a noose) were considered contraband.

"Thanks for coming to see me," he said.

"Of course." She tried to smile.

"Are you okay?" he asked.

She wasn't, but she didn't think it was particularly appropriate to unburden her emotional problems on her brother while he was in the psych ward.

"Shouldn't I be asking *you* that?" she said.

He smiled at the joke, but addressed her seriously. "You're allowed to have problems, too."

Not really, she thought. Not here, not now. Quinn looked around the room at the small groups huddled in conversation. Everyone seemed involved in an unspoken conspiracy of pretending these were the most normal circumstances in which to have a chat.

"You seem like you're doing better," Quinn offered.

"I had two rounds of electroshock."

She tried not to grimace. "What is it like?"

He shrugged. "They put you out. It's like nothing."

"But it really helps?"

"A lot."

She nodded. "What about memory loss?" she asked, as she knew it was one of the side effects.

"So far, so good," he said. "But who knows? I could forget we ever had this conversation."

She almost laughed, but caught herself—he wasn't kidding. "Are you worried?" she asked.

He shrugged. "If it happens, it happens. It's only temporary."

A man with a missing tooth asked if he could have the chair they weren't using, and Hayden said it was fine. Quinn studied her brother to see if it disturbed him to be in this strange place among mentally ill people, some of whom were delusional and possibly dangerous. But he looked calm.

"I wanted to tell you something," Hayden said to Quinn, after the chair was dragged off. "I guess you probably figured it out, but it was me. I was the one who moved the curio cabinet back." He paused. "And returned the paintings."

Yes, of course. Who else could it have been? But why? It was so bewildering Quinn couldn't imagine what his explanation would be.

"I don't understand," she said quietly.

"I don't, either, but"—he paused to run his fingers through his hair—
"I found the paintings in Cordell's closet."

"What?"

Hayden looked agitated. "Please don't freak," he said.

Talk about shock therapy. Quinn was reeling, but she steadied herself.
"I'm not freaking," she said evenly. "Tell me what happened."

Hayden took a deep breath. "He left for Los Angeles to film that show
and I went into his closet looking for a shirt I thought he might have borrowed. Instead, I found the paintings. I nearly passed out."

"Why would he do that? Why would he steal the paintings?"

"I don't know. And I don't want to know. As soon as I found them I
changed the locks on my apartment . . . and then put the paintings back
in Mom's studio."

"Why did you keep it a secret, Hayden? Why didn't you call me?"

He pulled a tissue from the box next to him and blew his nose. He took
another tissue and dabbed at his eyes. It took him a few minutes before
he could respond.

"I was afraid you would call the police. I didn't want him arrested."

"But if he stole the paintings—"

"Please," he interrupted. His voice sounded desperate.

She backed off. "Okay," she said, but knew that when he was feeling
more stable she would bring it up again. If Cordell stole the paintings, he
deserved to be arrested.

"Anyway, I haven't spoken to him since," Hayden said. "He keeps
calling but I don't answer. You should see my cell phone. I have sixty-six
messages." His eyes watered and he paused, waiting for it to pass. "How
could he do this, Quinn?" he whispered, as if this were the one thing he
didn't want anyone else to hear.

"I can't imagine," she said.

"I loved him."

"I know."

"He's back in New York now—I heard it through the grapevine. He's staying with some friends on West Fourth."

"Does he know you're here?"

"Probably. But even if he comes to visit, they won't let him in."

"That's good," she said.

"Is it? I can't stop thinking about him. I keep imagining him walking through the door, holding flowers. I try to imagine a plausible explanation so I can forgive him, but I can't make it work." He paused, sighed. "Anyway, now you know. Now you know what pushed me over the edge."

She reached for his hand. "It's going to be okay," she said.

"I guess."

Quinn changed the subject. "Do you know when you're getting out of here?"

"A few days, I think. I'm eager to get back to my students. Some of them sent me get-well cards."

She smiled. "They're good kids."

"The best."

"You're going to be okay," she said to her brother.

"So are you."

She nodded and wished she could believe it.

WHEN QUINN GOT OFF the elevator in the lobby, an older couple in warm-up suits approached her and asked if she knew where the maternity ward was.

"Maternity?" she said.

The woman's rheumy eyes filled. "Our daughter had a baby," she said. It seemed as if her joy might cause her to detonate if she didn't get the words out.

The husband held up the flowers he had brought, as if that constituted all the proof Quinn might need.

Quinn couldn't help smiling. "Congratulations," she said. "Your first grandchild?"

They nodded simultaneously, which Quinn found so adorable she almost laughed. She wanted to adopt them.

"Let's find out where you need to go," she said, and walked them over to the security guard. As he gave directions, pointing toward the elevator they would need to take, he put his hand on Quinn's back. It occurred to her that he assumed she was with the couple, perhaps their other daughter—the new aunt. She enjoyed the fantasy and decided to go with it. After all, she had time to kill. Quinn was meeting an old friend from Baston's Books uptown for lunch, and had an hour or so with nothing to do.

She got on the elevator with her pretend parents, and when the doors opened they thanked her and said good-bye. Quinn stepped out into the wide hallway and watched them walk away, feeling bereft. She wasn't quite ready to go back to being a sad and frightened pregnant woman whose mother was dead.

Quinn eyed the double doors to the maternity ward and felt a pull. New mothers. New babies. So much joy. She wanted to get close to it, to breathe it all in like pure oxygen.

Why not, she thought, and walked through the doors as if she belonged there. She didn't want to stop and ask any questions that might arouse suspicions about her presence, so she got in step behind a nurse pushing a newborn in a bassinet. Just as she expected, the woman led her straight to the nursery.

Quinn got close to the glass and looked inside. The brightly lit room was similar to the one at North Shore Hospital in Manhasset, where she had given birth to Isaac. Tiny babies swaddled in the hospital's flannel receiving blankets were on display in acrylic bassinets. Each had a little sign with the baby's name and gender. New moms and other proud relatives stood outside the window, smiling, laughing, cooing and even crying. Emotions were high, and Quinn felt her heart contract. This is it, she thought. This is where joy lives.

Quinn turned and saw a woman in a bathrobe waddle to the nurses' station dragging an IV pole, her eyes swollen and red. She asked to be directed to the NICU. Neonatal intensive care unit, Quinn thought, the other place. The one where hope and sorrow fought a daily battle. When hope was defeated, the losses were unimaginable. The tiniest fallen soldiers, Quinn thought, could leave the most giant hearts battered and broken.

I shouldn't do this, Quinn thought, as she followed the woman to the NICU. But she had to. She had to get a glimpse of her future.

Quinn stood to the side as the woman had her wristband checked and was let into the room. Though the window was smaller here, Quinn could see the woman take a chair toward the back, and watched as a nurse carefully picked up a small baby and placed it in the woman's arms. All she could tell about the infant was that it was much too small. The mother, Quinn sensed, was saying good-bye.

It was a private moment, and Quinn looked away, focusing instead on an infant in front of the window. He or she—it was impossible to tell here—wore a white cap and had ruddy skin. Quinn intuited that this was a boy. There was an oxygen tube in his nose, a piece of tape on the side of his face holding it in place. Another tube protruded from what looked like a cuff on his birdlike arm. The baby opened his eyes, blinked, closed them again. This went on for several minutes, and Quinn could feel this child fighting. She didn't even realize she was crying until a nurse stopped by and asked her if she was okay.

Quinn shook her head and the nurse waited for her to elaborate.

"I'm pregnant," she began, and didn't mean to let it all tumble out, but it did. Once she started, she couldn't stop. She explained about the encephalocele and the MRI. She told the woman that her mother had committed suicide and that her brother was upstairs in the psych ward.

She explained that she wasn't supposed to be there but had followed a couple inside.

"I'm sorry," Quinn said. "I couldn't help it."

The nurse, who was a head shorter than Quinn, had listened intently. And now that Quinn was done, she expected the woman to be apologetic about kicking her out. Perhaps she'd give Quinn some medical advice or tell her to seek counseling. But she didn't.

"Come here," said the nurse, and she led Quinn into the NICU, where she instructed her to wash her hands and put a paper gown over her clothes. Then she pushed a chair next to the little fighter by the window and asked Quinn to sit down. The nurse lifted the baby and gently placed it in Quinn's arms.

"This is Carly," she said.

Quinn stared at the tiny face. "A girl?"

"Yes."

"Is she going to be okay?"

"Two days ago we thought we were losing her. But she's surprising everyone."

Carly seemed to weigh almost nothing. Quinn brought the tiny body close to hers and felt a tug in her breasts, as a primal chain reaction of hormones urged her not-quite-ready milk ducts to let down. She felt washed in a blissful, protective, "dear God, don't let anything happen to this baby" emotion she could only describe as love.

Quinn touched the tiny hand and four impossibly small digits wrapped around her finger. "Carly," she whispered. "You show them, little girl. You show them what you've got."

Carly's eyes blinked open and she seemed to stare into Quinn's face. It was magical. Suddenly, everything but this one potent connection was irrelevant.

"I feel like I've just been sprinkled with fairy dust," Quinn said.

"That happens a lot in here," the nurse said.

23

QUINN ASCENDED FROM THE SUBWAY ON THE WEST SIDE OF Manhattan and buttoned her coat against the chill. Home, in the suburbs, she would be wearing a big coat on a day like this—something puffy and unflattering. But for the city she had donned her wine red wool jacket with gold buttons, accented by a fashionable scarf. It felt good to be back in the city, dressed like she belonged.

She headed in the direction of Baston's Books, where she was meeting her friend and former coworker, Meredith Huff, a lanky blonde who had taken over her old position as events coordinator and was now running the whole store.

Meredith, Quinn thought, had found the best possible job for herself. The woman adored writers. Particularly male writers. Particularly male writers who were willing to get naked with her. When they first met, Meredith had confessed to Quinn that she was "kind of an author groupie." After they got to know each other better and Quinn had endured hundreds of conversations regarding her friend's exploits, she told Meredith that the groupie analogy wasn't quite accurate. Groupies were teenage girls who eventually outgrew their infatuations.

"You," Quinn had said to her friend, "are more of a fetishist."

Meredith laughed and owned up to it. "God help me, it's true. The very idea of a writer's dick makes me shiver. I think it's the crazy twisted ego behind it—the way they are always imagining their own lives in twelve-point type. Seriously. You haven't lived until you've gone down on a guy who has already decided how he's going to describe the color of your nipples. It's *so hot*!"

Quinn was thinking about all this as she headed for the bookstore. She smiled, anticipating the stories Meredith would tell, and the guessing game they would play. She wondered what it said about her that she wound up with friends like Georgette and Meredith when her own life was so tame. Was she subconsciously trying to re-create her relationship with her mother? Quinn's head was so filled with unraveling that she walked toward Baston's on autopilot, tuning out the sounds of the city. Then a truck stopped short and the taxi driver behind it leaned on his horn for so long it tore her from her reverie. She looked around and realized that she was about to walk down the block where she and Eugene had lived in her other life. She paused, almost causing a pileup of pedestrians. They jostled along as she thought about which way to go to avoid walking past their co-op. She looked left and right, considering her options, then realized it was silly. In this life, the building had no meaning. Eugene didn't even live there.

She continued straight, giving the entrance a quick glance as she passed. Jean-Claude, the elegant doorman with a Salvadore Dali–esque mustache, was helping a woman with packages. Quinn realized that if she walked up and said hello, she would be a complete stranger to him. The thought gave her a charge. It was like having a special power.

As a child, Hayden would sometimes ask Quinn what kind of magic power she would most want to have, given the choice. Her brother always chose invisibility, which seemed downright icky to Quinn. She had no desire to know what people were doing or saying behind closed doors. Likewise, she didn't care about X-ray vision. Even superhuman strength didn't appeal much to her. But flying. Flying was perfect. Quinn liked to close her eyes and imagine the freedom of being able to soar through the air. Up there, none of her problems would trouble her, and everything would look so condensed and flawless.

Quinn thought she heard someone calling her name. Was it her imagination? She turned toward the building. Jean-Claude was now obscured by a short, stocky man who stood in front of him, waving to her.

She stopped. "Walt?"

He jogged over to her.

It was Eugene's friend Walt St. Pierre, the former *Saturday Night Live* writer who had been sitting on the sofa with him the other day when she hurried past to return home to Isaac. To him, of course, that never happened, and he hadn't seen her in ten years. She marveled at the coincidence of running into him, but then realized that since he lived in this building in the other life, he probably did in this life as well.

"I thought it was you," he said. "You look *fantastic.*"

She wondered how he would know how she looked when his focus was somewhere in the vicinity of her right shoulder. Walt had never been able to make eye contact with her or, as far as she knew, any woman. The guy was funny, smart, and very talented, but had massive insecurities when it came to the opposite sex.

"Thanks," she said, and moved to kiss him on the cheek, but he turned his head at the wrong moment and she sort of grazed the corner of his mouth, which embarrassed both of them. "It's good to see you, Walt."

"How long has it been?" he asked.

"Ten years, at least."

"You look fantastic," he repeated.

"You, too," she lied.

"You lost weight, right? You look fantastic."

Quinn considered telling him that if he wasn't careful she might get the impression he thought she looked fantastic. But she wasn't sure how well the joke would go over, so she just said, "Actually, I'm pregnant. With my second."

"Oh! Congratulations. Are you still with that taxi driver?"

That, Quinn surmised, was the story Eugene had told all his friends. She could imagine him weaving a tale about her running off with a cabbie. *She didn't have money to pay the fare so he invited her to his apartment and she never left.* Or something like that.

"He's not exactly a taxi driver," Quinn said.

"I also heard you moved out to the suburbs," he said, as if this chance encounter proved that rumor false as well.

"I did. I'm here to meet a friend from Baston's for lunch."

A gust of wind disturbed his comb-over and he struggled to keep it in place. "I never thought of you as a bridge-and-tunnel girl."

She smiled. "But I am! I have a house in the suburbs, a husband, a kid, and a Volvo."

"A bona fide soccer mom."

"That's me."

"You should run for vice president."

She laughed. "I think I'd have to be a *hockey* mom."

"Soccer mom, hockey mom—either way, it gives me a boner. Housewives are *hot*."

Quinn blanched.

He covered his mouth. "That was inappropriate, right?"

"A bit."

"The good news is that my reputation as king of the awkward moment remains untarnished."

"Part of your charm," she said, and changed the subject. "You live here?"

He glanced back at the building. "A few years now. I love it. Can't beat the location."

"Or the views," she said, and instantly realized her gaffe.

"You've been inside?"

"No, I . . . uh, just figured the apartments facing the park would have beautiful vistas."

He nodded. "You know, I tried talking Eugene into taking an apartment here years ago, but he wasn't interested."

Of course. The memory was there, imprinted by her visits to the other life. She was the one who had talked Eugene into taking the beautiful apartment overlooking the park. He had, at first, insisted it was just "too glam."

"You still keep in touch with him?" she asked.

"Sure," he said, and took out his cell phone. "You want to talk to him? I have him on speed dial."

She most certainly did not. What on earth would she have to say to him? In all likelihood, Eugene still seethed with bitter resentment over the break-up. "Thanks anyway," she said.

"You sure?"

He seemed about to press a button, and she raised her voice. "No, don't! *Please.*"

"Oh, sorry," he said. "I guess that might be kind of uncomfortable, huh?" He shook his head, as if trying to rattle some sense into it.

She smiled and tried to make eye contact, but he was focused somewhere near her left ear now. He looked embarrassed, so she changed the subject, trying to put him at ease. "I've been reading your books," she said. "I'm so impressed, Walt."

After leaving *Saturday Night Live,* Walt wrote a nonfiction book about his tenure there. It was funny, honest, and self-effacing. The critics were charmed by it, and it did pretty well. He followed it up with several novels, and was gaining a sizable readership.

"Coming from you," he said, and didn't finish the sentence. Telling her he got a boner had slipped right out, but thanking her for a compliment was nearly impossible. His eyes were now focused on the sidewalk. "Hey, remember that fund-raiser your parents came to? Your mom was a trip."

In her single days, Quinn had been involved with Planned Parenthood, and had attended a number of big fund-raising parties for them. On one occasion, she brought her parents, and her mother had gotten into a row with one of the protesters out front. Someone from the *Daily News* seized the opportunity and snapped a photograph of Nan and a right-to-life woman screaming at each other, face-to-face, their angry, openmouthed expressions nearly mirror images. It was quite a picture.

Of course, what the photograph didn't show was the dialogue that went along with it. As Quinn, Eugene, Nan, and Phil had tried to pass the protesters, the woman shouted at them, "How would you feel if *your* mother had an abortion?"

The moment captured in the photograph was when Nan turned and responded, "I wish she had. Then I wouldn't have to suffer piss-brains like you."

"Ah, wit," Eugene had said. "It's like living in a Noël Coward play."

Immediately, Nan's anger was defused and she laughed at herself.

The irony wasn't lost on Quinn that she had once been an active supporter of Planned Parenthood, and now here she was, faced with the option of getting an abortion and choosing life instead. But of course, it only served to prove what Quinn had believed all along—that there was nothing inconsistent about being pro-choice and anti-abortion. In fact, now more than ever, she was thankful that the decision to carry this child could be hers, and not the government's.

"She was," Quinn agreed. "She was a trip."

"How is she doing?" Walt asked.

"She passed away several years ago." It was her standard line. No need to elaborate unless pressed.

"Not well, then, I guess."

She grimaced.

"I'm sorry," he said. "Bad joke. How did she die?"

Quinn sighed. It was her most dreaded question. "She overdosed on prescription medication." She tried to say it matter-of-factly, but her throat constricted and it came out high-pitched.

"Oh, God. That's rough."

"Yeah."

"Did you know Jackie died?" he asked.

"Jackie?" The name sounded familiar but she couldn't place who it was.

"My fox terrier."

His dog? Was he making a comparison? "I'm sorry," she said.

"I know it's . . . you know, not the same thing. Hey, do you want to come to a party next week?"

"Excuse me?" Talk about odd transitions.

"It's another fund-raiser," he said.

"Um . . ."

"A good cause. I'm donating a portion of the profits on my new book to St. Jude Children's Research Hospital, and we're having a launch-party fund-raiser next Thursday. You should come. I got some big names. There'll be paparazzi and everything."

"Sounds interesting, but . . ."

"No angry protesters out front at this one. Well, maybe a few cranky book critics."

"I don't know, Walt."

"Eugene won't be there, I promise."

"It's not that," she said, though it was certainly part of it. "I just—"

"Tina's going to be there," he interrupted.

"Tina?"

"Fey."

"Ah."

"And possibly Adam," he added.

"Adam?"

"Sandler."

"I was never really that starstruck," she said.

"Oh, and Janeane."

Her eyes went wide. "Garofalo?" Okay, so maybe she was a little starstruck.

"You know her?" he asked.

"No, but I've always wanted to meet her."

He pulled a glossy postcard from his pocket and handed it to her. "This has all the details. You can bring whomever you want. The more, the merrier."

She put it into her purse and told him she would think about it. Quinn managed to successfully kiss him on the cheek as she said good-bye, and then went off to meet her friend Meredith.

OVER MASSIVE SALADS at a publike restaurant near the bookstore, Meredith caught Quinn up on all the latest gossip at Baston's, and then told her about her most recent conquest, an established author of murder mysteries. Instead of revealing his identity outright, she gave hints—the names of his characters, the settings, his overall reputation—until Quinn figured out who it was. This made Meredith feel as if she had free license to kiss and tell. After all, Quinn had *guessed* his name. What was Meredith to do?

Quinn wanted to know if he was as exciting in the bedroom as he was on the page.

"He's all verbs and no adjectives," Meredith said.

"That sounds very clever," Quinn said. "What does it mean?"

"It means he touches, pets, kisses, bites, thrusts. But he pays no attention to whether it's sweet or passionate, tender or wild."

"So this isn't a lasting relationship?"

"Let's just say I'm not buying the sequel."

Quinn stirred her salad and speared a slice of zucchini. "I thought you had sworn off genre writers, anyway," she said.

"Just sci-fi," Meredith corrected.

Quinn laughed. "What's wrong with science fiction writers? I figured they were very imaginative."

"Look, I'm not saying they *all* live in their mothers' basements, but maybe they should. Tell me what's new and exciting in *your* world."

Quinn would have preferred to focus on Meredith's carnal adventures, but she owed her friend some entry into her life, so she started by catching her up on the pregnancy and the results of the MRI.

"Are you . . . having the baby?" Meredith asked.

"I am."

"That's very noble."

"No," Quinn said. "Not noble at all. In fact, it might turn out to be the most selfish decision I've ever made."

"Selfish?"

Quinn looked into her friend's eyes. "How do I know this baby isn't going to spend her whole life suffering?"

Meredith thought about it. "I guess you don't," she said.

"And yet I'm bringing her into the world."

Meredith reached over and gave Quinn's hand a squeeze.

"Do you think I'm making a mistake?" Quinn asked.

"I think the only mistake would be ignoring what your own heart is telling you to do."

Quinn nodded and went back to her salad. She changed the subject and told Meredith the whole story about Hayden and how he had found their mother's paintings in Cordell's closet.

"Why did he steal them?" Meredith asked. "Did he need money?"

"I guess so."

"But what was he planning on doing with them? How do you sell stolen paintings?"

"Beats me," Quinn said. "Maybe he has contacts."

They moved on to other topics, and were almost finished with lunch when Quinn brought up what happened on the way over.

"Have you ever met Walt St. Pierre?" Quinn asked, worried that he might, in fact, already be a notch in Meredith's Coach belt.

"No, but we've been trying to get him to do an event at the store. Wasn't he a friend of Eugene's?"

Quinn nodded. "And I just ran into him."

Meredith's face lit up. "What's he like?"

Quinn laughed, as she knew where this conversation was going. "Forget it," she said. "He's not your type."

"Gay?"

"No, just seriously uncomfortable around women."

"Like the characters in his books," Meredith offered.

"Exactly."

"I'd *love* to do a guy like that."

"Why?"

"Are you kidding? He'd be all shivery and grateful. I'd feel like a goddess."

Quinn pulled out the invitation Walt had given her and passed it to Meredith. "Here's your chance," she said.

"What's this?"

"He invited me to a party. You can go in my place."

Meredith read the card. "This looks cool. We should go together."

"I don't think I'm really up for a party these days, Mer."

"You're allowed to have fun, Quinn."

Was she? Most days Quinn felt like she was already in mourning for Naomi . . . or the healthy girl she might never get to be.

She sipped on her straw. "I'll think about it."

QUINN DECONSTRUCTED, NO. 7

Nan had been able to find only one photograph of Quinn with her leg in a cast. She was on her bed, reading a book and not looking at the camera. Nan would have to imagine—or invent—her expression.

It was a pivotal moment in Quinn's young life, as she had just touched the other side for the first time. Yes, she had known about it since she was practically a baby, but Nan had managed to push it from her daughter's consciousness. Now the truth was unavoidable.

Nan knew she had done this to her daughter, had created this rift in her world by straddling life and death at the moment of her birth. But was it a curse or a gift?

For Nan, escape was a seductive visitor who whispered softly every time things got too dark to bear. So simple. So easy. Just leave. Open a vein, take some pills, go to sleep in the car with the garage door closed and the engine running. The solution was always there.

For her daughter, a different kind of escape beckoned, and Nan had to wonder if it was sweeter or crueler than the lure of death. Could Quinn manage life's difficulties with more grace, knowing there was another version she could choose? Or did it taunt her with a decision no one should ever have to make?

For this portrait, Nan would paint Quinn contemplating her choices. But what expression would she wear? Nan took out her sketch pad to try some different faces. She experimented with fear, love, confusion, joy, sorrow, anger.

Nan looked back at the photograph of her daughter. If she could speak to that girl right now she would ask, "How do you feel about what I have done to you?"

24

QUINN GOT UP FROM THE KITCHEN TABLE, WHERE ISAAC WAS having his snack, and looked out the front door. Nothing. Her brother was already almost an hour late. Hayden had been released from the hospital a few days earlier and was trying to get his life back on track without Cordell. He still felt too shaky to face him, and so had asked Quinn if he could empty Cordell's things from his apartment and store them in her garage. She said it was no problem, and that she'd be glad to make the call to Cordell and arrange for him to come by and retrieve everything.

She picked up the phone and called her brother's cell, but got his voice mail. "Hey," she said. "I'm wondering where you are. Hope everything is okay."

"Is he coming?" Isaac asked. He loved his uncle and was eager to see him.

"He's just running a little late," she said, and hoped she was right.

Her fear was that he had changed his mind at the last minute, which she thought would be a disaster for him. Hayden needed to move on. His mental health depended on it.

Quinn was also anxious about the conversation she needed to have with her brother. She was determined to convince him to turn Cordell over to the police. Letting him get away with what he had done was just wrong, no matter how much Hayden had loved him.

Isaac finished his snack and ran to the front door. "Why isn't he here yet?"

"Let's play a game," Quinn suggested, hoping it would distract them both.

Isaac chose a board game called Guess Who?, in which one player picked a card with a person's face on it and the other would ask yes-or-no questions to try to determine who it was. Isaac was getting so good at it that Quinn no longer had to let him win. After a few rounds he got bored and wanted to draw his own people, so Quinn went back to the kitchen and tried her brother again. This time she hung up without leaving a message.

The card the police detective had given her was resting on her counter next to the phone. She had planned to give it to Hayden so that he could make the call. But now she worried whether she would get a chance to talk him into it. He was so late she was sure he had changed his mind. Maybe he even went to see Cordell.

She fingered the card, considering her options. Should she make the call herself? Previously, she had decided Hayden should be the one to do it. She thought it would be empowering for him to make the move. Also, she didn't want to be accused of butting in again. But was butting in so terrible if it meant doing the right thing? Cordell needed to face the music, and Hayden just might need to be saved from himself. Cordell was like an addiction, and placing the phone call could be her way of launching an intervention.

She went to the front door and looked out one last time, and then went back to the kitchen and made the call.

"He's here!" Isaac yelled just as Quinn put the phone down. She went to the front door and watched as Hayden backed his car into the driveway. The driver's door opened and Isaac ran from the house.

"Is that Vincent van Gogh?" Hayden said when he saw his nephew.

Isaac laughed. "No!"

"René Magritte?"

"No!"

"Don't tell me," Hayden said. "Norman Rockwell?"

"It's me, Isaac!"

Hayden knelt and wrapped his nephew in a hug. "Did you make a picture for me?"

Isaac smiled and nodded. "But I'm not done."

Hayden looked up at his sister. "Everything is in the trunk. Should I put it right in the garage?" He rose and hugged her.

"You're so late," she said.

"It took me forever to get everything loaded into the car."

"I tried calling you."

He patted his pockets. "I guess I forgot my cell. Is everything all right?"

She waved his question away. "I'm just glad to see you. I'll give you a hand unloading."

"The hell you will."

"Hayden—"

"You can point and give orders. If I see you lifting anything I'll call the authorities."

The remark vexed her. She was going to have to find a way to tell him she had just given Cordell's name to the police.

Isaac tugged at his uncle's sleeve. "I'll help."

"You got a deal, Leonardo."

Quinn let Isaac press the button that opened the automatic garage door. It rose slowly, making a terrible racket as metal rubbed against metal. Hayden grimaced, which made Isaac laugh.

Quinn shouted over the noise to tell Hayden where he should put Cordell's things. He opened the trunk of his car and started hauling cartons and other items, letting Isaac drag some of the lighter things, such as shopping bags filled with clothes. As Hayden worked, Quinn asked him if he was doing okay.

"I have good moments and bad," he said while heaving what looked like a pile of wooden bookshelves from the car, "but I'm ready to start a new chapter in my life."

It sounded to Quinn like a rehearsed line, but she figured that was the first step in this long journey of healing.

After all the shopping bags were unloaded, Isaac tried to reach for what looked like a small black suitcase.

"Better let me get that, buddy," Hayden said. "It's a laptop. Kind of fragile."

When the trunk was finally empty, Hayden slammed it shut and dusted his hands. "That's that, then," he said. He was trying to remain stoic, but Quinn thought he looked like a pot with a lid that was fitted too tight. Any increase in pressure, and the thing might blow right off.

"You sure you're okay?" she asked.

"I could use a cold drink."

They went into the kitchen, where Quinn got her brother a Diet Coke. Isaac went into the den to work on the drawing for his uncle.

"Is he still trying to contact you?" she asked.

Hayden shrugged. "I haven't checked my cell phone messages this afternoon."

"I'm really proud of you, Hayd. I can imagine how hard this must be." She poured herself a glass of cold water from the dispenser on the refrigerator door and sat down with her brother.

"I told our mutual friends to let Cordell know you'd be calling about his things."

Despite the November chill, Hayden was sweating from the exertion and Quinn handed him a napkin, which he used to blot his forehead. "I know you think I'm being very strong," he said, "but I'm not. It's the opposite. I'm weak—too weak to face him. I still love him, still think that maybe one day we'll be together again."

"But he did such a terrible thing."

"Maybe," he said.

"Not maybe. Definitely."

Hayden shook his head. "There's still a part of me that thinks there has to be some explanation."

"But he was hiding the paintings in his closet, Hayd."

He looked down. "I know."

"And don't forget that he was with us after the break-in," she said, "folding Dad's sweaters and straightening up, not letting on that he was the one who had created the whole mess. His performance was Oscar-worthy."

Hayden wiped the back of his neck and nodded. Quinn continued. "He had every opportunity to tell you the truth that day, but he never said a word. He pretended he was just there to help. And as if that wasn't bad enough . . ."

"I know. He was such a jerk that day."

They heard the front door open and Lewis's voice call, "I'm home."

Isaac ran to greet him first and Quinn rose and gave him a kiss. He said hello to Hayden and gave him a hug.

"It's all done," Hayden said. "Everything's in the garage. Thanks for letting me store it here."

"I thought you were going to wait and let me help you," Lewis said.

"It wasn't that big a deal."

"I helped!" Isaac said.

"Couldn't have done it without him," Hayden said.

Lewis asked his brother-in-law if he was staying for dinner, and Quinn said he wouldn't have it any other way. She got started with the preparations, while Isaac went back into the den and Lewis asked Hayden how he was coping.

"So-so."

"Must be hard," Lewis said.

"It *is* hard," he said. "I thought we were going to get married. Part of me . . . part of me still thinks that."

"Then why did you take this step?"

"I just needed some space, some time apart to get stronger. Once I'm feeling better I'll talk to him again and find out what really happened."

Quinn cleared her throat. "You might get your chance in court."

"What do you mean?" Hayden asked.

Quinn pulled out a chair and sat. "Listen, before you got here I made a call . . . to that police detective. I told him. I told him how you found the paintings in Cordell's closet."

"What!"

"I had to, Hayden. It was the right thing to do."

"Are they going to arrest him?"

"I would imagine so. The detective asked me where I could find him, and I told him where Cordell was staying."

"You didn't!"

"He broke into the house and stole the paintings. He needs to answer for that."

"But he could go to jail!"

Quinn nodded. Hayden rose and started to pace.

"I don't think I would have done that, Quinn," Lewis said.

"Why not?"

"You know how I feel about Cordell. He can be pretty obnoxious. But I've been thinking about it all week, and the thief piece just doesn't fit. I don't think he did it."

"Are you serious?" Quinn asked.

"Honey, you know my track record. My business hinges on the ability to size up a man's character. Cordell is annoying, but he's not a criminal."

"You sound so sure," Hayden said.

"Not one hundred percent . . . but pretty close."

"It never made sense to me, either," Hayden said. "I don't know if I ever told you this story, but a couple of years ago a woman sitting next to him on the subway left a shopping bag behind. It had two new pairs of shoes inside, so Cordell found her name on the credit card slip, looked up her phone number, called her, and then met her on a street corner to return the package. That doesn't sound like someone who would steal, does it? But I couldn't come up with a plausible explanation for finding those paintings in his closet. I figured he was getting ready to sell them on eBay or something."

"That actually makes sense," Quinn said. "I was wondering how he was planning on unloading stolen artwork."

"It just doesn't jibe for me," Lewis said.

"But he spent all his free time on those sites," Quinn said. "Even when I was over there he was wheeling and dealing online."

Lewis rubbed his cheek, which was sporting stubble after a long day. "I wonder . . ." he began.

"Wonder what?" Hayden said.

Lewis bit his lip. "Maybe that's where he *found* the paintings. Maybe the thieves were dumb enough to sell them online. I mean, let's say you're a criminal who normally steals and fences stolen jewelry. Suddenly you find yourself with a stack of paintings to unload and you know nothing about art. The easiest thing to do would be to list them online."

Hayden's face lit up. Clearly he was thrilled at the prospect of exonerating Cordell. Quinn felt a nervous tug in her gut. She didn't want to see him get his hopes up only to face crushing disappointment.

"It all seems so unlikely," she said. "Even if he spent hours and hours at those sites, what are the chances he stumbled across a listing for the stolen paintings?"

"Maybe he went looking for them," Lewis suggested.

"We could check his computer," Hayden said to Lewis. "It's in the garage."

"Wouldn't that be an invasion of privacy?" Quinn said.

"I don't think he'd mind very much," Lewis said, "since we're trying to clear him."

A short while later, Cordell's laptop was on the kitchen table, with Lewis sitting in front of it. Hayden and Quinn watched from over his shoulder as he tried to access Cordell's eBay account, which was password protected.

"Any ideas?" Lewis asked Hayden.

"Try *julios*. It's the name of the restaurant where we had our first date, and I know it used to be his e-mail password."

Lewis tried it but couldn't gain access. Hayden suggested his own name, Cordell's sister's name, and his niece's name, but no luck. They tried matching up ages and dates of birth with the names, but were still denied. Hayden came up with the name of Cordell's beloved Bichon, who died years ago, several of his ex-boyfriends, and even the name of the soap opera part he had recently landed. Still nothing. They switched over to craigslist and tried all the same passwords, but still couldn't access the account.

"Maybe there are some clues in his e-mail," Hayden suggested.

"You said he uses *julios* for that one?" Lewis asked.

"He used to," Hayden said. "But he might have changed it."

The tension was palpable as Lewis accessed Cordell's e-mail account and typed *julios* into the password prompt. It was, they all felt, their last shot. They held their breath as Lewis hit enter.

Incorrect password.

Quinn looked at her brother's face. Hope had given way to misery. "I'm sorry," she said to him.

Lewis continued typing, determined to go through the whole list of possible passwords they had tried for the other accounts. Quinn knew it was futile and wrapped her arms around her brother to comfort him.

"Wait!" Lewis yelled. "I'm in!"

Quinn turned to the computer. A list of names and subject lines appeared. Lewis scrolled down until he found a correspondence between Cordell and someone called bellofek1978@aol.com with the heading "paintings." They read from the bottom up. The first e-mail was from Cordell, dated several days after the theft.

> I saw your ad on craigslist for a portrait by Nan Mazursky. Do you have any other paintings by this artist?

The response from bellofek1978 came within an hour:

> Yes, we have four. Are you in the New York area? If so, call my cell phone and we can discuss.

It was signed by "Bello" and included a 917 number.

"Oh, my God!" Hayden cried. "He's innocent! I knew it."

"I don't understand," Quinn said. "Why didn't he say anything? Why would he keep this a secret?"

"Maybe he was waiting until he got back from Los Angeles," Lewis said.

"Right!" Hayden said. "I just remembered. Before he left he asked if we could get together with you two when he got back. He said he wanted to make amends for the misunderstanding. I thought he was going to make a production of asking you to be in our wedding party, but I bet he was planning to make a big deal of returning the paintings and surprise us all."

"He wanted to be a hero," Lewis said.

"A hero!" Hayden repeated, his face flushed.

Quinn lowered herself into a chair. "I feel like such a jackass. I got him arrested."

"I'll take the laptop straight to the precinct right now," Lewis said. "I bet they'll release him."

"I'll go with you," Hayden said. The rosiness had given way to a glow. Hayden was beaming.

Quinn squeezed his hand. "I'm glad it worked out this way. And I'm so sorry for calling the police," she said. "I really thought—"

He cut her off. "Never mind," he said. "It's a happy ending."

"I can make it even happier," Lewis said. "His password was *Hayden*."

QUINN FELT LIKE A DOG FOR HAVING CAUSED CORDELL so much misery. The police had shown up at the friends' apartment where he was staying and led him away in handcuffs. He was at the precinct, in the middle of being booked, when Lewis and Hayden arrived with the laptop, insisting on speaking with the detective. An hour later, they walked out the door with the freed suspect and went out for beers. The following day Cordell and Hayden came over and loaded all the things from the garage back into Hayden's car. Quinn apologized two or three hundred times, and Cordell joked that the next time he was tempted to call her a homophobe, he would keep it to himself.

Quinn stood at the curb as her brother slammed the trunk of his car closed. She hugged him good-bye and then turned to Cordell.

"I've been apologizing so much I forgot to thank you for retrieving the paintings."

"You're welcome."

Quinn wanted to make plans to take the two of them out to dinner, but it would have to be a very special restaurant to both thank him for what he had done and make up for getting him arrested. She thought about her schedule for the week ahead and realized that she and Lewis already had plans for a night out—they were going to Walt St. Pierre's party with Meredith. Then she had a great idea.

"What are you guys doing next Thursday?" she asked.

THE NEXT FEW DAYS found Quinn bubbling with anticipation about the party. It was exciting to focus on something a little bit glamorous instead of obsessing on her problems. She also thought it would be fun to walk in with her very own posse—Lewis, Hayden, Cordell, and Meredith. She allowed herself to indulge in the fantasy of rubbing elbows with the rich and famous . . . and making an impression. Maybe she and Janeane Garofolo would exchange e-mail addresses and become cyber pals.

Since nothing in her wardrobe would do, she had gone shopping and splurged on a new black V-neck sweater, roomy and flattering enough to hide her expanding belly. She put it on over a push-up bra, which accomplished the task of heaving her swollen breasts higher than she thought possible. The result was enough cleavage to embarrass her.

"You are smokin'!" Lewis said, sneaking up from behind and wrapping his arms around her waist.

"I feel like I've borrowed someone else's breasts."

He laughed. "You look great, but if you feel self-conscious . . ."

As she viewed herself from the side, debating whether or not to change into a different bra, the phone rang and Lewis answered it. Quinn could tell he was speaking to Georgette, and that she had come down with a cold. Her heart sank. Lewis covered the phone with his hand and spoke to his wife.

"She's running a little fever but said she'd be happy to come stay with Isaac anyway, if we didn't mind exposing him."

She has to, thought Quinn. I just can't take another disappointment. Sure it was just a bit of frivolous fun, but when would she get another chance like this? After all she had been through these past weeks, she felt she deserved it.

On the other hand, Isaac. He had just gotten over a very bad cold, and it was irresponsible in the extreme for Quinn to allow him this exposure.

She sighed and pulled off her earrings. "Tell her thanks anyway and we hope she feels better." She sat on the bed, dejected.

Lewis relayed the message and got off the phone. He sat next to his wife.

"You go," he said.

"What?"

"Go without me. I'll stay home with Isaac."

That hadn't even occurred to her, and Quinn felt a buzz of excitement returning. "Are you sure?"

"Absolutely. There's no reason we both have to miss it. You'll have fun with your little gang. Just report back to me on who Meredith leaves with."

She threw her arms around him. "I will!"

"And promise me you won't make out with Adam Sandler."

She laughed. "Not to worry. But you'd better cross your fingers that Jon Stewart isn't there."

THE FOURSOME HAD ARRANGED to meet up at Penn Station. Quinn's train was a few minutes late getting in, so Hayden, Cordell, and Meredith were already at the information booth waiting for her when she arrived.

They exited Penn Station among the throngs, and were greeted with a wave of umbrellas popping open against the freezing rain. Quinn huddled beneath Meredith's as they walked slowly and carefully to the taxi line, hobbled by high heels and slippery pavement.

All four of them piled into the back of an SUV taxicab and gave the driver the address. Because she was married to a fleet owner, Quinn knew they were in a favorite model of New York City taxi drivers, as it brought them more fares on slow nights, when passengers sometimes passed up the smaller vehicles in favor of these roomier cabs.

The taxi drove north and east through the slick streets, and Quinn was glad she had opted to leave the car at home and take the train. She hated driving in icy conditions.

As they approached the party venue, Quinn asked Meredith if she knew anything about the place, called simply Ohm.

"I was at a party there once before," Meredith answered. "It's sort of an Asian-fusion restaurant-lounge-dance-club with a screening room upstairs."

"I get it," Quinn said. "Kind of like a Chuck E. Cheese for grown-ups."

"And lookee," Hayden said, pointing to a line of limos out front, "must be a class trip."

The facility was closed to the public for the event, and admission required a $150 charitable donation per person, and at least one member of the group had to show a printed invitation. Pricey for a night of fun, Quinn thought, handing over her credit card, but for a good cause.

The foursome entered the main dining room of the restaurant, which was dimly lit and elegantly appointed in minimalist Asian fashion. A sleek bar ran the length of the room, and a jazz quartet in the corner played soft music. Quinn was surprised by the thin crowds and low-key atmosphere, but the hostess who offered to take their coats and umbrellas quickly explained that most of the guests were upstairs, where there was dancing and a DJ.

Quinn, Meredith, Hayden, and Cordell followed her directions to the staircase in the back, trying to be subtle about scanning the small groups they passed for famous faces.

They could hear the loud, pounding music through the speakers before they even reached the room. It was a cavernous space, with a loft-height ceiling and lighting even dimmer than what was downstairs. Quinn squinted at the crowd, looking for someone recognizable. She had the odd feeling of being watched, and turned around. When she saw no one she knew, Quinn realized it was probably just a reaction to her self-consciousness. She hadn't been to a party like this in so long.

"Look!" Cordell said to Hayden. "There's Jennifer!"

"Aniston?" Quinn said, struggling to see.

"Martinez," he corrected. "Our Pilates instructor."

Cordell and Hayden took off in her direction, and Meredith told Quinn she was set on getting an introduction to Walt St. Pierre. She suggested they push their way to the bar in the back for drinks and then try to find him.

On their way, Quinn still couldn't shake the creepy feeling that someone was watching them. She kept looking behind her.

"What's the matter?" Meredith shouted over the music.

"I feel like someone is following us."

"Best news I've heard all day."

"What if it's an ax murderer?" Quinn asked.

Meredith shrugged. "Is he single?"

Quinn laughed. "I think you might need higher standards."

"I think *you* need a drink."

"I'm pregnant, remember?"

A cute guy with dark curls pushed his way through the crowd and embraced Meredith. She introduced him to Quinn as Steven Marsh. He smiled, glanced quickly at Quinn's breasts, and then looked back at Meredith with a lewd squint.

"A writer," Meredith added as part of her introduction, giving Quinn a look that was easy to interpret.

After chatting for just a few minutes, Meredith dismissed him with a flirty squeeze of the arm. "I'll catch up with you later," she said.

"I think he likes you," Quinn said as they continued toward their destination.

"Not as much as he likes himself."

Before they reached the bar, they ran into three more acquaintances of Meredith's, two of whom were conquests.

"I wonder what you'll do when you run out of writers in this city," Quinn said. The driving, heavy-beat pop song had ended and was replaced with a ballad, which was a little easier to talk over.

"Please. The easiest way to understand the concept of infinity is to start sleeping with writers in New York."

At the bar, Meredith ordered something called an electric martini, a funky blue drink served in a stylishly retro glass. Quinn got a club soda with a twist of lime, served in an oversized, inelegant tumbler. The two women remained by the bar for several minutes as they scanned the room, trying to catch a glimpse of Walt St. Pierre. When Quinn's eyes reached the right side of the room, she saw a man's head turn away quickly, as if he didn't want her to see him looking at her. Was it just her imagination? She tried to get a better look at the man, but he disappeared into the crowd. All she could tell from that one quick glance was that he was bald. She took a deep breath and tried to relax. Even if someone had been following them, he was probably looking at Meredith, and not at her. Given her friend's history, there was a good chance she had some screwy admirers.

"I see Walt," Meredith said, pointing to the left of the room. "There, near the DJ booth."

The two women took their drinks and pushed their way through the crowd to Walt St. Pierre, who was chatting with another man. Quinn kissed him on the cheek—successfully this time—and shouted over the music to introduce him to Meredith.

"She runs Baston's Books," Quinn said.

"I love that store," said the other man. He introduced himself as J.D., and Quinn wondered if Meredith would make a play for him instead of Walt. He was young and handsome, with short blond hair, a pretty smile, and what Quinn assumed was a spray-on tan.

They made small talk over the music, chatting about the weather and the party. J.D. smiled at Quinn several times, and she was surprised that he seemed more interested in her than in her leggy friend. Or maybe it was her cleavage. She caught his eyes wandering to her chest more than once. Quinn cursed herself for not changing out of her atomic-powered bra.

J.D. asked what everyone was drinking and then went off toward the bar.

"I'd love for you to do an event at our store," Meredith said to Walt, laying a hand on his arm. "I heard you give great . . . book talks."

Quinn cringed. Her friend was laying it on so thick.

"That's because I really enjoy giving . . . book talks," Walt answered, giving Meredith's lithe body the once-over.

She moved closer. "So many authors just go through the motions."

"That just never pays off," he said.

"A good book talk can really move people," Meredith said.

Quinn wanted to tell her friend that this banter sounded like the script of a bad porno movie, but she didn't want to cramp her style, and was glad when J.D. showed up with the drinks a few minutes later. She thanked him and asked what he did for a living, happy to extricate herself from Walt and Meredith's verbal tango.

"I'm an underworld crime boss," J.D. said quickly. A well-rehearsed joke, no doubt.

"I could tell you were Sicilian," Quinn joked back. He had translucent blue eyes and blond lashes.

"Actually I'm a nuclear physicist," he said.

"I think I'm more inclined to believe the crime boss story."

"I'm a Manhattan district attorney," he said.

"Nuh-uh." She didn't believe that, either.

"Retired general?"

She laughed. He was in his late twenties.

"I'm a dot-com millionaire," he said.

"I suppose you're going to tell me you invented Yahoo! or something."

"Don't be silly. I would never insult your intelligence with such a ridiculous lie."

"Thank goodness."

"I invented Windows."

She folded her arms. "I think that was Bill Gates."

"Help me out here," he said. "I'm trying to figure out what would impress you."

"The truth," she said.

"I've never tried that."

"Always a first time."

He cleared his throat. "The truth," he said, "is that I'm an actor. An *aspiring* actor."

"That I believe," she said.

She asked about his career, and he told her about finding an agent and going on auditions. She told him about the career of her soon-to-be brother-in-law, and it turned out J.D. had once auditioned for the same soap. They continued talking until a song with a fast beat came on and J.D. asked Quinn to dance.

"Why not?" she said, and followed him to the dance floor, where they moved and sweated to three different songs before Quinn said she needed to sit down.

J.D. found an empty table for them and left Quinn while he went to get more drinks. By the time he returned, Quinn was so thirsty she downed half her drink in one long gulp.

"This is just club soda, right?"

"With a little Rose's Lime Juice for kick," he said.

"Is there alcohol in that?" she asked.

"In Rose's? No. It's just a tangy mixer."

"That's all?"

"Promise."

She finished the rest of her drink while J.D. talked about the ups and downs of his career. By the time he got to a story about getting a bit part on *Law & Order,* Quinn realized she was having trouble following his story.

"Are you okay?" he asked.

"Just a little dizzy," she said. "Probably my pregnancy hormones telling me to slow down."

He looked shocked. "You're pregnant?"

"Five months."

He looked at her drink. "Oh, fuck."

She sniffed it. "You didn't."

"Vodka," he said. "The lime juice is so concentrated it masks it."

"Oh, my God!"

"I . . . I didn't know. Walt didn't tell me you were pregnant."

"But I *asked* you what was in it!"

"I thought you were in on the joke."

Without thinking, Quinn threw what little was left of the drink in his face and stormed off. She wobbled downstairs to the main level, where she found herself pacing, trying to shake off the effects of the vodka and think. What should she do? Had she consumed enough alcohol to harm the baby? She looked around. In the shadows by the staircase she could make out the figure of a man. Was it the bald guy who had been watching her upstairs?

To hell with him, she thought, taking a seat at the bar. *If he comes over here, I'll tell him to get lost.*

She asked the bartender for a glass of water, thinking it might be a good idea to try to flush the alcohol from her system. Had she heard about that someplace? She couldn't remember, but at the very least it wouldn't hurt.

She drank it quickly and got a refill. As she sipped it, she started to get an odd feeling, as if there were a portal nearby. Was the alcohol clouding her judgment? She looked left and right, but couldn't get a sense of where it might be.

She closed her eyes for a moment, trying to focus on what she was picking up from the other side. Nothing came, and Quinn dismissed the sensation as imaginary. She was probably just thinking about her single days with Eugene because this party reminded her of that lifestyle.

Suddenly, Quinn became aware that her bladder was so full she had to get to the bathroom immediately. When she stood, her head was spinning, and she held on to the bar for a minute to steady herself. She glanced in the direction of the ladies' room and thought she saw the bald man again. She looked harder and saw nothing, so she dismissed the notion as drunken paranoia. Quinn went into the bathroom, pushed her way into a stall, and peed with relief, feeling as though she could fall asleep right there on the toilet. But she forced herself to stand and managed to go through the motions of washing her hands before leaving the bathroom.

In the narrow hallway, she smelled something appealing—a familiar aftershave. Was it her imagination, or was it the scent Eugene wore? Maybe she had caught a whiff of it earlier, and that was why she thought she had sensed a portal nearby. Perhaps it was just some man wearing Eugene's cologne.

She leaned against the wall for support and closed her eyes. She was still so damned dizzy.

"Hello."

It sounded like Eugene's voice, which made her shut her eyes even tighter. How could she be hearing Eugene? Was there a portal nearby after all? This was all too much. After the mess of accepting his proposal and sleeping with him, she wanted to forget all about it. She wanted to be a normal person with one life, one husband, and decisions that couldn't be undone.

She had to get out of this place, to put some distance between herself and the very bewildering portal she sensed.

Quinn opened her eyes and stepped forward, almost crashing into the man standing in front her.

"Excuse me," she said, without looking at his face.

The man grabbed her shoulders. "Quinn," he said.

She looked up. It was the bald man. She recognized him immediately, but it took her a few seconds to find her voice.

"Eugene?" she said.

"You look so shocked—like you've just seen a ghost. I haven't aged *that* much, have I? Except for the shaved head, that is."

"I . . . I didn't expect to see you here. Walt had said you couldn't make it."

Eugene made a face. "He can be such a fuckwit sometimes."

Quinn tried to reconcile the two realities. There was the Eugene she had made love with in Fiji a few days before, and the man standing in front of her now. She took a deep breath, slowing her pulse. "I guess . . . I guess he assumed I wouldn't come if you were here."

"Is that true? Would you have stayed away on my account?"

She pictured the scene in their apartment ten years before, when she told him she was moving out. At first he didn't believe her—he just couldn't accept it. Then he tried to change her mind with a massive guilt trip. When it became clear that wouldn't work, he got angry and told her that if she left him he would never speak to her again.

"I don't know," she said. "Maybe."

"Why?"

"I figured you hated me," she said. "You were pretty angry when I left."

There was one small overhead light in the dark vestibule where they stood, and it shined directly in Eugene's face. He seemed to be remembering. "I don't hate you anymore," he said.

"You don't?"

"I just dislike you intensely."

She felt stricken. Why had she ever agreed to come to this party?

"I'm kidding," he said.

"You are?"

"It was ages ago. I'll admit I was furious for a long time. But what guy would be able to handle his girlfriend leaving him for Louie the taxi man?"

"Lewis," she corrected. "Not Louie. And he bears no resemblance to the Danny DeVito character from *Taxi.*"

"Do you mind if I go on picturing him like that?"

She laughed. "Suit yourself."

"I was actually worried you wouldn't want to talk to *me*, especially if you were here with . . . whatever his name is. I tried to stay out of your way until I could figure out if you were alone."

So that was why he had been tailing her all night. "Was there something you wanted to say to me?" she asked.

"Just that everything is okay now. That's all."

"I'm glad," she said, and left it at that. She didn't want to ask him about his career, which she figured was a sore point. She was just happy to know he didn't bear a grudge and that his life was okay.

"I've got a pretty good gig upstate. I never knew I would like being in a small market, but it's not bad."

"Less stress?"

"That's the key," he said. "I don't feel like I have to prove anything. I get to be the hottest ticket in town."

"That sounds perfect."

"And then there's Linda."

"Your girlfriend?"

"Almost five years now. What about you? How's married life? I think I heard you had a kid."

"Isaac. He's six. A beautiful, amazing boy. And get this—my mother's artistic talent skipped a generation and went straight to him."

Eugene was quiet for a moment, then he reached out and squeezed her shoulder. "I read about your mom in the paper," he said. "I'm so sorry. She was a great broad."

Quinn nodded. She was too choked to speak. She was accustomed to people asking about her mother, but it was rare to run into someone who knew her and loved her. It made the tragedy of her death seem so fresh.

"Are you okay?" he asked.

She wasn't. She wasn't okay at all. And the question was all it took to push her over the edge. She simply couldn't keep back the tears. Eugene took her in his arms and held her close. His tenderness felt like the permission she needed to let go completely, and her shoulders shook with sobs. She remembered how much her mother loved Eugene, how his teasing lit her up. At that moment, she couldn't help thinking she had made a terrible mistake. If she had only stayed with Eugene, her mother would be alive now. It didn't mean she didn't love Lewis and Isaac with all her heart, but the unfairness of the trade-off was too much to bear.

"You know, I still love you," he whispered.

She didn't say anything. She just held on tight, as if she might otherwise drown.

"Do you still love *me*?" he asked.

"It doesn't matter," she said.

"Then you do. I know you do."

She couldn't think of a response, but held him closer. She didn't know why she did it, and didn't know what she was thinking when Eugene put his lips on hers. Maybe she wasn't thinking anything. She was just feeling. And letting him kiss her seemed like a release from the dark force that was sucking her down. She got lost in the kiss. It was her past, present, and future colliding in one physical moment. She even lost sense of where she was. That is, until she heard a voice behind her.

"Quinn!"

Eugene released her and she turned to see Cordell standing three feet away, his mouth slack in shock.

Time expanded with the fraction of a second it took for her to look into Cordell's eyes and understand what he was thinking. Quinn tried to find language, to come up with words of explanation, but there was nothing to say. What Cordell had seen was very, very real.

Maybe it was her animal brain that kicked in at that moment, but Quinn did the only thing that occurred to her.

She ran.

"Quinn!" Eugene shouted. "Where are you going?"

Without even stopping for her coat, she pushed open the front door and ran outside, into the icy-cold night, where she was pelted by freezing rain. She had to keep going, had to put space between her and what had just happened.

When she reached the curb, Quinn glanced behind her and saw Eugene and Cordell at the door.

"Stop!" Cordell shouted, but she didn't. She ran into the street and looked up just in time to see it coming toward her. She heard a screech of brakes and quickly turned to step out of the way. She could make it. She knew she could! But she hadn't counted on the car's tires losing traction on the slick street. The last thing she heard before the impact was the sound of her own scream.

26

QUINN DREAMED THAT NAOMI HAD BEEN SWADDLED AND placed in her arms. All the nurses said she was the prettiest girl ever born in that hospital, and Quinn had to agree. She was filled with joy. All mothers thought their baby was the most beautiful, but hers truly was. Quinn wondered if she was born with hair, and she started to remove the baby's cap, but a nurse grabbed her wrist.

You don't want to do that.

Why? Is her head open?

Yes.

Quinn looked at the sleeping baby again.

Is she alive?

We don't know.

The dream changed then, and she wasn't looking at the baby but a painting of her. Quinn was confused. Had her mother painted it? Where was she? Where was Naomi? She came to a long corridor and frantically

looked around for someone to ask, but she was alone. She ran to the end
of the corridor and pushed open a door. Dr. Bernard was there.

Who are you looking for? the doctor asked.

Quinn wasn't sure. Was she looking for her mother or her baby? She
felt it was crucial to tell the truth. Startling music played. It was Quinn's
alarm clock. She sat up and shut it off.

"How do you feel?" Lewis asked.

Quinn hesitated, still trying to separate dreams from reality. Yes, she
had been in a car accident the night before. No, she hadn't lost the baby.
She rubbed her rounded belly. You're okay, Naomi, she thought. We're
both okay.

Though the impact from the car knocked Quinn down, she had been
able to rise on her own. Both her knees were bloody from hitting the
street, but nothing seemed broken. Most important, her middle hadn't
taken a hit. Thank God, she thought, as a crowd gathered. Thank God
the baby is okay. Nothing else matters.

Cordell and Eugene tried to talk Quinn into going to the hospital, but
she refused. She knew she was okay, and was afraid they might insist on
taking X-rays just to cover themselves. The thought of exposing Naomi
to radiation was too much to bear. She simply wouldn't do it. Bad enough
that she had consumed alcohol. One assault on her baby that night was
more than enough.

The owners of Ohm had insisted on paying for limo service to drive
her all the way home to Long Island, and she accepted. Hayden and
Cordell went along for the ride to be sure she was okay.

Cordell didn't say a word about what he had witnessed. In fact, he
tried to lighten the mood by talking about all the celebrities they had seen
at the party. She had managed to miss all of them.

Quinn looked out the window as their conversation drifted into a
back-and-forth between Hayden and Cordell. They were dishing and

gossiping about who looked Botoxed and who didn't, and how gorgeous, hideous, smashing, butt-ugly, slammin', gawdy, or fabulous each outfit looked.

"You know who else was there?" Cordell said to her.

Quinn couldn't take the evasion any longer. It was like trying to ignore the elephant in the limo.

"Eugene," she said. "Eugene was there."

"Quinn," Cordell said, "you don't owe me any explanations."

"But I don't want you to think I don't love my husband."

Hayden looked down, picking at his cuticles. Clearly, Cordell had already told him what he saw.

"We all make mistakes," Cordell said.

"I've never . . ." she began, and stopped. She had planned to say she never cheated on Lewis, but knew that on some level what happened in Fiji did indeed count. She rested her head in her hands.

"Don't worry," Cordell said. "I'm not going to tell him. Forget about it."

She kept her head down. "Thank you," she mumbled. Surely, Lewis didn't need to know about this. If Hayden and Cordell would keep the secret, she would, too. Still, the knot inside her wasn't unraveling.

Hayden rubbed her back. "You okay?" he asked.

At last she looked up. "I made the right choice," she said. "Marrying Lewis, I mean."

"Of course you did," her brother said. "No one suggested otherwise."

"Mom did," she said.

He put his arm around her and Quinn rested her head on her brother's shoulder. No one spoke for the rest of the ride.

When she got home, Quinn had put in a late-night emergency call to Dr. Sally Bernard to ask about the alcohol's possible effect on the fetus. The obstetrician assured her that the baby would not suffer fetal alcohol syndrome as the result of one drink. And though Quinn swore to her that the car's bumper hit her in the back of the legs and that she hadn't suffered any impact to her torso, the doctor said she was more concerned about the accident than the alcohol. "It was more like falling down than getting hit by a car," Quinn insisted. Still, Sally made Quinn promise to get lots of rest the next day, and to call her immediately if she had any problems.

Quinn sat up and swung her feet over the side of the bed. She felt tired and a little stiff, but otherwise okay.

"I'm fine," she said to Lewis. She put on her bathrobe and went downstairs to make pancakes for Isaac. She didn't usually prepare such an elaborate breakfast on a weekday, but she wanted to make up for her absence the night before, especially since he was still recovering from the trauma of getting off the bus to find himself alone. Quinn was intent on assuring him that she was not going to disappear again.

Lewis came downstairs just as she was stirring a handful of chocolate chips into the batter. He kissed her on the back of the neck.

"How are your knees?" he asked.

"Not too bad. I'll change the bandages in a little while."

"Why are you fussing with breakfast? Didn't Dr. Bernard say you should rest today?"

"I will," she said. "I promise. I'll get back in bed after you guys leave."

"Do you want me to go wake Isaac?"

"It's okay," she said, putting down the spoon. "I need to let the batter rest, anyway."

"At least let me finish making the pancakes," he said.

Ordinarily, she would have turned down this offer without a thought. But her visits to the other side were having an impact on her. Quinn's psyche was starting to believe what her intellect had been telling her all along—it's okay to accept help.

"Deal," she said, and went upstairs.

Quinn stood over her son for several minutes, watching him sleep. He was so still, lying with his mouth open and his head tipped back on his pillow. She had to watch carefully to discern the subtle rise and fall of his chest beneath the covers. Quinn leaned in, intending to kiss his smooth forehead, but stopped to breathe in his scent. It filled her.

"Isaac?" she whispered after touching her lips to his head.

He stirred but kept his eyes closed.

Quinn took off the bulky bathrobe she wore over the pale green pajamas that had been a birthday present from her mother-in-law, and climbed into the warm bed with him.

"Scooch over," she said. He nestled in to her.

"You want pancakes?" she asked.

His eyes opened. "Chocolate chips?"

"Yep."

He smiled and let his eyes close again. "How was the party?"

What a kid. She pulled him close. "It was fine. Should we stay in this bed all day and snuggle?"

"Yeah."

"How about all week?"

"All year," he said.

She laughed. "You'll miss your birthday party."

"We'll have it here."

Quinn was cozy and comfortable next to her son, and felt as though she could easily fall back asleep. It wasn't like her to be this tired in the morning. Then again, it wasn't like her to go out drinking and get hit by a car. She really would need some time to rest that day.

Quinn forced herself to sit up and lay out Isaac's clothes for him. She put her heavy bathrobe back on and went downstairs. The three of them had pancakes, and then Lewis took Isaac to the bus stop before heading off for work.

Quinn sat at the kitchen table for almost an hour, reading the newspaper. She was just too tired to move. The only thing she wanted to

accomplish that morning was changing the sheets, but even that seemed
like a massive effort.

Finally, Quinn pushed herself away from the table and went to her
bedroom, where she stripped the sheets and dropped them into a laundry basket. She put on clean bed linens and carried the laundry basket to
Isaac's room to do the same.

When she pulled back the covers on his bed she noticed a strange stain
in the middle of the sheet. It looked like blood. Was it hers? Had a wound
on her knee opened up and bled straight through the Band-Aid while she
was lying there?

Quinn opened her robe and sat down on the edge of the bed. There
was no blood seeping through the knees of her brand-new pajama bottoms. Where had that mysterious stain come from? She stood up too fast
and felt dizzy. The night before had taken more of a toll on her than she
realized. She decided that she would just put clean sheets on Isaac's bed
and leave the laundry for Lewis. She really did need to lie down.

She pulled the bloody sheet off, still confused about that spot. Did he
have a nosebleed he forgot to mention? She took a clean sheet from the
linen closet and shook it out over his bed. As she was tucking it in, she felt
woozy again, only this time it was worse. She left the bed unmade and
headed to her room to lie down. But she got so dizzy she had to stop in
the hallway and hold on to the wall.

Quinn didn't think she could make it to her room without fainting.
She sat cross-legged on the floor and put her head between her knees.
And that's when she saw it—a dark crimson circle spreading through the
pale fabric of her pajamas right between her legs.

27

EVERYTHING HAPPENED SO FAST AFTER THAT. QUINN CALLED Lewis, who was already at work. He made her stay on the phone with him while he called 911, and then Georgette, who arrived within minutes. By then Quinn had already changed out of her bloody pajama bottoms and was wearing clean sweatpants with two sanitary napkins stuffed inside her panties.

Georgette—still in pajamas herself—held Quinn's hand while they waited for the ambulance to arrive.

"Everything's going to be okay," Georgette said.

Quinn was crying. "I'm so scared."

"I know, cupcake. I know."

Two uniformed paramedics arrived—a bulky man with a round face and a woman with her hair pulled back in a loose ponytail. Quinn explained about finding the dark blood soaking her pajamas as the woman wrapped a blood pressure cuff around her arm. The man asked a barrage of questions. Did she have any allergies? Was she on any medications?

Was she having trouble breathing? How many weeks along was the pregnancy? Had she ever bled before? Was this her first child? Did she know her blood type? And on and on.

"Are you under a doctor's care?" the woman asked.

Quinn nodded. "The baby has an encephalocele," she said. "They told me she might not make it to term."

"We'll do everything we can," the woman said. She squeezed a pump to get Quinn's pressure and then ripped the Velcro cuff off her arm. "I'm going to start you on a saline IV now," she said, "just to keep you hydrated."

Both paramedics went to work on her. The woman put a tourniquet on Quinn's arm and quickly found a vein. The man asked her to open her mouth and inserted an electronic thermometer under her tongue. Once the IV was in place, the woman opened a box and started sticking small disks onto Quinn's torso and hands. As she worked, a strand of blond hair escaped from her ponytail and hung over her face. She blew the hair out of the way and explained to Quinn that they would be monitoring her heart rhythm.

"Routine procedure," she assured her. "Nothing to worry about."

While the woman spoke, the man asked Georgette a question Quinn couldn't hear. "I don't know," Georgette said, and turned to Quinn. "Have you gone to the bathroom?" she asked.

Of course. She had gone there to peel off her bloody bottoms, which she dropped into the sink. But she knew what they were after, and it made her queasy. They wanted to know if a fetus had been expelled into the toilet and flushed away.

"I'm so dizzy," Quinn said.

"Your blood pressure is low," the woman said. She turned to the man. "Let's get her on the gurney and start two liters of oxygen." She turned back to Quinn and repeated the question about the bathroom.

"I didn't use the toilet," Quinn said. "I just took off my bloody clothes."

"Where are they?" the man asked.

"In the sink."

"Where's that?"

"Off the master bedroom," Quinn said.

Georgette offered to show him where it was, and he grabbed a red plastic bag from his kit and followed her upstairs. When they came down the bag was filled, and Quinn was able to make out the lettering on it: BIOHAZARD.

As they took Quinn away in the ambulance, Georgette said she would get dressed and meet her at the hospital.

Slow down, Quinn thought as the ambulance rushed through the streets. Please. She didn't want to get to the hospital before Lewis or Dr. Bernard. She couldn't go through this without them. Sally should be the one to tell her the baby was gone. Lewis should be there to hear it, to take her hand, to hold her.

Quinn imagined some strange doctor 'snapping off his gloves after examining her.

We'll have to schedule you for a D and C.

What? What about my daughter?

Baby's dead, ma'am.

Dead?

It's for the best.

That, she knew, was what everyone would say. It's for the best. It wasn't meant to be. Nature's way. God's will.

The ambulance pulled to a stop at the hospital. Quinn wanted to tell them to turn around and take her home, that she had changed her mind. She didn't want to go through with any of this. But it was too late. She was a cog in a giant machine that wouldn't stop turning, and it was all beyond her control. She was pulled out of the ambulance on the gurney and pushed through double doors that had opened automatically. It reminded Quinn of the haunted house ride at the amusement park, in which the wall parted in the middle just when it seemed that crashing into it was inevitable.

A woman doctor took her chart and conferred with the paramedics. Quinn was then wheeled to a curtained area in the emergency room and moved to a bed.

A nurse with olive skin and a blunt haircut pulled the curtain closed and put another blood pressure cuff on her arm. The doctor stayed on the other side of the curtain, finishing her conversation with the paramedics.

"My name is Milena," the nurse said.

Quinn paused, momentarily short-circuiting. How was she supposed to respond to that? "Nice to meet you" seemed entirely inappropriate.

"I'm Quinn," she finally said.

"Dr. Kanterman is very nice."

"Good," Quinn said, but couldn't manage to change her expression.

"We're going to need you to undress from the waist down. Can you manage that?"

Quinn lifted her bottom and pulled off her pants and panties, but left the sanitary napkins pressed against her crotch in order not to soil the bed. She handed her clothes to the nurse.

The curtain opened and the doctor entered. She was sixtyish and pale, with stiff hair and dark circles under her eyes. And she was tall—very, very tall. Doctors, Quinn thought, should be required to pass some sort of anti-intimidation test.

"I'm Dr. Kanterman," she said. "We're going to take good care of you."

"Where's Dr. Bernard?" Quinn asked. She wanted her small, gentle doctor. Her friend.

"She's on her way."

"And my husband? He should be getting here about now."

"What's his name?" Milena asked.

"Lewis. Lewis Braverman."

Milena said she would check, and left.

"I need to do an internal exam," the doctor said, putting on gloves. "Try to relax."

Quinn pulled the sticky sanitary napkins from her crotch and looked at them. The blood was still dark, but there wasn't much of it.

"I think it's stopping," Quinn said. "I was bleeding so much more before."

"Well, you're lying down now."

Gravity. Of course. Quinn felt her heart contract. The doctor took the pads from her and stared at them for a moment before setting them aside. Quinn put her legs in the stirrups.

"Try to relax," the doctor repeated, her gloved hand inside Quinn.

Relax. Sure. She grimaced as the doctor felt around.

"You're not dilated," the doctor said. "Not effaced, either."

"That sounds . . . positive," Quinn said. She didn't want to get her hopes up, and knew this doctor wasn't about to give her false hope.

"Let's find out," Dr. Kanterman said, snapping off her gloves. "I'll be right back."

Quinn waited alone, trembling, with nothing to look at but the cold tile of the ceiling and the garishly colorful clown-striped curtains. She kept both hands on her belly, trying to get a sense of whether her baby was still alive. She was the mother. She was supposed to know. Why was this so hard?

Nurse Milena came back, pushing a cart piled with electronic equipment.

"Your husband is filling out the insurance paperwork," she said.

"What is that?" Quinn said, pointing to the cart.

"We're going to check for a heartbeat, and at the same time monitor any contractions you might be having."

"Heartbeat?" Quinn said. "No! Please don't."

"Don't?"

"I . . . I want my husband here."

Lewis had been there at Isaac's birth, and she needed him here for this. She simply couldn't get this news alone.

Quinn remembered that confusing moment after Isaac was born and the doctor announced, "It's a boy!" Instead of feeling elated, Quinn was bewildered. Everyone had predicted she would have a girl, and Quinn hadn't imagined it any other way. In her heart, she was already in love with her daughter. In fact, all that back-and-forth with names had felt like a game. Making two lists was just a matter of going through the motions. She was having a girl. There was just no doubt.

Then they presented her with this stranger—a boy. How could she possibly love this child? She wasn't prepared.

A panic was starting to take hold when she looked up at Lewis's face. Joy lit his features. There was no equivocation—he was consumed with love. This softened Quinn's heart, and by the time they laid the tiny squirming newborn on her chest, she had been split open.

Yes, she thought, as she watched his tiny face turn, rooting for her nipple, I'm your mother. She put him on her breast, and just like that, it all made sense. He was the baby she was meant to love.

She turned to Lewis then, weeping. "We have a son," she said, and what she meant was, *I will never be the same.*

"Those insurance forms can take a long time," Milena said, "and it's not a good idea to delay this."

"Please," Quinn said. She was desperate. If the device couldn't pick up a heartbeat and Lewis wasn't at her side, there would be nothing to hold on to. She thought about the glass of vodka she drank last night, and about running into the street without looking. Quinn realized that if the baby was dead, it was probably her own fault.

"I'm sorry," the nurse said, "but I have to follow protocol."

"I'm sure he'll be here in a minute," Quinn said, crying.

The nurse looked at Quinn's face and softened. "I shouldn't do this," she said, putting the equipment down.

The tightness in Quinn's chest began to loosen. "Bless you," she whispered.

Milena waved the comment away. "We never had this conversation," she said, and slipped out.

Alone again, Quinn's hands went right back to her belly. But she was too tense to get in touch with any sensation beyond her own fear. She tried counting the ceiling tiles to calm her nerves, but it was useless. On the other side of the curtain another patient was being examined. They tried to speak in hushed tones, but Quinn was able to hear that it was an old woman complaining of chest pains.

At last, the curtain by Quinn's bed opened and four people entered together—Dr. Kanterman, nurse Milena, Dr. Sally Bernard, and Lewis—turning the tiny space into a sad parody of a crowded cocktail party.

"Are you okay?" Lewis asked, and that's when Quinn realized that the dam holding back her fear was made of wishes. It gave way instantly and she wept in great torrents. Lewis embraced her.

"I'm here," he whispered. "We'll be okay."

Quinn didn't want to let go. But she was acutely aware of the audience waiting for them to finish, so she patted her husband on the back to let him know she was ready. But she wasn't. She was terrified.

Lewis stood and backed away. Sally Bernard squeezed Quinn's hand and released it. The nurse asked her to sit up so that she could wrap a band around her middle, then adjusted it so that the monitor attached to it was near the center of her belly.

Dr. Kanterman turned on the machine and the sound of static filled the room. Beneath it, Quinn could detect a faint steady noise.

"That's *your* heartbeat," the doctor said.

Milena repositioned the monitor and then there it was: the fast familiar *woosh-woosh-woosh-woosh* of the fetal heartbeat.

Could it be? Quinn swallowed hard. "That's the baby, right?"

"Right," Dr. Kanterman said.

Naomi was still alive. Tears of relief traveled down Quinn's face toward her temples. Lewis took her hand and smiled, but it looked more as if he were trying to cheer her than experiencing real happiness.

"Thank God," Quinn said.

"Does this mean we're out of the woods?" Lewis asked the doctors.

"It might," Dr. Kanterman said. "We still need to do an ultrasound to figure out what caused the bleeding."

"I'll see what's holding up that equipment," Milena said, and left. When she came back, she was pushing a cart with a sonogram monitor on top.

Dr. Kanterman repositioned the band on Quinn's belly to get it out of the way, and then squirted ice-cold gel onto her flesh. Quinn winced.

"Sorry," the doctor said. "In the ER, we don't get warmers for the gel like they do up in radiology." She switched on the screen, and then picked up the transducer, which she ran over Quinn's middle. She held her face close to the monitor as she moved the wand back and forth. Dr. Bernard stepped in for a closer look.

The room was quiet as the doctors concentrated, trying to find something as mysterious to Quinn as wormholes in space. What were they looking for?

At one point, both doctors moved their heads forward simultaneously. Dr. Kanterman froze the picture with a click of her mouse.

"You see that?" she said to Dr. Bernard.

"I do."

"What is it?" Lewis asked.

"Just another minute," Dr. Kanterman said. She continued moving the tool around Quinn's middle. After several minutes she asked Dr. Bernard if she wanted to have a closer look, and the two switched places.

The images on the screen meant nothing to Quinn, so she focused on Dr. Bernard's face, which was somber. At last, she put the instrument down. The nurse wiped Quinn's belly and put the fetal monitor back in place. Naomi's heartbeat once again filled the room.

Dr. Sally Bernard cleared her throat and spoke. "We believe you have a partial abruption, which means that a portion of the placenta has torn away from the uterine wall. That's what caused all the bleeding. It seems to be clotting. And as far as we can see, the baby is getting enough blood and enough oxygen right now."

"How did this happen?" Quinn asked.

"It's usually the result of trauma or a fall."

"So it's from the car accident?"

"Most likely."

Quinn went cold. This was all her fault after all. "Am I going to lose her?"

"Honestly, Quinn, we don't know. We'd like to monitor you for a few hours, then assess the situation again."

"What's the best-case scenario?" Lewis asked.

"Well," Dr. Bernard said, "if the baby's heartbeat stays strong and the bleeding stops, we can assume the placenta successfully clotted. In that case, if you choose to continue with the pregnancy, we'll recommend bed rest to minimize the chance of another tear."

If you choose to continue with the pregnancy. The words shook Quinn from the safe place she had retreated to after hearing the heartbeat.

"Is it dangerous for Quinn?" Lewis asked.

"It's not life threatening, but . . ."

"But?" Lewis said.

"The further along the pregnancy progresses, the harder it is to terminate. And if the fetus dies in utero after twenty-four weeks, the safest course of action is to induce contractions or wait for Quinn to go into labor naturally."

"What are the odds?" Lewis asked. "What are the odds of that happening?"

The two doctors exchanged glances.

"Fairly high," Dr. Bernard said.

Quinn's scalp prickled. She couldn't imagine anything more horrific than giving birth to a dead baby. She put a hand over her mouth to suppress a wail, but it was too late.

28

QUINN KEPT HER ARM OVER HER EYES, SHIELDING HERSELF from the light. She and Lewis were alone in the cubicle, listening to the steady sound of baby Naomi's heartbeat.

"I can't do this," Quinn said. "I can't give birth to a dead baby."

He sat on the edge of her bed. "Do you want to terminate?" he said softly.

She should have known he was going to ask that, she should have been prepared. But she wasn't.

"I can't do that, either," she said, and moved over, making room for him to lie down. He did, and she rolled toward him, holding the monitor in place so it wouldn't slip. She put her head on his chest, and they lay there silently, listening to the sparrow-fast beat of Naomi's heart.

"Honey, I know this is hard," he finally said. "But I think today is decision day."

Quinn rolled onto her back and stared up at the ceiling tiles again. She remembered the delivery room scene on the day of Isaac's birth, her adrenaline getting her through the pain of contractions. "Push!" Dr. Bernard had said when she reached ten centimeters. I can't, she thought. I'm just too tired. But she somehow found the strength. When the doctor said, "Harder!" Quinn was furious and frustrated. Didn't they realize how exhausted she was? It had already taken everything she had and then some. But she thought about the new life winding its way down her birth canal and summoned energy from someplace she didn't even know existed. "Again!" the doctor said. *Impossible,* she wanted to cry. *I'm depleted.* But she did it anyway. And then she did it again. And again. Until finally the baby emerged, a slippery new life. Her son.

What would it be like to go through all that to give birth to a dead baby? Her daughter, lifeless and blue. Quinn imagined driving home from the hospital with Lewis, the backseat empty. They would pull up in the front of the house and slam the car doors shut, the still air of their suburban street muffling the lonely sound. Later, there would be a funeral. A tiny coffin.

The steady heartbeat continued to pulse. *Woosh-woosh-woosh-woosh.*

Quinn turned toward Lewis. "I don't know what to do. Tell me. Tell me what to do!"

"You want me to make the decision?"

"Yes. *Please.*"

He rose from the bed and sat on the small metal stool in the corner, as if he needed some physical space for his thoughts. He began to rock, just a bit, which Quinn recognized as deep concentration. Finally, he got up again and approached her bed.

"You are my world, Quinn," he said, his eyes now red and watery. "You matter to me more than anything. I hate to see you go through all this, and I wish I could fix it. I wish I could make the baby well. I wish I could make this pregnancy easy and healthy. But I can't." He wiped his nose with the back of his hand. "I think . . . I think it's best to terminate now while we can. And I think that deep down that's what you really want . . . isn't it?"

"Deep down I want her to be alive and okay. That's what I want."

"I know."

Quinn put her hands behind her head, her fingers interlocked. She remembered being in the same position on a lounge chair in Fiji, overlooking the crystal blue Pacific Ocean. What an easy life. What a stupid, easy life. And how cursed she was to know she could so easily slip away.

She didn't want to terminate this pregnancy. She wanted to have this baby. But the very real possibility of losing her later—of having to give birth to a lifeless little girl—was more than she could bear.

Quinn sat up and unbuckled the strap holding the fetal heart rate monitor in place. She took it off and laid it next to her.

"Okay," she said. "We'll terminate."

•

29

QUINN WASN'T SURE WHY SHE WENT DOWN INTO THE BASE-
ment when she had no intention of leaving. She only knew that at three in
the morning, when she was still wide awake in bed, she felt compelled to
face the beast in her life and rail at it about the unfairness of it all.

Why? Did she feel that it was the portal's fault?

No, that wasn't it. She was furious that a part of her was still tempted.
It would just be so easy. She could slip through and all of this would be
gone. There would be no appointment for an abortion in the morning.
No pregnancy at all. But of course there would be no Lewis and no Isaac
in her life, either.

Until now, it was something she had avoided contemplating, because
leaving her husband and son was unthinkable.

Wasn't it?

But what if she did? What would it be like to leave all these problems
behind? Would she and Eugene enjoy a perfect life filled with friends and
money and traveling and parties and fame?

Quinn remembered a joke from one of her favorite films, *Annie Hall*. Diane Keaton's character was trying to get Woody Allen's character to abandon the East Coast for the West Coast, where they would just sit around all day watching movies. "And gradually you get old and die," Woody responded. And everyone understood the pithy joke. Life was meaningless without some struggles.

But of course she never felt her life with Eugene was carefree. He needed constant attention. And it was never enough.

"I'm kidding myself," she said out loud. She loved her husband. She loved her son. If she simply had to choose between her life here and her life with Eugene, there was no contest.

The wild card was Nan.

Quinn opened the ironing board, put her hands on either side of the fissure, and wept. She missed her mother so much. If only she were here, Quinn thought. If only . . .

"Mommy?"

It was Isaac. Quinn hadn't even heard him come in.

"What are you doing up?" She was angry. Isaac was the last person in the world she could deal with right now.

His tongue traveled around his dry lips, a bad habit that got worse when the weather turned cold. This time of year Quinn usually put Vaseline around his mouth before putting him to bed, but tonight she had forgotten.

"I had a bad dream," he said.

How could she comfort him and be the sweet, tender mother he deserved when she couldn't even give the baby inside her a chance at life? And, worse, how could she be a mother at all when she was contemplating leaving this life altogether?

"Go back to bed," she said to him.

He didn't move. He just stood there, in his SpongeBob pajamas, staring at the fissure. "What is that?" he said, pointing.

"It's nothing. Go back to bed."

"Is the wall broken?"

"A little, yes."

"I want to feel it."

Quinn thought about the day she first discovered a portal in her life and dared to touch the other side. She wasn't much older than he was now. What would have happened if she had gone through and relived her life without breaking her leg that day? Would everything have been different? Would the tiny shift in her life have changed what followed? If she hadn't spent those weeks in bed reading and falling more and more in love with books, would she have gone to work for Baston's as an adult and eventually met Eugene and then Lewis? Or would she have had a different life entirely, with a different child, a different husband, different everything? Would she, at this moment, be standing in a cold basement on the last night of her unborn daughter's life?

Would her mother still be alive?

Nothing about the choices she had to make in her life seemed fair. She wished Isaac wasn't standing before her now, poking at the part of her heart that was throbbing in pain. She needed to be left alone.

"I want to touch that," he repeated, taking a step forward.

"No!"

He reached toward it. "It looks silver."

Quinn grabbed his hand before it reached the fissure. "Did you hear me?" she shouted. "You get back upstairs this minute!"

"Why are you yelling?"

"Because you're not listening to me. Now, go! I don't want to *see* your face, I don't want to *hear* your voice! And I don't want you *ever* touching this wall. Have I made myself clear?"

Isaac's eyes went wide. His mother had never spoken to him like that before. Ever. His face turned bright red and a terrible grimace transformed his pretty features into an ugly mask.

"Mommy!" he wailed as he started to cry.

And just like that, Quinn's fury morphed into the acid of self-loathing, and she collapsed onto the floor, where she rolled herself into a ball, sobbing. Isaac put his tiny hand on her back. "I'm sorry," he said. "I'm sorry!"

But Quinn couldn't stop crying.

"Go back to bed," she said. "Just go."

Isaac turned and left, sniffling. Quinn wept as she listened to the sound of his footsteps on the stairs.

The weight of Quinn's sorrow was heavier than the total of everything she had ever lifted. It did, in fact, feel like a physical force that threatened to crush her, and she didn't have the strength—or even the desire—to push it off.

Quinn kept her eyes shut tight, wishing that when she opened them everything would be different. But it wasn't. She was still there on the floor of the laundry room in her basement.

But then Quinn noticed something she had never seen before. It was another fissure—a new crack in the foundation wall starting from the floor and reaching up two and a half feet. At once, she knew exactly what it was—a portal to the life in which she had made the decision not to terminate the pregnancy.

The weight bearing down on Quinn doubled. How would she be able to go on with this life, knowing that she had also made the opposite decision? There was no chance for peace. She would spend the rest of her life second-guessing this choice.

She reached toward the fissure and let herself feel her life on the other side. It was just as tortured. There she worried whether she had made the right decision to go through with the pregnancy. Her other self was consumed with the fear of giving birth to a dead baby, but equally terrified of the tragic life her damaged daughter might have.

Then a more horrific thought occurred to Quinn. If her daughter was born alive in the other life, would she be satisfied staying in this life? Or would the temptation to cross over just be too great? Would she spend the rest of her days crossing between two lives, the one with a disabled daughter and the one without? How could she—how could any mother—cope with such a daily struggle?

The longer she lay there on the cold floor, the more she felt consumed with a madness she couldn't fight. It was all simply too much.

She remembered, then, what her mother had said about the depression that drove her to attempt suicide. It wasn't just sadness, it was blackness. That was exactly how Quinn felt. The darkness was so complete, she couldn't imagine a pinhole of light could exist anywhere.

Quinn didn't know how long she had been on the cold tile floor. She was barely even aware of rising. But the next thing she knew, she was climbing onto the ancient ironing board and crawling through.

30

THE JOURNEY WAS TERRIBLE, COLD, NAUSEATING, BUT IT WAS the last time she would make it. Each time Quinn crossed over, the passage back had become harder, and now, she knew, it would be impossible. For not only had the opening to her basement become smaller, her body had grown larger. So even if she could make it as far as the foundation wall—which seemed unlikely, as the temperature of the bathwater would have to be so cold now that Quinn doubted she could even survive it—she would be unable to fit through.

Quinn emerged from the bathtub in her Manhattan apartment, shivering. She wrapped herself in a big towel and tiptoed into the dark bedroom, where Eugene was asleep. There was enough light from the window for her to discern his form. He was on his side, facing the wall. She quietly opened a drawer to find some clothes, and heard the rustle of sheets. Quinn froze, watching as he turned over and threw his arm over her side of the bed. Would he awaken? She listened until she could make out his breathing, deep and steady. She dressed and slipped out of the bedroom carrying her shoes.

The kitchen was dimly lit by the glow of the microwave clock. She switched on a small counter light, picked up the phone, and dialed her parents' number on Long Island.

"Hello?" Nan's voice was hoarse with sleep.

"It's me," she whispered.

"Quinn? What's wrong?"

"Can you meet me at the Blue Bird?" It was a diner in Queens, about halfway between Quinn's Manhattan apartment and her parents' home on Long Island. Best of all, it was open all night.

"When? Now?" her mother asked.

"In about half an hour. I'll drive straight there."

"What time is it?"

Quinn looked at the digital clock. "Almost four."

"Is everything okay?"

"I need to talk to you."

There was a brief pause while Nan considered the request. "Okay," she said. "I'll see you in thirty minutes."

Quinn gently returned the phone to its cradle and walked toward the front door, still carrying her shoes. She put them down and opened the closet. It squeaked. She held her breath. Nothing. Quinn sighed, relieved. She pulled out her coat and slipped it on, then bent over to put on her shoes. When she rose, Eugene was behind her.

"Where are you going?" he asked.

Her hand went to her heart. "You startled me."

"It's four in the morning," he said.

She stuck her hands in the pockets of her coat so that he wouldn't see them trembling. "I have to go see my mother," she said.

Eugene folded his arms. He was wearing print pajama bottoms and no shirt. "Are you having an affair?"

"For God's sake, Eugene."

"You are. You're having an affair. I knew it."

"I'm *not* having an affair."

"Why would you be going to see your mother at four in the morning?"

"Why would I be going to see a *lover* at four in the morning?"

"To get laid."

She rolled her eyes. "You have to trust me."

"Something very bad is happening," he said. "I feel it."

She turned and opened the front door. "Take a Xanax and go back to bed," she said.

"Please, don't go." He looked frightened and desperate, as if he suspected he might never see her again.

"I have to," she said, and shut the door behind her.

"Are you even going to say good-bye?" he shouted through the door.

DRIVING TO THE DINER, Quinn tried to reconcile seven years of longing with the reality that her mother would now be in her life. The problem was that the most agonizing moments of missing her had a direct connection to what she had just given up.

She remembered the night she had given birth to Isaac. She was so depleted. It had been almost two days since she'd had any sleep. Lewis had gone home and Quinn was alone in her hospital room. She was weak, hormonal, emotional. The epidural had worn off and her bottom was throbbing in pain where she had been stitched. Still, she was sure she would fall fast asleep. How could she not? She was as spent as she had ever been.

And yet. Sleep would not come. It felt as if her body had forgotten how to shut off. Quinn teetered on the sharp edge between restlessness and anxiety.

The other bed in the room was empty, so she was free to turn on the television, which usually had a soporific effect on her. This night, it did nothing. She turned it off and an hour later she was still awake. She switched on the light and picked up the book she had brought with her. After a few chapters, the paragraphs stopped making any sense, so she put it down and finally drifted into a light sleep.

Minutes later, though, a noise woke her. They were bringing another new mother into the room. The woman and the nurse were trying to be quiet, but it was too late. Quinn was wide awake.

After the nurse left, her roommate picked up the phone to make a call, and Quinn put her pillow over her head, trying to fall back asleep. It was no use. The new mother talked as softly as she could, but she was only a few feet from Quinn, with nothing but a curtain to separate them.

"It's a boy," the woman whispered. "Eight pounds, three ounces. I know. Yes, Benjamin Jacob. He's so beautiful. Like you, I think. Okay. I can't really talk—I'll call you in the morning. Yes, deliriously! Love you, too, Mom."

A small noise escaped from Quinn's throat.

"Sorry if I woke you," the woman said. "But my mother would have killed me if I didn't call her."

"It's okay," Quinn said, as she tried to convince herself she had nothing to be depressed about. So what if the first thing this other woman did after giving birth was call her mother? It didn't imply that Quinn's existence was bereft of meaning. She didn't need her mother's approval to validate the birth of her son. Nan's reaction was *not* the period to every statement of her life. She could have a happy life without her mother.

Normally, she might have been able to convince herself that all that was true. But on that night, depleted of every resource, she was laid bare.

"Congratulations," Quinn choked out.

"Thanks," said her roommate. "You, too. What did you have?"

"A boy. Isaac Nathan."

"That's sweet. You must be so happy."

Quinn's face was soaked. She wiped the tears with her hand. "Yes."

The next day, the staff looked the other way as Quinn's bedside was surrounded by more visitors than she was supposed to have at one time. Lewis was there, of course, and so was her father, her brother and Cordell, Lewis's parents and sister, and two of Quinn's girlfriends. There was barely enough room for all the flowers; with all the joyous chatter, it was as festive as a celebration could be.

"I bet you wouldn't trade this moment for anything in the world," Cordell had said.

Quinn strained to hear her roommate talking to the one person who was visiting her at that moment, her mother, and then looked back at Cordell.

"Right," she lied.

NAN WAS SITTING in a booth with a steaming mug in front of her when Quinn arrived. She had the look of someone who had been roused from sleep—her eyes still puffy and her hair barely combed. Quinn slipped in across from her and ordered a cup of coffee.

"You must have something pretty heavy to tell me," Nan said.

"I do." Quinn was determined not to beat around the bush, but now that she was actually face-to-face with her mother, the words flitted around her as if caught in a breeze.

Nan folded her hands, waiting.

It was warm in the diner, but Quinn was still chilled from the outside air. She shivered and wrapped her arms around herself, then closed her eyes tight. She opened them and decided she would have to start at the very beginning.

"You remember that guy Lewis I met about ten years ago?" she said.

"Of course," Nan said. "You were going to leave Eugene for him."

The waitress set Quinn's coffee in front of her. A drop splashed onto the table and Quinn put her finger in it, thinking about Isaac drawing chickens with spilled milk. She started to cry.

"What is it?" Nan asked.

Quinn shook her head. She couldn't speak.

"Tell me," Nan said.

"I *did* leave Eugene for him, Mom."

"What?"

"I married Lewis. We have a house in the suburbs. And a little boy. His name is Isaac and he's six years old." She watched her mother's face as it became clear.

"I don't—" Nan began, and stopped. "My God," she said.

"He's got your artistic talent. And your eyes."

"My God," Nan repeated.

"All these years," Quinn said, "I resisted going through the portal and visiting this . . . this other life."

Nan's hand was over her mouth, as if she had to seal herself shut to absorb it all.

"And then . . ." Quinn said, and stopped. She couldn't talk about it. She couldn't explain about the baby. Not yet, anyway. "How did this happen to me?" she said instead. "Why do I have these separate lives? These portals? I know it has something to do with that day you cut your wrist, but I still don't understand."

Nan stared into her coffee cup, but her eyes looked unfocused and far away.

"Please," Quinn said. "Tell me."

Nan looked up. "I died that day," she said. "We both did. I know I was dead because I saw that perfect light. You know the one I mean. People describe it as beautiful, but they never tell you it's a kind of beauty you've never seen before. You can't help but be drawn to it. You were with me, of course—inside. We were traveling together but you didn't want to go. You wanted to be born—you were pushing toward life, and I was pulling you toward death. And then, in one discrete moment, you entered both worlds. I felt it. I felt the split. You were both alive and dead. And in that instant I had to make a choice to join you in one place or the other. But you . . . you had no choice. You had already gone in two opposite directions."

Nan paused and looked out the window. It was still dark, and the only things visible were the headlights of cars and trucks traveling on the service road. She looked back at Quinn and continued. "It was a terrible decision for me. I had to either abandon you in life or in death. Up until the very last second I thought I was choosing death. It was what I wanted. And it was so much . . . easier. But my maternal instinct took over. You needed a mother, so I came back." She used a paper napkin to blot the tears running down her cheeks. "I hoped you would never find out, but you knew. A part of you always knew."

"I guess I did."

"I'm sorry I never spoke to you about it before."

Quinn shrugged. "What would you have said?"

"I don't know."

"Were you ever sorry you made the decision to come back?"

Nan shook her head. "The only thing I'm sorry about is that I lost a part of myself that day. I tried to recapture it through you and Hayden, but I never could."

"What did you lose?"

"It's hard to explain. I used to think of it as the happy part of me, but that's not it. I still experience my share of happiness . . . joy . . . rapture—whatever you want to call it. It's more like I lost a color palette. I lost the cotton candy colors, the sorbets. All those lovely hues that dance with light."

Quinn understood the portrait of her mother that Lewis had bought for her in the Berkshires. The reason it didn't exactly resemble her was that the artist had captured the part of Nan that had died.

"Maybe you left behind the lightness to stay with the version of me who passed away," Quinn said. "Maybe you didn't abandon that baby after all."

Nan reached over and squeezed her hand. "I hope that's true."

Quinn stared down at her coffee mug, trying to connect with her new existence. There would be no other life from now on, just this one. She took a sip, and mentally followed the trail of the hot liquid down her throat and into her belly. She needed to accept this physical reality.

"Did you suspect this?" she asked her mother. "Did you suspect that I had another life?"

"I knew something was going on but I couldn't put my finger on it. Maybe I knew on a subconscious level. Perhaps that's what I've been trying to figure out with those paintings. Maybe I sensed there was another Quinn, and that was my way of trying to get to you."

"I don't think that's it," Quinn said, shaking her head. "That thing you were trying to capture—that essence that kept eluding you—it wasn't me. It was you."

Nan paused to consider that. "Maybe you're right," she said. "Maybe it was my own light I was after." She paused and sighed. "I was so different then."

"I know," Quinn said. "I saw you."

"What do you mean?"

"Well, not *you*, exactly, but a portrait of you. It was painted a long time ago by a fellow student."

Nan furrowed her brow in concentration. "I remember that painting," she said. "Where did you find it?"

"At a gallery in the Berkshires . . . with Lewis." She felt a terrible sorrow of longing. She would miss him so much.

"Quinn," her mother said, "why are you here?"

She closed her eyes, trying to block out images of Lewis and Isaac. "I had to leave that other life," she said.

"Why?"

Quinn rubbed her head, trying to figure out how to explain it all. "You didn't want me to marry Lewis," she said.

"That's not true."

"It is," Quinn insisted.

"I liked Lewis. I thought he would be good for you."

"Then why did you tell me not to marry him?"

"I said that I didn't think you *would*. I was playing devil's advocate. I wanted you to marry him. I knew it would be a better life for you. But I also knew that your need to be needed was so strong that you might not make the right decision. So I pushed in the opposite direction, hoping you would push back."

"But I *did* marry Lewis! And you were so depressed about it you practically wore black at my wedding."

Nan sat back, thinking about that. "I was depressed at your wedding?"

"Like you were in mourning."

"Was I taking my meds?"

"I don't know," Quinn admitted.

"Maybe I was just having a bad day."

Quinn shook her head, avoiding her mother's eyes.

"What then?" Nan asked.

"I can't say it."

"Look at me," Nan said.

Quinn picked her head up and looked straight into her mother's amber-flecked eyes. "You killed yourself," she said. She didn't mean to sound angry, but it came out like an accusation.

"What?"

"You killed yourself because I married Lewis."

"No!"

"Yes! You took an overdose of pills and killed yourself. Dad found you in the bathroom. He tried to resuscitate you but you were already gone."

"Oh, no."

"You left him. You left me. You left all of us."

"Maybe it was an accident."

"You pushed me away."

"I couldn't have."

"Right before you died you painted a scene. It was supposed to be a portrait of me, but it showed the two of us on opposite sides of a wall. You sat on a stool, looking straight ahead. I was on the other side, trying to get in."

Nan chewed on her lip, and Quinn could tell her mother was envisioning the painting. She could probably imagine colors and shadows, see the expressions. Nan stared out the window at the darkness and then looked back at Quinn.

"If I was depressed when I painted it," Nan said, "I must have been thinking about suicide. I was probably thinking that if I killed myself, you wouldn't miss the real me, but the mother you wished I could be. My darling, I probably painted that because I was thinking you were better off without me." She sat back, exhausted.

Quinn put her trembling hands around her coffee cup. "That's why I left, too. Because they're better off without me."

"You mean your husband and your son?"

Quinn took a jagged breath and nodded. "My daughter, too," she said softly.

"You didn't say anything about a daughter."

"Because she'll never be born. I was going to call her Naomi, but . . ."

"But?"

"She's damaged. She has a crack in her skull. And they said I would probably lose her."

"I'm so sorry, Quinn."

"I needed you so badly."

"Like she might need you?"

"No. I couldn't go through with it. I made an appointment for an abortion and then I left. I left Naomi and Isaac and Lewis. It's better this way."

"Do you really believe that?"

"You should have heard the way I spoke to Isaac."

"God knows I was never mother of the year, Quinn. But did you ever think you were better off without me?"

"Never!"

"I can't tell you what to do about the baby, Quinn, but your husband and your son need you. That's one thing I'm sure of."

Quinn looked out the window. There was a pink glow on the horizon as the sun started to rise. She thought of Isaac looking out the window and then running into her bedroom to wake her. What had she done!

"Oh, God! It's too late. I can't do it. I can't go back!"

"Why not?"

"Because every time I cross over it's harder to get back. And now . . . I just don't think I can."

"You have to try."

"But, Mom, there's something else. Something too horrible."

Nan went pale. Was it possible she sensed what Quinn was about to tell her?

Quinn grabbed her mother's warm hands with her icy fingers. "The fissure between my two lives is closing," she said. "And if I go back—if I can somehow manage to make it through—the opening will disappear behind me, leaving nothing but a solid concrete wall. This life . . . I think this life will be gone, too."

Nan's breath came in steady puffs through her nose. Her face changed, hardened. Her eyes became steely. "You have to go anyway."

"How can I?"

"You have to. You have to try. I'll help you."

"But, Mom . . ."

"How old is Isaac again?"

Tears rolled down Quinn's face. "He's six."

"He needs you."

The trembling that had started in Quinn's hands now overtook her. "He does!"

Nan rose. "Let's go."

"Are you sure?"

Her mother nodded.

"But you're sacrificing everything."

She wrapped her arms around her daughter. "I'm not."

31

DURING THE CAR RIDE BACK TO THE CITY, QUINN TOLD NAN about the other journeys, and how the water had to be colder every time she went back. She told her about the fissure in her basement, behind the ancient ironing board, and how she had sensed its presence from the first moment she approached it.

Nan wanted to know more about the house and her life. Was Lewis good to her? How was their marriage? Was Hayden okay? Was he still with Cordell? Did she speak to her father often? Had he moved on? Question after question tumbled from Nan, and Quinn had to struggle to keep up.

As she drove across the Fifty-ninth Street Bridge, Manhattan's magnificent skyline rising in the distance, they both went silent. The crisp early-morning sky provided a perfect backdrop, and Quinn's eye, as usual, went from the Empire State Building—easy to spot with its spire reaching high above the jagged silhouette—to the Chrysler Building, perpetually celebrating in its chrome Art Deco tiara. Today, though, the vista felt different, and she knew why. Her mother would never see it again.

Quinn glanced to her right. Nan was staring, tears running down her face.

"I don't have to do this," Quinn said. "I can stay here with you."

Nan shook her head, resolute. "No."

Quinn gripped the steering wheel, trying to pull strength from wherever she could.

"Tell me about Isaac," Nan said. "Start at the beginning."

And she did. She told Nan that she took a home pregnancy test one morning while Lewis was still asleep. When she saw it was positive, she removed Lewis's toothbrush from its holder above the sink and replaced it with the test stick. Then she woke him for work. She sat on the bed, waiting for a reaction, and laughed when she heard a loud whoop from the bathroom. She knew she would later get complaints from the mean couple in the apartment next door, but she didn't care. She told Nan about her labor and delivery, and how Isaac was a little jaundiced when they brought him home, and had to be kept by the window in a bassinet, which they moved hourly to follow the sun.

She told her mother how quickly he got fat, his little hands turning into meatballs. She explained how he started to slim down as soon as he learned to walk, and now was so skinny she had trouble finding jeans that didn't slide down his bottom. She told her about the time he had to get stitches in his forehead when he was only two, after falling in a playground. She told her that he was a gifted little artist who had been drawing from the time he could wrap his tiny hand around a crayon. She told her Isaac had an infectious giggle, and liked playing with action figures and building sets more than with cars and trains.

"He likes believing in the tooth fairy," Quinn said, "but he's skeptical. The wrestle between his heart and his mind is something to see."

"Did he ask you about it?"

"He did. But it was funny how he phrased it. He didn't come right out and ask me if she was real. He said, 'If the tooth fairy wasn't real, would you tell me?' It was like he wasn't sure he wanted the truth. He just wanted to know if he could trust me."

"What did you say?"

"I think I gave him the right answer. I said, 'If you *asked* me I would tell you the truth.' Then I waited for him to respond, but he didn't, so I said, 'Do you want to ask me?' It took him about a full minute to answer."

"What did he say?"

Quinn smiled thinking about it. "He said no, and then took out his crayons and started coloring."

Nan laughed. "What a delightful boy. And I'm glad he turns to art for comfort."

"I gave him a sketch pad from your studio," Quinn said. "It's his favorite thing to draw on."

"Give him everything," Nan said. "My paints and brushes, my palettes, my canvases, my charcoals. Whatever I left behind."

"I will."

"And don't give him art lessons too soon. Let him just create."

Quinn felt she could barely breathe. "Okay."

"Make sure he gets to experience the natural world. He needs to see mountains and lakes."

"Right."

"Bring him to Jones Beach in the winter," Nan said. "He'll love the light."

"Yes."

"Do you take him to the art museums?"

"Of course."

"What does he like?"

"The moderns. I mean, he likes everything. But twentieth-century art drives him wild."

"Good. He's reacting viscerally. Is he smart like his mama?"

"Smarter."

"Does he call Phil 'Grandpa'?" Nan asked.

"Calls him Papa Phil, and he loves him to pieces."

"I bet Arlene eats him up," Nan said, referring to Lewis's mother.

Quinn could tell that her mother was trying to be strong, but her voice had gone soft. Quinn glanced at her face. This had to be so hard for her.

"They're very close," she said.

Her mother nodded. "I'm glad he has a grandma."

"I'm sorry . . ." Quinn began, and had to stop. She was crying too hard to get the words out. She took a long, jagged breath. "I'm sorry you never got to meet him."

"Me, too."

It was a Saturday morning and traffic was pretty light, so they made it to Manhattan quickly. Quinn parked the car in the garage beneath her apartment building but wasn't ready to get out. There was still so much to talk about. She cut the engine and turned to her mother.

"I found something in your room. A package with a newborn outfit inside. You had written my name on it."

"I remember," Nan said. "I was getting rid of your baby clothes, packing them up for charity. Your father kept telling me to save them in case we had another daughter one day. But you were growing out of things so fast and I was overwhelmed by the clutter. You know me—if I'm not using something, it's *out*. Anyway, I had a rare moment of sentimentality when I was packing up that tiny outfit. I had brought you home from the hospital in it and it felt so precious, like you were still in it. I just couldn't give it away. So I wrapped it and stuck it someplace, but I never remembered where I put it."

"You put it in a dresser drawer and it fell behind. Must have been back there all these years. It's in my house now. I thought . . . I thought it might bring Naomi good luck."

Nan grabbed Quinn's hand. "I hope it does."

"I'm scared, Mom. I'm scared that she's going to die." She paused to swallow. "And I'm scared that she's going to live."

"You're stronger than you think."

"Am I?"

"I'm not saying it will be easy," Nan said, "but you have a hell of a partner there."

"I know."

"You'll get through it together."

Would they? Quinn still couldn't imagine what it would be like to spend the rest of their lives as parents of a damaged girl. "Do you think I can do it? Do you think I can be a mother to a disabled child?"

Her mother touched her face and Quinn closed her eyes. She didn't want her to stop. She wanted to stay in the car underground with her mother's hand on her cheek for the rest of her life.

"When did you fall in love with Isaac?" Nan asked.

Isaac. Just thinking about him made Quinn feel that she would be pulled apart. How she wanted to hold him again! And yet. She took her mother's hand and kissed it.

"Right after he was born," Quinn said. "They cleaned him off and put him on my chest. He turned his little face and . . . I was flooded."

"Did you love him because he was perfect?"

Quinn shook her head.

"You'll feel the same way about Naomi."

"I will!" Quinn said, crying.

Nan leaned in and embraced her. "Let's go," she said.

Quinn took a deep breath, and then another, trying to gather strength with each one. "Okay," she whispered.

By the time they reached the apartment, it was empty, as Quinn had expected. Eugene was obsessive about getting to his Saturday-morning appointment with his personal trainer.

Quinn led her mother straight to the bathroom, where she turned on the tub's cold water tap.

"I'm going to need to add ice," she said.

Nan followed her into the kitchen, where Quinn held a glass under the ice dispenser on the refrigerator door and filled it to the top.

"Is that going to be enough?" Nan asked.

"Not by a long shot, unfortunately."

"Then let's not fool around," Nan said. She opened the freezer and removed the entire bin from the ice maker.

They went back into the bathroom and dumped all the ice into the tub. What had looked like a large quantity seemed dwarfed in the deep bathwater.

"I don't know if that's going to be enough," Quinn said, testing the water with her hand. "What are we going to do?" She knew of a store three blocks away that sold ice by the bag, but she was afraid that even if she ran there and back, Eugene would beat her home. She didn't want to have to try to explain any of this.

"Doesn't have to be ice," Nan said, and went back to the kitchen. She opened the freezer and started rummaging around. She found the three ice packs Quinn and Eugene used in their beach cooler. She also pulled out several unidentified packages of meat in plastic bags, a bottle of Grey Goose vodka, and four bags of frozen vegetables. "I think this should do it," she said.

"It's like some crazy frozen stew," Quinn said, as they stood over the tub with the strange assortment of items floating in it. She took off her shoes and socks and put her right foot in the water to test it. The cold was so painful it felt like a burn, but Quinn kept her foot in until it started to go numb. She pulled it out, and as her flesh thawed in the warm air of the bathroom it felt as if she were on fire.

She threw her arms around her mother. "I don't think I can do this!" she said, weeping.

Her mother held her tight for a long time. Quinn felt her resolve weakening. Maybe she should stay here after all. Nan pulled back and looked into her daughter's eyes.

"You're going to do this," she said.

Tears dripped over Quinn's lips and into her mouth. "Mom . . ." she began.

"I know," Nan said. "I love you, too."

"I can't say good-bye to you."

"Then don't. Just get in the water."

Quinn did as her mother said, stepping into the cold bathwater amid the strange assortment of objects. She left her clothes on, even though she knew they wouldn't really do anything to keep her warm. She sat.

"Oh, God. It's so cold." Her teeth chattered.

Her mother leaned over and kissed her forehead.

"I guess this is it," Quinn said. She kissed her mother back. "Thank you," she whispered. She took a long, deep breath and lay down, submerging herself in the icy bath.

She kept her eyes closed, fighting the instinct to sit up and escape the terrible pain of the cold. Her limbs were on fire. How long would it take before she felt a tug? And what if she didn't? She could die of a heart attack or hypothermia within minutes.

I should sit up, she thought. To hell with this!

"Give Isaac a kiss for me," she heard her mother say.

Isaac! Of course. If she didn't die first, she might get to see him very, very soon.

The burning was giving way to numbness. If she could only hold on! Her chest began to feel heavy and Quinn wondered if she was having a heart attack. She wanted to sit up and take a breath, but worried that she wouldn't be able to force herself down again.

And then she felt it. It was just a slight tug, but Quinn recognized the sensation. She was leaving. She opened her eyes. It wasn't too late to change her mind. Her mother was still there, hovering above her.

I can't do this! Quinn thought. I can't leave my mother! She tried to sit up but couldn't. She realized, then, that her mother had her arms pinned to the bottom of the tub. Nan was holding her down.

"Good-bye, Quinn," Nan said.

Quinn felt herself sucked into darkness with a powerful, violent jerk. She opened her mouth and took a hungry breath. She was alive.

But just like that, her mother was dead. Quinn could sense it immediately. There was no more Nan. Period.

Quinn was now naked and shivering as she barreled back toward her other life. Soon she would reach her basement wall and find out whether she could squeeze through and get back to her family, or if she would be stuck in this dank, hellish mid-place forever.

Light. It was Quinn's first bit of hope. The fissure hadn't sealed completely.

When she was upon it, though, she couldn't imagine how she would be able to squeeze through. It was so small.

Still, she had to try. Quinn put her head through, but her shoulders were just too big. It wasn't going to work. But maybe if she put her arms over her head like a diver she could make it.

Quinn backed out and tried again, leading with her hands and squeezing her head between her arms. She scratched the skin of her arms and back on the rough concrete, but she did it—she managed to get her shoulders through. She winced in pain as she pulled her tender breasts over the scratchy surface. Her bloated belly would be the hard part. It was just too large and round for the narrow slit. Quinn grabbed onto the ironing board with one arm and pulled as hard as she could, ignoring the ripping of flesh on her middle. At last, her belly was through, then her hips and her legs. It was over.

Quinn had made it. She was home.

32

QUINN STOOD IN HER LAUNDRY ROOM, NAKED, WET, AND cold. She closed her eyes and put both hands on her belly. Her injuries were all surface wounds. Naomi was still alive. She could sense it.

Quinn gathered her pajamas and went into the bathroom, where she took a luxurious hot shower. She dressed her tender wounds, put her pajamas back on, and climbed into bed with Lewis. She expected to feel happy to be alive and grateful to be safe and warm. But as she stared at the ceiling, grief hit her in a giant wave. Her mother was dead. Gone forever. And Quinn felt that she might drown in her own sorrow.

She tried to muffle her weeping but couldn't. Lewis awoke and turned to her. He took her in his arms, stroked her back.

"You feel okay?" he asked.

She shook her head.

"Is there anything I can do?"

Quinn tried to speak but couldn't. She shook her head again. Isaac appeared at the door of their bedroom.

"Mommy?"

"Mommy doesn't feel so well, buddy," Lewis said, rising. "Let's go downstairs and let her rest. I'll make you breakfast."

"Wait," Quinn said. She put her arms out and Isaac came to her. "I love you," she said into his soft hair.

"You were so cranky last night," he said.

"Yes," she said, laughing and crying at once. "I *was* cranky last night."

Lewis took him downstairs to let Quinn rest. Alone in the bedroom, she thought about the day her father called to say that her mother was dead. At first, she couldn't understand what he was saying, and he had to repeat it three or four times for it to break through. Much of what happened right after that was hard to recall, as her brain shut down in some critical way. What she did remember, though, was discovering that grief was a physical illness, like the flu. Everything in her body felt slow, tender, achy. Not just her heart, but her blood, her bones, her flesh.

She felt like that now, and it made her so very tired. Within minutes, she fell into a heavy sleep, as if gravity itself were pulling her into unconsciousness.

She awoke sometime later to the smell of toast and eggs wafting up from the kitchen. She was groggy enough to go right back to sleep, but hunger pushed her out of bed, as she had hardly eaten a thing the day before. Besides, there was something urgent she needed to tell Lewis.

"Feeling better?" he asked when she entered the kitchen.

"Coffee," she said. She needed to clear the cobwebs and regain the power of speech.

He set a cup in front of her, followed by a plate of eggs—scrambled easy, the way she liked them—and whole wheat toast. Had Lewis forgotten that she was supposed to fast this morning in preparation for her procedure? Whatever. She was famished, and still too sleepy for the conversation, so she ate greedily, gaining energy and strength as she sat across from him.

At last she downed the last sip of her coffee and cleared her throat. Lewis looked up from his newspaper.

"I'm not doing it," she said, speaking quickly. She had so much to say and she wanted to get it all out before he interrupted. "I'm not having the abortion. I want to give this baby a chance. I know that if she makes it to term we'll love her to pieces and we'll feel like we can't imagine how we ever lived without her. And if she doesn't live, well . . . it's impossible to predict how broken we'll be. But we'll get through it. Are you with me on this? I feel like you are. I *hope* that you are. And I also hope you don't think this is some misguided attempt to make up for whatever issues I had about my mother and her death. It's not. It's really not. I just feel . . . I feel like I'm already Naomi's mother and I have to do this. So we need to call it off, Lewis. We need to call and cancel the appointment. I'm not going through with it."

"Relax," he said. "I already did."

"What?"

"I know you didn't stay in bed last night," he said. "I heard you get up and go into the basement. I don't know what you do down there, but I respect your privacy. You need alone time. I guess I do the same thing with my weather equipment. In any case, after you left, I noticed that you had taken out that little baby outfit we found in your mother's dresser. But you didn't just look at it and fold it back up. You laid it out on a pillow, like you were picturing a baby inside it. It was such a tender thing to do. I knew then that you wanted the baby. And as soon as I processed that, I knew that I wanted her, too."

Quinn had almost forgotten about that, but he was right. After lying in bed for several hours, unable to sleep, she had unfolded the little pink stretchie with the matching hat and booties. She laid it all out, trying to picture her newborn there. It was as if she owed it to Naomi to try to think of her as a live baby.

But of course it was just clothing—empty pieces of fabric. And she was too distraught for it to give her comfort one way or the other.

There's your comfort, she told herself, looking at Lewis. *Right there.* How grateful she was that her mother had played devil's advocate all those years ago and pushed her to make the right choice.

Then Quinn saw something she hadn't seen since the day Isaac was born. Lewis was crying.

"So a little while ago," he continued, "when Dr. Bernard's office called to confirm your appointment, I told them we had changed our minds. Actually, I told them we would need a few more days to think about it, but I knew we wouldn't."

"Oh, Lewis." She went to him and sat on his lap. "Thank you."

He wrapped his arms around her and put his hands on her belly. It was too early to feel the baby move, but the gesture felt so reassuring.

"I have this very strong feeling that we're going to get to hold her in our arms and love her," Quinn said. "Beyond that, I just don't know."

THAT AFTERNOON, Isaac was scheduled to play his last soccer game of the season. Quinn wanted to go, but was under strict instructions to rest.

Isaac stood before her in his uniform, pouting, his ridiculous jersey hanging down to his shin guards.

"I'm sorry," she said. "There's really no place in the world I'd rather be today than at your game, but I have to do what the doctor says."

Isaac folded his arms. He wanted his mommy there, and that was that.

"I have an idea," Lewis said. "I'll take a video of the whole game and Mom can watch it when we get home. Sound good?"

Quinn could see that Isaac liked the idea, though he wasn't quite ready to release his resentment.

"Tell you what else," she said, taking him on her lap. "As soon as the doctor says it's okay for me to be active, I'm going to take you to Nana's studio so we can get her paints."

"For me?"

"For you. I think she would want you to have them." Quinn paused and swallowed, trying not to cry. "I *know* she would."

He laid his head on her shoulder. "I'm sorry I got you mad last night," he said.

"Oh, honey. That wasn't your fault. I was very sad and it was wrong to take it out on you. I'm so sorry."

He shrugged.

"Do you forgive me?" she asked.

He nodded, and she kissed him.

"Can I have the brushes?" he asked.

"What?"

"Can I have Nana's brushes, too?"

And just like that, she knew that Isaac had moved on. Last night's scene was history that would fade into the tapestry of his memory. "Of course you can," she said.

LATER, AFTER LEWIS and Isaac had left, Georgette dropped by with a plate of mini-muffins and a pile of paperbacks. Quinn was happy to have the company. It was as if the grieving process that had begun seven years before were starting all over again, only this time there was no formal period of mourning with visitors dropping by to distract her. And no one knew how fresh with grief she felt. This visit was a welcome diversion.

"I saw Lewis on his way out," Georgette explained, "and he told me you would be confined to bed for a while. Thought you might need some reading material."

Quinn glanced at the titles. They were all erotica, written under

Georgette's various pen names. "Is there anything here I don't have to hide from Isaac?"

"Nope."

Quinn smiled, grateful for Georgette. "Thank you, my friend. Can I get you a cup of coffee? Tea?"

"You sit, I'll get it."

Georgette went into the kitchen. When she came back into the den, carrying the beverages, she asked Quinn how she was feeling.

"Tired, but okay."

"Lewis didn't tell me much. Is everything okay?"

"We don't know yet. For now, I'm just glad we didn't lose her."

Georgette squeezed her hand. "I'm sorry I never made it to the hospital. My car wouldn't start and I had to have it towed to the shop. Turned out that was just the beginning of my problems yesterday."

"What else happened?"

"Esteban broke up with me."

Quinn thought about that for a moment. She didn't know one could actually break up with a cyber lover. "I'm . . . sorry," she said.

"Apparently he got tired of waiting around for me all morning and hooked up with an old flame. So now they're at it, hot and heavy."

"Are you upset?"

"I was."

"How did you get over it so fast?" Quinn asked as she peeled the paper off one of the muffins.

"I killed him."

"What?"

"There's a character based on him in my work-in-progress. But instead of a landscape architect, I made him a professional dog walker. Yesterday he got eaten by sharks."

"How does a dog walker get eaten by sharks?"

"A crazed cockapoo chases him off a pier."

Quinn laughed.

"It was very satisfying," Georgette said, smiling.

"Do you miss him?" Quinn said.

"He's already been replaced."

That took Quinn back. "You have a new cyber lover already?"

"Yes!" Georgette said, her hand to her heart. "Can't you tell? I feel like I'm glowing."

"You're incorrigible. What's his name?"

"Pamela."

Quinn almost choked on her muffin. "Pamela?"

"She's hot."

"But, Georgette, you're the most heterosexual person I know."

Her friend shrugged. "I'm not switching over to the other side, just taking a turn at bat."

"But why?"

"It occurred to me I'd tried just about everything else."

"I'm sure you have," Quinn said, laughing. "Honestly, I don't know what I'd do without you."

"You'd probably find a less crazy friend."

Quinn shook her head. "That wouldn't do."

"Why not?"

"Because I need your . . ." She paused to think about it. "Your light."

Georgette beamed. "I like that."

"Me, too," Quinn said, and tried to smile, but there was so much pain mixed in with the gratitude that her eyes teared.

"You sure you're okay?" Georgette asked.

Quinn shrugged. "I don't know. I've been thinking about my mom." She paused. "Never mind. I'm just having a rocky day."

"That's okay," Georgette said. "There's no statute of limitations on missing someone. I'm sure there are still times when it feels like only yesterday."

It was only yesterday, Quinn thought. "Thank you for understanding," she said.

"Do you want to go over there?" Georgette asked. "I'd be happy to drive you there if you think it would help to spend time in her studio."

Quinn shook her head. "Thanks, anyway," she said. The thought of going to the studio now was just too much to bear. Soon, though. Soon she would go back and clear the place out. "I've decided to sell off most of the artwork."

"That must have been a painful decision."

"I thought it would be. I mean, for so long I couldn't even consider it."

"What changed?"

Quinn pursed her lips, considering how to answer this. "I never really understood what my unfinished business was. I thought I was trying to understand why she killed herself. But really, what I needed to do was forgive her."

"And have you?"

Quinn thought about the weight of the sacrifice she had made by deciding to leave her mother behind, and how very close she had come to changing her mind. But her mother. Her mother's sacrifice was infinitely larger.

"Yes," Quinn said. "I have."

33

QUINN SPENT THE NEXT TWO WEEKS RESTING, ALLOWING Lewis to do just about everything around the house. The other moms picked up the slack in carpooling, and Georgette was happy to be the one to walk to the bus stop every day to meet Isaac, who seemed to understand finally that his mother was not going to disappear. Quinn liked to think it was simply a matter of maturing, but knew it was possible he sensed that she no longer had access to a portal that could take her away from him. Indeed, the crack in the basement wall behind the antique ironing board had fused shut, leaving nothing but a faint scar. And the new fissure she had seen that night had disappeared, as if it had never been there at all.

For Quinn, accepting the help she now needed was as hard as it ever was. But at least she was able to override her instinct to reject it. *For you*, she whispered to her womb every time she had to fight the urge to get up off the sofa and tidy the house or throw a load of laundry into the washer.

Two weeks later, when she went to see Dr. Sally Bernard and was told she was no longer confined to complete bed rest, Quinn was thrilled.

"This doesn't mean you can run a marathon," her doctor cautioned. "I still want you to take it easy. And if you feel cramping, you must sit down immediately and get some rest. And of course if you start to bleed—"

"I'll call you right away," she promised.

Sally smiled. "I know people think being a mom is the hardest job in the world, but it's nothing compared to being forced to sit back and let others do the work for you."

"So true," Quinn said.

"One day, they'll appreciate the sacrifices we make for them," Sally said.

At the word *sacrifices*, Quinn felt a sudden chill, as if she were back in the ice-water bathtub. She shivered, realizing that her mother's spirit would always be with her.

"MOM?" ISAAC SAID a few days later as he was having his after-school snack. "When can we go to Nana's studio and get her paints?"

A fleck of dark chocolate from the Mallomars cookie he was eating stuck to his face like a beauty mark—a little-boy version of Marilyn Monroe—and it made Quinn smile. She wiped it with her thumb.

"How about today?" she said.

His eyes went wide. "Really?"

"Really."

That morning, Quinn had finally called Ellis Everett, the art dealer, and told him he could have a number of her mother's paintings to sell on consignment. She would keep the landscape Nan had been working on when she died and hang it over the sofa in the living room. Hayden would get his portrait, which he wanted to put in the guest room in his apartment, but Cordell insisted it go on the wall in their bedroom, right over his computer. Her father wanted to hang his portrait in his Florida home. Quinn was still deciding what to do with *The Wall*, the painting of mother and daughter together yet apart. She didn't want to give it to

Ellis, but she couldn't bring herself to hang it in her home as a constant reminder of her mother's suicide. Perhaps she would get it framed and leave it in the studio until she could figure out where it belonged.

"Can I have the easel, too?" Isaac said as he dashed into the sun-drenched room.

"I don't see why not," Quinn said. She and Lewis were planning to finish the basement in their home and turn it into a playroom, and she could imagine making one corner of it a studio for Isaac. It wouldn't have the lovely natural light of her mother's space, of course, but it would do.

"Are we taking Nana's paintings?" he asked.

She looked around at the stacks of framed canvases lining the room. "Afraid not," she said. "Most of them are going to be sold."

He looked surprised—almost affronted. "To *strangers?*"

She nodded. "Art lovers."

He thought about that for a moment and seemed satisfied with the response. "Can I look at them?"

"Of course."

Quinn helped her son go through the stacks of paintings on the floor, most of which were landscapes. When they got to one that looked like a depiction of Jones Beach bathed in winter light, she pulled it out. In the foreground there was a pale gray shack with a sign by the door that said LIFEGUARDS ONLY. Early-morning shadows stretched long on the sand, and the sky and sea seemed to go on forever.

"What do you think of this?" she asked.

"I can smell the beach," he said.

Quinn laughed. "I think I can, too."

"I like it," he said, tilting his head in a way that made Quinn want to squeeze him.

"Do you want to keep it? We could hang it in your room."

Isaac clapped his hands, and Quinn turned over the canvas to read the back. There was a label that said *Morning Light on Empty Beach*.

She went through the rest of the paintings with him, enjoying his reactions. Quinn explained that they would get to keep slides of all the pictures, so he would be able to look at them whenever he wanted.

"Uncle Hayden!" he squealed when they got to a stack of unframed canvases.

"Do you like it?"

"It's pretty."

She laughed. "Pretty? I guess it is."

She showed him the portrait of her father and tried to quickly pass over the painting of her and Nan, together yet apart, but Isaac stopped her.

"Wait," he said. "That's you."

"Right," she said. "And Nana's on the stool."

"I think she's waiting for you," he said.

Quinn didn't respond. She couldn't. Lately, she had been trying to comfort herself with the idea that her mother's spirit would always be with her. But the reminder that she would never again see her in the flesh brought fresh pain.

"Mommy, are you crying?"

"A little bit."

"Why?"

She swallowed over the swelling in her throat. "Because . . . I miss her."

"I think we should take this painting instead of the beach one," he said.

This was hard. Isaac wanted the picture. Her mother probably wanted her to have it. And yet. "I don't know, kiddo," she said.

"But it's my favorite," he said.

"Why is it your favorite?"

He furrowed his small brow and licked his dry lips. "When I look at this, I don't know what's going to happen. Maybe you'll go in the door and maybe you won't. It's like the beginning of a story."

"I never thought of it that way," she said, and it was true—she hadn't.

Quinn stared at the picture and thought about taking it home. Could she possibly appreciate this painting as something other than a suicide note? Could it even be a comfort, reminding her of the choices she and her mother had both made?

Quinn pulled the canvas from its place in the stack and placed it on the easel so that it was eye level. She took a few steps back to get a better look.

"Can we take it, Mom? Can we take it instead of the beach picture? Please?"

Quinn continued staring at the picture—at her mother's face, looking directly at her. It did, in fact, seem as if Nan were waiting for something.

"No," she said to Isaac as she walked back and removed the painting. She put a hand on his shoulder. "We'll take both."

WITH NO PORTAL to distract her and bed rest no longer mandatory, Quinn's days were filled with the normal, albeit scaled-back, activities of a wife and mother. But she allowed herself the indulgence of occasional trips to the store, preparing for Naomi's arrival with secret optimism. She didn't dare tell anyone and risk looks of concern and pity. She wanted none of it. Quinn believed with all her heart that she would bring baby Naomi home from the hospital. She didn't know how sick she might be, but she knew they would get to love her.

She picked out a soft cream paint color for the walls of the nursery, and bought pale pink valances for the windows to match the patchwork bumper set she had chosen for the crib. The tiny outfit she had worn the day her parents brought her home had been washed, wrapped in tissue paper, and set in a drawer.

Throughout all this, Quinn pictured her mother at her side, and imagined her reactions and encouragement. She wondered if perhaps she was doing it a little too much. Shouldn't she, after all, be experiencing some sort of closure? Maybe she needed to take a trip to the cemetery and say good-bye again . . . this time for good.

On a December morning bright with bitter cold, Quinn drove to the New Montefiore Cemetery in eastern Long Island to visit her mother's grave. The tombstone was a simple gray block of granite that read:

NANETTE GILBERT

WIFE • MOTHER • ARTIST

1946–2002

Quinn picked up a smooth rock and placed it on top. She ran her gloved fingers over the year of death and looked around. There was little life on the grounds that day. In the distance ahead of her a couple stood over a grave. Beyond them someone who might have been a caretaker was kneeling, perhaps picking up trash. Quinn pulled her scarf over her nose and mouth and hugged herself against the breeze.

She heard car doors shut and looked to her right. Several rows down, a hearse and cars were pulling over, and people were getting out, slamming the doors and walking slowly toward the grave of the loved one being lowered into the ground.

Quinn pulled off her glove and touched her mother's name, as if there might be some magic in the engraved letters. But it was just stone.

A woman at the burial cried out in anguish and the wind carried the sound across the flat terrain. Quinn recognized the pain. It came from the place where loss met fury. *It's all so unfair,* the cry seemed to say. *I love this person too much for her to be gone.*

That was exactly how Quinn felt when her mother was buried. Now, though, the fury was gone. Her sorrow was mixed with gratitude.

Quinn kissed her fingers and touched her mother's name.

"Love you, Mom," she said. "Thank you."

———————

AT BREAKFAST the following Sunday, Lewis announced that it would be an unseasonably mild day for December—a rare gift of warmth just before the weather turned coldest.

"We should take advantage of it," he said. "Do something outdoors."

"The zoo?" Quinn suggested.

"The beach!" Isaac said.

His parents looked at him.

"Not quite *that* warm, buddy," Lewis said.

Quinn smiled. "I think we should go."

"Are you serious?" Lewis asked.

"Just to see the light," she said. "Like that painting my mother made, *Morning Light on Empty Beach*."

"It'll be empty," Lewis said, "that's for sure."

A short while later, wearing extra layers to compensate for the wind off the ocean, they piled into the car and headed to Jones Beach, cruising past the toll booths, which were closed for the season. They pulled into a lot, which would have been packed on a summer day. Today, there were only two other cars in the vast, lonely field.

They didn't bring much for this outing. Lewis had a single folding chair strapped to his back. It was for Quinn, who wasn't supposed to take long walks without resting. She was carrying a small tote bag containing a thermos filled with hot chocolate in case they got cold, a digital camera, and a paperback. Isaac held a football.

"It's cloudy," Quinn said, disappointed that the long, dramatic shadows of her mother's painting were nowhere in sight.

Lewis looked up. "It'll pass," he said.

"Are you sure?"

"I'm sure."

They walked toward the water and looked out at the ocean, which put on a grand show. The waves rose and crashed, rose and crashed, as if intent on demonstrating the power and chaos of nature. It was humbling, beautiful. Lewis stood in the middle, one arm around his wife and the other around his son. Quinn had her hand on her belly, feeling Naomi react to the strange, rhythmic sounds.

Isaac looked up and down the shoreline, and then pointed to something in the distance.

"Is that it?" he asked.

Quinn followed the line of his finger, but couldn't figure out what he was pointing at.

"What do you see?" she asked.

"That," he insisted. "That little building."

"You mean the lifeguard shack? From Nana's painting?"

He nodded. "That's it, right?"

"I don't know," she said. "Let's take a walk and find out."

"You sure you're up for this?" Lewis asked.

"It's not that far," she said. "And, besides, you've got the chair. I could always stop and rest."

They walked along the beach, listening to the ocean, occasionally stopping to inspect an interesting shell or stone, a few of which found their way into Isaac's pockets. When they reached the little building, they walked around it and sure enough there was a stenciled sign by the door that said LIFEGUARDS ONLY. Beneath it there was a bit of unintelligible graffiti, but other than that it looked exactly like the one in Nan's painting.

"This is it!" Isaac said, excited. He ran back a few feet and looked at it from a distance. "Come here! Look!"

Quinn and Lewis stood behind him to view the shack from his perspective. Sure enough, he had found the right spot. Quinn snapped a few pictures so that they could compare it with the painting when they got home.

"You think there are any sharks in the water?" Isaac asked, and it was clear to Quinn he was done with the shack, ready to focus his excitement on something else.

Lewis set up the folding chair for Quinn, and she sat while he and Isaac threw the football back and forth. She took out her paperback and started to read, getting absorbed in the story. After a few minutes, a drop of moisture hit the page. Spray from the ocean, Quinn assumed, and kept reading. But she saw another spot and then another, appearing as if out of nowhere.

Quinn looked at her husband and son, who had stopped playing ball and were staring into the sky. She realized why her pages were getting wet.

It was snowing.

Tiny white specks quickly gave way to great flakes falling everywhere—the sea, the sand, the shack. Snow on the beach! The little family was surrounded. It drifted downward like magic confetti, melting on contact. It was so unexpected, it made Quinn laugh. Her husband laughed, too, and then Isaac joined in. Lewis hadn't predicted a snow shower. No one had. It was that very element of surprise that made it so wondrous. Quinn closed her book and turned her face toward the sky. Snow on a mild day in December may have fallen short of being a miracle, but to Quinn, Lewis, and Isaac, it felt like a gift sent just for them . . . a hiccup in nature that delivered as much joy as a family chose to receive.

EPILOGUE

"Don't start without me!" Quinn shouted from the kitchen. Everyone else was seated at the dining room table—Hayden and Cordell (the guests of honor); Edward and Brett (their best friends); her father and Jillian; Georgette and Roger; Meredith and Michael (her current lover); Cordell's sister, Tamara, and her seven-year-old son, Devin; and, of course, Lewis and Isaac.

Quinn's father had suggested they go around the table and toast the newlyweds, which she thought was a great idea. First, though, she needed to tell the kitchen staff to hold off serving until the final speech had been made.

The dinner party had been Quinn's idea. She wanted to do her part to help celebrate Hayden and Cordell's wedding, since she hadn't been able to attend the service. They had decided not to wait until summer after all, insisting they had simply changed their minds about having a big, elaborate affair. But Quinn suspected it had more to do with the uncertainty over the baby. And she couldn't blame them. The possibility of a critically ill infant—or worse—could have certainly laid their plans to ruins.

So in April the two men drove to Connecticut, where same-sex marriage was also legal, and had a small private ceremony. Quinn was in her ninth month and prohibited from traveling, so she couldn't be there. When she suggested a celebratory dinner at her house, Lewis agreed, on the condition that they cater it, as he knew cooking such a big meal would place too much physical stress on her.

"Okay," Quinn said, when she came back into the dining room. "Let's start." As she lowered her now massive body into the chair, she felt her panties dampen, which wasn't all that surprising. The baby was big and pressing on her bladder, necessitating frequent trips to the bathroom. She didn't want to delay the party again, so she squeezed her legs together, figuring she could hold it in until they were done. She had her little speech all prepared and wanted to go last, wrapping it up with a toast to the grooms, her guests, and to the one person she knew was watching over the whole affair.

Her father started. He stood and addressed his son. "I don't know if you remember this, Hayden, but when you came out of the closet to your mother and me, the first thing she did was turn to me and say, 'Don't be a macho jerk about this, Phil.'"

"I remember," Hayden interrupted. "Only she didn't use the word 'jerk.'"

Everyone laughed, including Phil. "I'm censoring," he said, with a nod toward the two children, Isaac and Devin. He needn't have bothered, as the boys were huddled together, whispering and writing secret notes on a pad.

"Anyway," Phil continued, "my point is that I don't think I was ever especially macho. Still, as enlightened as I like to think of myself, it was hard news to hear. Soon, though—thanks to your mother—I was able to let go of whatever prejudices had been ingrained over the years and accept it. But . . . I was scared. I worried about your future, Hayden. I didn't know if you would be able to find someone to share your life with—a partner who would love you and appreciate you as much as you deserved. Today, that fear is laid to rest as we celebrate your marriage and welcome Cordell into our crazy family. . . . God help him!" He lifted his wineglass and all the others did the same, including Quinn and the boys, whose glasses were filled with white grape juice. "To Hayden and Cordell!"

Everyone drank and, as if to punctuate the toast, Naomi kicked her heel into Quinn's lower rib cage, where it remained lodged. The discomfort was hard to tolerate, and Quinn tried to alleviate it by pressing down against her ribs. No luck. She knew from her previous pregnancy that these last days could get unbearably uncomfortable. It was, she imagined, nature's way of making the mother eager to push the new life into this world.

Her father's girlfriend, Jillian, stood and made a toast, telling Cordell what a great choice he had made marrying into this family. Edward and Brett went next, making a speech so filled with private jokes that no one but Cordell and Hayden knew what they were talking about. Still, everyone laughed, appreciating the sentiments. Meredith told the couple they were an inspiration, and her date acknowledged that while he didn't know them, their commitment to each other was evident, and he was honored to be a part of the celebration. Georgette talked about love and quoted from a George Eliot poem about two human souls joining together to strengthen each other. Her husband raised his glass and wished the couple a marriage as strong as his, which prompted Quinn to give Georgette a look.

Still uncomfortable, Quinn arched her back in an effort to elongate her body and relieve the pressure against her rib cage. But the shift in position put stress on her bladder again, and a bit more urine leaked out. She cursed her incontinence—yet another indignity of pregnancy no one talked about—and hoped the rest of the speeches would be brief.

Cordell's sister was up next. She cried happily, telling everyone how much she loved Hayden, and how exciting it was to see them tie the knot just as her brother was on the brink of becoming a famous actor.

Then it was Lewis's turn. "First of all," he said, rising, "I want to thank Quinn for putting together this party at a time when she could have been a complete couch potato and no one would have blamed her. But that's my Quinn. Thank you, sweetheart!"

All the guests raised their glasses and drank to that. Lewis turned to Cordell. "Now, I know you think Quinn and I can be a pain in the neck," he began.

"Don't be silly," Cordell said, "I think you and Quinn are a pain in the *ass.*"

The group laughed, but Hayden poked him and nodded toward the children. Cordell, realizing his gaffe, covered his mouth and looked toward Quinn, who couldn't find it in her heart to be angry. In fact, if she hadn't been afraid of losing bladder control completely, she would have burst out laughing like everyone else.

Mercifully, Lewis cut quickly to the end of his speech, toasting the newlyweds as the best brothers-in-law he could ever hope for. After everyone drank, he told Quinn it was her turn.

"Wait a minute," Isaac said, "what about us?"

"You guys have a toast?" Hayden said.

"We wrote it down," Devin said, waving a piece of paper.

"Let's hear it," Cordell said.

The boys read in unison, "Over the teeth, pass the guns, look out stomach, here it comes!"

"Guns?" Phil said, laughing. "It's supposed to be *gums.*"

Meredith's writer friend chimed in. "I always heard of little boys creating guns from toast . . . but never toasts from guns."

Quinn smiled. "I don't know if I can top that," she said, "but I'll give it a shot." She looked at the empty seat at the table and pictured her mother sitting there. This dinner would have meant so much to her. I'm not going to cry, she thought. I'm not.

Quinn picked up her juice-filled glass and stood. Before she could utter a word, though, her bladder gave way completely, drenching her pants, the chair and floor. As she looked down, horrified, a painful cramp spread through her and all at once she realized it wasn't her bladder after all. Her amniotic sac had broken. Quinn was in labor.

This is it, she thought, and felt a rush of love for the child she knew she would be holding in her arms in a matter of hours. She looked over at her son and felt the same beautiful ache. This wasn't just a feeling. It was a restructuring of her DNA—a permanent change in who she would forever be. Her children were the beating of her heart, the flow of her blood, the hardness of her bones, and the softness of her flesh. It drove her to accomplish the hardest thing she had ever done—crossing through the portal to get back.

For the longest time, Quinn wondered if her mother had felt the same way. It seemed impossible for someone who truly loved her children to make the decision to kill herself. But Quinn had been to the place where the black veil drops with an opaqueness so complete no light can get in. And so she knew.

She also knew that once the veil was lifted, her mother had felt the same love for her that Quinn felt for her own children. Maybe even more. Because in the end, Nan had looked into the light just as she had at the moment of Quinn's birth. And again, the choice she made was out of nothing but love. Only this time it was harder. The ultimate sacrifice.

She had let her daughter go.

"Are you okay, honey?" Lewis asked.

Quinn nodded and placed her hand on her belly. "It's time."

ACKNOWLEDGMENTS

This book would not have been possible without the advice, encouragement, and generosity of three spectacularly talented writers: Myfanwy Collins, Susan Henderson, and Saralee Rosenberg. Again and again, I went back to these women for help, and they always had the time and wisdom to find the light switch and turn it on for me. Thank you, my friends.

Additional illumination was provided by the medical professionals and other experts who patiently untangled technical information and sometimes even offered creative input. In particular, I thank Dr. Robert W. Marion for contributing such clear answers on the difficult subject of encephaloceles. Others who generously provided their expertise include Dr. Robin Cohen, Dr. David Cruvant, Alicia Gifford, Dr. Charles Goldberg, Michael Kitay, Melissa Michaels Meister, Roch Preite, Dr. Eric Shultheis, and Mindy Silverman.

I'm lucky to have friends in the writing community, both online and (gasp!) in person, who have given their support and advice, including Mary Akers, Terri Brown-Davidson, Don Capone, Louis Catron, Ramon Collins, Ron Currie Jr., Katrina Denza, Susan DiPlacido, Kathy Fish, Kelly Flanigan, Karin

Gillespie, Bonnie Glover, Ceci Grant, Andrew Gross, Carol Hoenig, Debbi Honorof, Tony Iovino, Brenda Janowitz, Elinor Lipman, Lisa McMann, Pam Mosher, Michael Palmer, Ellen Parker, Patricia Parkinson, Jordan Rosenfeld, Robin Slick, Maryanne Stahl, Vivian Swift, Amy Wallen, and Liz Willard.

Humblest thanks to my agents, Andrea Cirillo and Annelise Robey, who responded with such ebullience to the sharp turn my writing took with this novel. I'm a lucky author to have such champions. Indeed, the whole Jane Rotrosen team—including Don Cleary, Peggy Gordijn, Christina Hogrebe, Lindsay Klemas, Mike McCormack, Meg Ruley, and the rest—deserves a cheer. Ditto Joel Gotler . . . So glad you're on board.

Galaxies of gratitude to mission control, aka Rachel Kahan, my superstar editor, who understands readers as well as she understands writers. Without her wit, wisdom, and sage guidance, I'd be lost.

To Lauren Kaplan and the rest of the astounding gang at Putnam (whose names I hope to learn by the time you're reading this), thanks for moving mountains.

To my parents, Marilyn and Gerard Meister, thank you for believing I could walk on water, even as I struggled to stay afloat. To the smarty-pants trio, thanks for putting up with a mom who sometimes straddles two different lives herself. And finally, to my husband, Mike, who endures my mood changes round the clock and still manages to love me, a kiss and a squeeze.